Silv...

Stil...

Over 100 Great Novels of Erotic Domination

If you like one you will probably like the rest

New Titles Every Month

All titles in print are now available from:

www.adultbookshops.com

If you want to be on our confidential mailing list for our Readers' Club Magazine (with extracts from past and forthcoming titles) write to:

SILVER MOON READER SERVICES

Shadowline Publishing Ltd
No 2 Granary House
Ropery Road
Gainsborough
DN21 2NS
United Kingdom

telephone: 01427 611697
Fax: 01427 611776

NEW AUTHORS WELCOME

Please send submissions to
Silver Moon Books Ltd.
PO Box 5663
Nottingham
NG3 6PJ
or
editor@babash.com

First published 2006 Silver Moon Books
ISBN 1-903687-81-0
© 2006 Syra Bond

Trojan Slaves

By

Syra Bond

Also By Syra Bond
Roman Slavegirl

All characters in this book are fictitious, and any resemblance to real persons, living or dead, is purely coincidental.

This is fiction - In real life always practise safe sex!

*to the late
Professor Gordon Harrington*

Preface

In the summer of 2003, archaeologists recovered a manuscript, written in Attic Greek, from the library of the Villa of the Papyri in Herculaneum, Italy. It had been buried there since the eruption of Vesuvius in AD 79, but dated from an era much earlier. Its preservation was completed in the Museum of Antiquities Rome and then because of his reputation in the field, its translation was taken on by the internationally renowned anthropologist and classics expert, Professor Gordon Harrington of Mercy University, Houston, Texas. It was Professor Harrington who discovered its secret: a story about the sexual lives of some of the most well known characters who inhabited the histories of Ancient Greece; warriors, gods and heroes whose deeds were recorded by the first true scholar — Homer. Professor Harrington believes the author of this work to be the central character, Sappho, herself well known for her writing at this time, and here retelling in the third person, her own part in the Greek war against Troy.

I met Professor Harrington, at a conference on the discovery in Austin, Texas. In the raucous music district of the city, we spent several evenings together in a lively student bar inhabited by lovers of bondage and slavery. Here, I learned of his love of bondage, and he found in me an eagerness to submit to a variety of humiliations he had learned on his travels throughout the world. He kept me with him for two months early in 2004, at one time binding me with tape and shutting me in a small cupboard in his office for two whole days. I have rarely experienced the levels of joy that Professor Harrington brought about in me with his harsh techniques, humiliating and imaginative practices. Especially, he aroused in me a love for confinement in small spaces which, to this day, only continues to grow.

At last, after two more joyous and degrading visits to

him, he has agreed to my using his text, with some amendments, and it is reproduced here with his full permission.

Syra Bond
Houston, Texas, March 2006

Chapter 1

Humiliation on the beach at Troy

Eva swung on her painfully tight bonds, and shivered with uncontrollable fear as the greatest warrior in all Greece approached the beach. Achilles, son of the mortal Peleus — King of the Myrmidons — and the sea nymph Thetis, strutted along the lines of Greek ships pulled up on the shore at Troy. High off the ground, girls were suspended on ropes from the flattened paddle ends of outstretched oars. Some were only partially clothed, shivering in the morning light, their ragged garments tattered and torn by the vicious mistreatment of their cruel captors. Several were naked, red stripes marking their buttocks or breasts where, during a night of terror, flailing whips or leather straps had scourged them into agonised unconsciousness. All had their wrists bound tightly, the rough plaited rope carefully wound around twelve times before looping up between their hands and onto a bulky knot, itself the weighty base of a rope that dangled from the oars. These humiliated victims all hung on their tethers, twisting around slowly, completely vulnerable to their enslavers, and powerless to help themselves.

Eva, one of the youngest amongst them and, before her capture, a proud member of her own tribe's nobility, ached with the strain as she, one of the naked ones, hung pitifully on her rope. Wide-eyed and racked with gnawing pain, she stared into the sky, her mop of long red hair blowing slightly in the breeze. She swung slowly, her hands forced together by the securing rope, as if in prayer — an anguished supplicant bidding to deaf gods for deliverance. Her ribs were sore and her breasts, tender from the night of mistreatment at the hands of the vicious Greek soldiers, throbbed. Her smooth stomach, tightened and pulled in by the tension, dipped flatly between her hips only to rise again towards her tight-stretched slit. Light pubic hair curled above her crack, but it did not hide the shape or definition of her beautiful crack, nor the delicate folds of her soft, pink labia that surrounded it.

At the start, when they had first been hauled up onto the ropes, she had ached, and like some of the others, had cried out when the flails had been used. But, as the night went on, she felt the pain less — it became less acute, less penetrating. The sharp stings of the leather flails, so burning to begin with, first became duller, then heavier, then, as each stroke blended into the next, turned into a deep throbbing pulse of pure sensation. The pain was absent; the naked sensation filled her body. She listened to the exhalations of effort from her tormentors as they drew the whips back then released them, ever quicker, ever harder, ever more desirous to hear the squeals of their prey. Eva felt their effort, their desire to create pain, to cause their victims to cry out, but, as the punishment went on into the night, she became absorbed only in the sensation, how her whole body filled with it — the exquisite penetration of it.

Throughout the night, she remained suffused with the deep, exquisite sensation. Occasionally she drifted into sleep or into unconsciousness, she was not sure. When she came back, she jerked with the initial shock of pain again, or sometimes the pangs of her humiliation. But always she was rescued by the delicate folds of the sensation which again overcame her. As she drifted into a strange, brittle sleep, she had dreamed of her life before in Germany: her own servants dressing her, combing her hair, bathing her, massaging her with oils. Then the images of invaders violating her village. In her mind, she watched them tearing off her sisters' clothes. She saw them spreading the young girls' legs, thrusting their fingers inside them, forcing their cunts wide. She witnessed them again defiling them, making them scream in agony. She pictured them forcing them onto their hands and knees, thrashing them, filling their rectums with oil, driving their cocks in and spraying their semen into the frightened girl's gaping mouths. She saw them degraded in every way possible. She saw their tears mixing with semen as they were thrown on their backs and spreadeagled. She saw their faces contorting with fear as their legs were held wide and objects were forced into their wide-spread cunts. She watched their panic-stricken eyes as they were violated repeatedly, and she witnessed again their hopeless groans as they were tied down and whipped with flailing, leather scourges.

Eva shivered with fear and an involuntary jerk racked her taut, pained body. It was as though she felt again the sting of the invaders' brutal whips as she and the others had been driven like animals into captivity and subservience. Through the images in her mind, she felt again the humiliation of nakedness and the stinging pain of suffering, only to wake and feel the scourging sting of a whip as it laced across her back and buttocks.

Several of the girls looked towards Achilles, opening their eyes widely, entreating him to help them. They recognised his power and appealed to him, capitulating silently to his authority, offering him any favour for their freedom. He smiled at each one, himself imagining what degrading humiliation he could demand. Eva was not prepared to surrender yet — she was too proud. She turned her face down towards the sandy beach beneath her feet and others, seeing her defiance and gaining some strength from it, did the same.

Achilles, the handsomest, bravest and most fearsome of all warriors in the army of Agamemnon, stopped by the boats. He stared at this pitiful line of women as they hung suspended, waiting either for release or further torture, more pain or greater humiliation. He widened his eyes at Eva: red-haired, beautiful, barely matured, lithe and youthful. He saw she had authority, that the others, even in their tortured state, and notwithstanding her youth, respected her. And Eva felt his power and, trembling but still defiant, she dropped her head even lower.

He walked over to her, stretched out his hand and touched her legs. She quivered, enlivened by his touch, roused by the glance of his skin. She felt her cunt moistening. Achilles tightened his eyes with interest, circled his fingers around her knees, held her firmly, stretched forward and placed his lips against the backs of her calves. She tried to twist away, she did not really know why — his touch inflamed her like no man's had ever done — she was too weak, too ashamed, too humiliated to even try and resist. Her pathetic efforts increased his interest.

Tears of ecstasy flowed from her eyes as he ran his fingers up the insides of her thighs. Suddenly, she could not bear any more. She had hung on her bonds all night, and before that, she had been the sport of all the soldiers in the camp. As they had whipped her viciously, she had been forced to suck their cocks, one after another. She had taken them deep, as she had been instructed, but it had never been enough. They had held her head and forced themselves in as far as their length determined. But no matter what she was given, it was never enough. For a short while, she had kept the first simply in her mouth. She had held the throbbing glans between her tongue and the roof of her mouth, but she could not resist it, she could not keep it away from her throat. She allowed as much spit as possible to run around the cock in her mouth, to keep it wet, and allow it to slide in easily. But even though she was desperate for it to enter her throat, she was not prepared when it did. Its venous thickness clogged her throat completely, filling it, plugging it, then, as it went deeper she felt herself gagging. Her throat contracted against the shaft, tightening on it, making her choke, and she tried to pull back, but she was not allowed. They held her head in place and the cock thickened and squeezed inside her throat even more tightly. She felt vomit in her throat, but the cock stayed in, sliding up and down slowly — lubricated by her spit — but never coming out, the engorged glans was too swollen to allow it to be released. She retched, and fell forward but it only increased her torturer's ardour and his cock hardened even more, lengthened and plunged in deeper. She felt it stiffening for a last time and, as she choked and wretched, she felt his semen, hot and copious, flooding down her gagging throat. Suddenly it was out, the cock unplugged her and she let out a massive gasp. Her mouth filled with semen, spit and vomit and, struggling onto her hands and knees, she retched on the floor before quickly being flung back ready for the next.

And that was not all she had been subjected to. She had been whipped so much — more than the others and harder. She had been held over the back of one soldier while another flailed her. He pulled her face forward against his back, reached back and took hold of her wrists and, while another held her ankles, he bent forward. She was stretched over tightly, tensioning her muscles, tightening her buttocks, making her all the more susceptible to the stinging, writhing whip. She had jerked every time it fell, convulsing and retching and screaming out for them to stop. When one fell back exhausted, another took over until he also finally tired. When they had all finished with her, she was dropped to the floor, naked, red-striped and gasping. She had been forced face forward against a horse, tied by the arms and ankles around its girth, and caned as the horse bucked and whinnied. As it had reared up, she had been jolted and thrown heavily against it. Its skin had rubbed against her, covering her with its sweat and bruising her on the breasts and hips. The cane had come down hard and, as she twisted from side to side, and the horse was driven into a panic, the cane lacerated the sides of her breasts and her waist. After they cut her free, she fell to the ground barely conscious. They had thrown buckets of water over her to revive her. She had barely regained consciousness, when she had been pushed forward coughing and choking, headlong over a pile of armour, bent down and restrained with heavy thongs, then thrashed with a massive leather belt.

Suddenly, she felt an overflowing of fear as the images of her suffering and violation, flashing before her eyes like a terrible dream, burst in as though they were happening again. She twisted on the rope in a pitiful effort to save herself, as if somehow pulling herself away from her torturers, from their punishment, their pleasure. She looked up, her eyes wide-open, and saw Achilles staring at her. She twisted away from his touch, foolishly thinking she could escape. Achilles' hand was trapped between her legs as she spun around on the tight rope. Her muscles, already stretched, tightened more and, as a reaction to the sensation of the tightening, she tried again to pull away. But it was pointless — ridiculous.

Achilles let the backs of his hands slip against Eva's smooth skin until, stretching his arms fully up and parting her legs slightly, his fingertips touched her crack. Instantly, pleasure welled up inside her. Her blood pounded through her veins, her temples throbbed with anticipation, and her heart, already beating heavily in her chest, raced so much she could not catch her breath. She flinched as he ran his fingers along either side of her flesh. It was a flinch of expectation not fear. She could not believe what she was thinking. Would he penetrate her with his fingers? Would he open her up and pull her down onto his tongue? Perhaps he would simply lay the tips of his fingers against her flesh until, without applying any pressure, it would open up to him? Yes, she thought, if he just held his fingers there, her crack would part, only slightly, but enough to release her moisture, and that would be enough to allow his fingers in. Just the smallest pressure and the silky wet inner leaves of her crack would open up and fold against his fingertips, lubricating them, scenting them, encouraging them, to enter her. Yes, that is what he will do, she thought. She hung onto the anticipation and wanted him to wait, to prolong her expectation, to capture her with potential.

But Achilles did not wait. His fingers followed the contours of the delectable raised edges of her cunt, poking gently at the swollen flesh and finding, by pressing it apart, the wet softness between them. He found her clitoris — raised and hard, throbbing and wanton. He took it between his thumb and finger and squeezed. Her taut body tightened even more. He stared into her face and saw her pain as he pinched hard, digging his nails into the throbbing knob of flesh, crimping it, squeezing it, crushing it. Excruciating pain ran through her and, as spit dribbled from her mouth, a shock of pleasure joined it and she fell into a drooling ecstasy.

He pulled back and slowly she licked the spit from around her mouth. Her long, broad tongue poked down onto her chin — pink and fleshy with strands of spit bubbling at its tip. But he did not let her rest. Her pubic hair was soft and sparse and he curled his finger into its light loops. Now she sensed him as a lover might — his power, his heat, his passion. She knew she was a captive. She knew she was victim to his every wish, humiliated by his presence, degraded by his attention. But she could not ignore the swollen, moist flesh of her cunt that had opened up so easily with the lightest pressure from his hand. She realised he knew her desires, her needs, her wanton expectation. She shivered again with fear of her own yearnings and, as he felt them too, he drew back and smiled.

'You are indeed a beauty,' he said, massaging her ankles and quickly taking her toes, one by one, into his hungry mouth. 'And,' he exclaimed, pulling back abruptly, 'you taste like the most delectable summer fruit!'

Eva rose on his sucking lips, bending her elbows and, ignoring the pain, raising herself on her bonds. She could not hold back the sensation of pleasure. It ran up the backs of her legs, into her buttocks and across and within the flesh of her cunt. As she swallowed hard in an effort to control herself, she felt her breasts tingling, her nipples hardening and her throat filling with apprehension. But no amount of gulping could bring her to her senses. She bit onto her lips, offering herself more pain, distracting herself, giving herself an escape route and suddenly, and with a great effort, she shook her feet from his grasp.

He laughed loudly and stood back. He was just about to grab her again when he heard someone behind him. He swung around, his muscles tensioning with easy, athletic poise — he was, every inch, the graceful, assured warrior.

A heavily built man, tall with long black hair to his shoulders, stepped forward. His muscular chest glistened with oil and his burnished leather tunic shone in the light of the rising sun. He looked straight into Achilles' eyes. It was obvious he held Achilles in contempt, at the same time, it was clear that he dared not cross him.

'Ajax,' said Achilles, turning away from the still spinning Eva and reaching out his hand in friendship. 'Ajax, my friend, you have a fine row of pretty girls here. Especially this red-haired maiden. She must be from a great distance. We do not have such fair-skinned females like this in Greece.' He reached his hand up between Eva's thighs again. 'Nor do we have such tight clits, I'll wager.' He pinched her flesh roughly and she felt a wave of joy spreading deep into her stomach.

'You are right, my lord. They are fine indeed, and, as you say, tight. They say this one was a princess, from the north of Germany. And you are just in time to see how she suffers. She has not been fully tested yet, but I do not think she will disappoint. She how she scowls. It will be a treat for us all to hear her squeal.'

Achilles smiled.

'Do not be too harsh to start with, Ajax. I feel her promise will not be revealed until she warms to our ways.'

'You are strangely merciful, my lord. Has the beach at Troy made you soft?'

Achilles knew Ajax should not say such a thing. If the other men heard him, it would be seen as an obvious challenge to his authority. But he shrugged it off with a laugh, he knew there were different ways of controlling men than with the sword. Just as he knew there were different ways of controlling women than with the lash, or the flail. Ajax was too barbarous for Achilles' refined taste, but he was a fine warrior and Achilles needed him for that.

'Ajax,' you reveal my tender side, and for that I am grateful. Come, show me what these women have for us. You can teach me a lesson in cruelty. You are right. I need hardening!'

Ajax laughed and waved to some men who were resting at the bow of a boat. They sprang up, eager to please their chieftain and to show Achilles their willingness.

'Unhitch our prizes!' Ajax commanded. 'Bring them down so that we can show our general, the great Achilles, how we sport ourselves with them.'

Chapter 2

Eva's suffering

At Ajax's command, the soldiers sprang into action. Two of them ran to the side of the boat. Others clambered up ladders onto the deck. Draping their legs on either side to keep their balance, the men on the deck scrambled out along the oars from which the women were suspended. The oars bent under their weight and the hanging women bobbed up and down. As the women reached the top of the bounce, the strain was taken from their wrists and they felt the relaxation of the tension. Their elbows bent slightly and their breasts took up their normal rounded form. When they dropped again and bounced at the bottom, their arms tightened and pulled close to the sides of their heads, and their breasts flattened against their strained ribs. Some gasped under the strain as their weight dropped on the ropes. Fearing they could stand no more, others called out to their gods for mercy. Eva fixed her stare on the sand beneath, held her lips tightly together, clamped her jaw firmly, and remained silent.

Achilles looked up at her.

'Her name is Eva,' said Ajax with a wry smile. 'You have a special fancy for her, my lord?'

'She is becoming, yes. I fancy she could bring a man a good deal of pleasure. The right man, of course.'

'Then let us see if she is worthy of the greatest warrior in the land.' Ajax turned to his men and pointed up at Eva. 'This one. Rope her feet. I want her pulled taut. We will see how long she can remain so silent and tight-lipped.'

The men on the ground lashed a rope around each one of Eva's ankles, binding it many times before tying it off. They looked back at Ajax for further orders.

'Pull her down against the tension of the rope. Do not cut her free from the oar yet,' he shouted. 'Bring her feet to the ground. I want to see her body stretched. A beautiful way to behold a woman's body do you not think, Achilles? Pulled tightly between opposing ropes. Stretched until the body will stand no more.'

The two men pulled on the ropes, lying back on the sand and winding Eva down against the stiffness of the barely flexible oar that held her wrists. Slowly it bent, and gradually they brought her down until finally her feet touched the ground. They held her there as, with her mouth wide open, she gasped for breath.

'Keep her tight!' ordered Ajax. He removed an object from beneath his tunic and held it up before Achilles. 'Look, Achilles. I took this from Praxis, the Persian slave-master, at the battle of Ixia. That was before I pierced his eyes with a dagger and threw him to the hounds of Troy! I can still see him now. Trying to staunch the blood. Swearing his revenge as they dragged him away. I hope he died miserably. He had a fine reputation though. He was the cruellest master ever, they say. He invented so many torture techniques that King Priam granted him his own palace. I have been told that no slave could disguise their shiver at the utterance of his name. Even at the thought of him! Let us see if our little maidens will learn to quake at the name of Ajax!'

'What is it?' asked Achilles. 'This prize.'

'A training device, my lord. Praxis called it the mouth-cock. I will show you how it works. I think we shall soon have this fiery-headed maiden begging for her release. Though I do not see how she will tell us.' He laughed. 'See? It is a man's cock, fashioned perfectly and covered in fine leather. Any of our men would be proud to have such a thing of their own! But this has a thong driven through it, about halfway. This is what makes it so effective.'

Ajax stood in front of Eva. She gave an involuntary shiver, but her body was stretched so tightly between the rope that hung down from the oar and the ropes wound around her ankles, that it was not apparent. Her bright blue eyes flashed from side to side. Her mouth gaped.

Ajax held the mouth-cock in front of her. Eva gasped at its size, widening her eyes, quickening her breath and pulling back as far as she could against the straining ropes.

'Now open wide, my northern beauty,' said Ajax. 'Let us see how you respond to Praxis' mouth-cock.'

She closed her mouth, breathing heavily through her flared nostrils. Ajax pushed the end of the leather cock against her lips, but she kept them tight shut. He tried again, pressing hard, but still she resisted, twisting her head from side to side and fixing her jaw. He grabbed her cheeks between his finger and thumb and squeezed hard. Her eyes bulged and slowly her full lips widened but, when he tried to insert the end of the mouth-cock, it was still too big to enter.

Suddenly, Eva spit out at him. He looked angrily at her as he wiped it from his face. She stared at him and spit again.

Achilles laughed.

'Ajax, I have seen you glorious in battle against the fiercest enemy. But now I think I see you brought down by a woman. Can this be true?'

Ajax stared hard at Eva.

'No, my lord. It is not true, he said, seized with anger.

At the same time that he squeezed Eva's cheeks hard, he gripped her bottom lip, pulled it down and forced her mouth open. He forced the cock against her lips then drove it in. Her startled cough was immediately suppressed as he pushed it in as far as the thong would allow. He wound the thong around the back of her head, pulling her chin down towards her neck, before tying it tight and binding it in a knot.

'Now, my lord,' he shouted, 'you will see how Ajax controls any who oppose him.'

Achilles laughed loudly.

Ajax stood back and unbuckled his heavy leather belt. Its glistening surface shone in the sun, its massive buckle reflected the light from the sea and its edges glinted as he wielded it behind him.

Eva gulped heavily. The bulbous end of the mouth-cock pushed against the back of her throat. She tried to widen her throat, so that it would not touch, but, when she tried, it just allowed the mouth-cock to pull back tighter, and penetrate further. She gagged on it and felt vomit in her throat. Suddenly, she twisted sideways as a shock of pain cut deeply into her buttocks.

Ajax brought the flat of the heavy belt down viciously. It smacked against Eva's buttocks causing an instant redness to appear where it made contact. She wanted to scream but she could not. Her mouth opened involuntarily and her head pulled back in shock, the mouth-cock went in further. She gagged again, her throat tightened and she felt herself heaving. She heard Ajax laugh, and she heard the swing of the heavy belt as he drew it back. She held herself tight, bracing herself for more, but when it came, she could not hold back the shock and once more she opened her throat and raised her head. The thongs that attached the mouth-cock dug into the sides of her mouth and spit bubbled from the indentations that the pulling thongs caused.

The belt came down again. She strained to react, to save herself, somehow pull away, but she was so tightly secured at the wrists and ankles that all she could do was move her head. The tautness of her body accentuated the pain and heightened her feeling of captivity. She felt completely under Ajax's control. She was his victim, and his to humiliate. She could only receive the pain he gave her.

Again the belt came down. Again she gulped, again her head went back and again the mouth-cock was driven deeper. The bubbles of spit became a dribbling froth, running down her chin, onto her chest then down each breast until it dripped from the end of her hard throbbing nipples.

Another hard blow came down. The loud smacking sound filled her ears, and the pain it inflicted filled her body. Then another blow, and another. She heard the laughter of the soldiers as they watched and she was consumed by humiliation. Another blow and she twisted slightly against her bonds. Her thighs squeezed together and the flesh of her cunt was tightened. She felt the edges of her flesh, their heat, their softness. Another blow. More laughter. More pain. More humiliation and she twisted again, but this time, not because if the pain, but because she wanted to feel the tightness of her slit. She wanted to feel the hardness of her clitoris as her flesh pulled against it. She wanted to feel the moisture that ran from her swollen crack. With each blow, with each surge of pain, with each wave of humiliation, her pleasure built.

Another blow and she felt the wetness from her cunt on the insides of her thighs. Another and another. Each stroke of the belt, each wave of pain was filling her with increasing joy. She bit down on the mouth-cock, sucking at it, drawing it in. She felt hungry for it. She wanted it in her throat. She wanted to swallow it, to consume it. Another blow and her excitement built even more. She was filled with pain and joy at the same time. She was consumed by her violation and yet lifted by the sensation of her degradation. She wanted another stroke, another lash, another burning surge of pain. She wanted to hear the smack. She wanted to feel the tension of her body. She wanted to be humiliated.

She bit down harder on the mouth-cock, and sucked at it as much as she could. Spit ran from her mouth then, as a rain of blows cut across her taut buttocks, she tightened her legs together and let her pent-up ecstasy run through her. She shook and quivered and, as Ajax kept whipping her with the belt, she drew the mouth-cock in as far as she could and was overcome by a convulsion of breathless ecstasy.

Ajax tightened his belt back around his muscular waist.

'Surely, you do not think she has had enough,' gibed Achilles.

'Of course not. Her pleasures have only just begun, my

lord.' Ajax called up to the men straddling the oars. 'Cut them down!' he shouted. 'Now we shall have some real pleasure!'

Eva's legs were released and she bounced up quickly on the rope at her wrists. The man sheared the ropes that held the women to the oars and they all dropped to the ground with a jolt. Eva fell sideways, still biting hard onto the mouth-cock, still jerking with the convulsions of her orgasm.

Ajax grabbed her roughly and untied the mouth-cock. It burst from her mouth, covered in spit. Eva let her legs fall wide apart and gasped for breath.

She was not given time to recover. She was grabbed and carried forward to a narrow wooden rail, supported by two posts about knee high. She and the other women were forced onto their hands and knees before it. Eva waited, still panting, not knowing what would happen, wondering if she could stand any more.

The men gathered behind the women, kicking at them, pushing them, smacking them. The women edged forward towards the rail.

'Tie up our ponies,' commanded Ajax.

One after another, the women were taken to the rail. The first had her mouth put against the edge of it. She was ordered to open her mouth. When she did, she was made to grip the rail in her mouth. It pulled at its sides, stretching it wide. Thin ropes were used to fasten her against bar in her mouth. They were wound around her head until she was so tight she could not move. The next woman was tied up in the same way and finally, Eva was made to grip the rail and was secured like the first two. They waited, motionless, their elbows slightly bent, their heads fixed to the rail, their buttocks raised.

Eva stared ahead, letting her spit dribble from the sides of her mouth. She raised her buttocks higher, exposing the shape of her cunt, its pink crack and swollen, fleshy edges. She relaxed and showed her anus, feeling the air against it, allowing it to open slightly. Still heated by her pleasure from the beating, she felt aroused, in need.

The first lash surprised her — a multi-tailed flail struck hard across the soles of her feet. The next stung deep and she bit harder onto the rail. The next made her tighten her body. The next made her part her legs. The other women groaned as each was whipped across the bottoms of their feet by a different man. Their moans only inflamed Eva more and, as the punishment continued, she felt again, her cunt moistening with desire, its flesh swelling with the urgency of her growing pleasure.

When the flails were turned onto her buttocks, Eva opened herself more, She allowed her anus to dilate and her cunt to spread. She took the tails of the flail against her anal ring and labia as much as she could. She was filled with excitement — the pain was transformed into total pleasure. When, finally, the whipping stopped, she writhed for more. She bit into the rail, and moaned like an animal. Then, when she felt the heat of a throbbing cock entering her cunt, she forced herself back onto it. She squeezed it tightly, pressed herself down on it. When she brought out its splashing rush of semen, she tightened her cunt onto it and consumed it thirstily. She took the next one into her anus, pushing back and drawing it deep into her rectum. She pulled its venous heat into her bowels, riding it then consuming its copious splatter of semen like a starved beast.

Each man took a turn, until all had experienced the pleasure of all the women's cunts and anuses. When they were exhausted, and when Ajax gave them permission, they cut the women free from the rail and threw them onto the ground. Eva fell back and her eyes filled with tears. She was overwhelmed with despair and yet it was the very hopelessness and the mistreatment she had received, which had stirred in her needs more than she could ever have dreamed. Her violation had inflamed her. Her punishment had drawn her into an ecstasy like no other she had known.

Her body ached and, as she pulled her knees up to her chin, and held her legs for comfort, she felt the wetness of semen dribbling along her crack and running between the smooth, taut skin of her buttocks.

One of the soldiers, inflamed by the sight of her wet exposed flesh, pulled her legs wide and pushed his face between her thighs. Her eyes rolled up as he licked at her wet cunt, poking the end around her sore clitoris and delving deep inside her semen-filled cunt. She felt her stomach tensing and, without warning, she jerked, widening her legs then gripping them around the man's head, as her orgasm burst like a breaking dam. As she convulsed, she pulled his face onto her flesh. She tightened her legs around him, pulling his tongue in, sucking in his spit, mingling it with the semen that still ran from her. She opened her buttocks and let the delectable fluids run onto her anus, and she tightened her grip, even more so that he would not leave her without delving his tongue deep in there as well. She rode on his face, panting and gasping, yelling and screaming. She would not let him go, gripping him and pulling his tongue in ever more deeply, wriggling on it, opening her anus onto it, using it, fulfilling herself on it, being everything for it.

Another soldier dragged the man free and cast Eva down. She lay on her back, her hips still writhing, her cunt still glistening and open, her anus dribbling and her skin gleaming with sweat. She knew, even as she fought for breath, she had not had enough. She could not imagine ever having enough.

In the end, all the women's wrists were unbound. They lay on the beach, pained and exhausted. Fine yellow sand stuck to the sweat on their skin, covering their breasts, filling their eyes. Some of them groaned, some of them cried out, but Eva, who had suffered more than any and had reached greater heights of pleasure than any, remained silent.

Ajax instructed his men to drag the women to their feet and give them a final thrashing.

'And do not spare our wanton northern maiden,' he shouted back. 'I can still see defiance in her eyes.'

Eva took her place in the line, got down on her knees and waited her turn. Through tear-filled eyes, she watched Achilles, with Ajax behind him, walking away. Beyond them, in the reddening sunset, lay the plain of Troy upon which so many battles had already been fought. Beyond that, the great walls of the city, the defeat of which was the pledge of Agamemnon in his undertaking to rescue his brother's wayward and beautiful wife Helen from the arms of her magnificent lover, Paris, son of Priam, king of Troy.

Chapter 3

The pleasures of Troy

The great city of Troy sat behind its towering walls, impregnable, unviolated by the outside world, immersed in its own pleasures, degraded only by its own depravity. Its inhabitants made a study of gratification and pursued delights of the body and mind with insatiable eagerness.

The beautiful young Sappho ducked down behind the statue of Hera, the ox-eyed goddess. Pelador, the priest, wearing a ram's fleece on his back, his face covered by a mask, chanted rhythmically. He held a sharp, glittering knife to a ram's throat. The air was thick with incense and myrrh. White-robed acolytes, the palms of their hands pressed together at their chests, recited prayers and bowed low. Naked girls danced around them throwing flowers. When their baskets were empty, they stooped down and filled them from the floor, tightening their young buttocks and exposing between them the shape of their naked cunts. Young men ogled them with eager eyes, occasionally grabbing one by the breasts or between the thighs, and fondling them harshly before releasing them to the sound of mutual laughter.

Sappho loved watching these ceremonies. They excited her so much. She squatted low behind the statue. She drew up her loose robe and gathered it between her knees. She felt the draught of cool air from the inner temple against her exposed buttocks. It made her shiver and she felt goose flesh on the silky softness of her labia. She ran her fingers between her legs. For a second, she closed her eyes, imagining her cunt, picturing the sweet pink crack, raised at the edges, shaved and oiled. She pictured the glistening moisture at its centre — sparkling, sweet, available. She thought of her fingers, poking towards her flesh. She imagined them steadily working their way beneath her robe, across the front of her thigh then, slowly, nervously, finding their way into the sweet valley that lay at the base of her stomach. She touched the top of her slit and felt her clitoris hardening. She pressed slightly, and felt the petals of flesh that surrounded it opening, inviting, yearning. She licked her lips and opened her eyes, looking around quickly to see if anyone was watching. No, there was no one. She was safe.

Last week when she had been here, at the same place, doing the same thing, a young man had seen her. He had crept up behind her and grabbed her roughly by the shoulders. She had fallen back on the cold stone floor, her hands outspread, her fingers still sparkling with wetness from her cunt. He had glared at her hard, embarrassing her, humiliating her with his stare. He had threatened to tell Pelador, to expose her. She had said she would do anything to stop him. She had fallen to her knees and begged him. She had said she could not bear the idea of public humiliation. The young man had taken her into an alleyway behind the temple and thrashed her with a stick. He made her bend over and hold her ankles so that her buttocks were taut and her cunt was exposed between them. It had hurt so much. But, even as he continued her punishment, she did not pull herself away or beg for mercy. Even when the thin stick cut across the swollen flesh of her cunt, and the pain stung deeply inside her, she felt something within herself that drove her to submit to more. The fear of humiliation — of exposure — mingled with the pleasure of subordination to his control, with the joy of the punishment he was inflicting on her. As the beating went on, she widened her legs a little, and thrust her buttocks higher, exposing her fleshy slit to the cutting strokes, increasing the pain, heightening her humiliation, and intensifying her pleasure. After he had finished with her, she lay in the alleyway, her fingers pressed between the stinging flesh of her slit, gasping, panting, recovering from her overwhelming joy.

Sappho got down lower behind the statue of Hera. She

bit hard onto her bottom lip. In her mind, she still felt the sting from the young man's stick and winced as she remembered it. It had burned her — scorched her flesh — and she had run home with tears flowing from her eyes. But it had not stopped her coming back. Indeed, the idea that she might be discovered again filled her with a fresh flush of excitement.

She loved watching others like this, feeling herself, suppressing her cries of ecstasy as she brought herself first to the edges, and then to the depths of her jerking ecstasy. This place was so exhilarating: the scents, the worshipping followers, the sacrifice, the howling of the ram, the chanting of the priest, and always the fear of discovery, of humiliation. The delectable exposure to the glare of others, made her shiver with delight. The fear of being found made her heart bound with thrilling expectation. She delighted in being where the threat of being found was always present. And she was here again, doing that.

Sappho squatted down behind a statue of Aphrodite. She liked this position, it opened her buttocks and squeezed at the edges of her cunt. She pulled up her robe and hitched it around her waist. Now, anyone who came past, who discovered her would see her nakedness, see her crouching as though she was urinating, and they would see whatever it was she was doing. She parted her knees and felt again the cool draught of air on her flesh. She placed the flat of her hand against her fleshy cunt and massaged it gently, feeling its warmth, its wetness, its heat. She felt the hardness of her clitoris and ran her fingers around its base, squeezing it, provoking it, making it yearn.

Pelador thrust the blade of the knife into the ram's throat. It squealed loudly, gurgling, bleating, crying out for release. He twisted the knife and the animal was silenced. He held his arms up high and allowed the blood of the sacrifice to run in red streams down his wrists and arms.

The young girls danced around him, reaching up high in

imitation of him, stretching their firm breasts and tightening their already taut bodies. They touched his blood-soaked arms and rubbed themselves with it, smearing their pale skin with wide red lines, rubbing it around their breasts, down their flat stomachs and onto their thighs.

Two of the girls dropped to their knees, and began smearing each other with the blood. They seemed in a trance, rubbing each other's faces and breasts. They embraced each other, kissing and squirming wildly as excitement seized them and took control. Another girl joined them, holding onto the first two, licking them, smearing their blood-soaked bodies with her spit, pressing her cheeks against their breasts.

Sappho realised her fingers were deep inside her cunt. She felt the heat of her flesh around them, and the wetness that ran from her, on the upturned palm of her hand. She dropped her head forward as, gasping with delight, she drove them further. She parted her knees, allowing room for her hand, and thrust her hips forward to gain every bit of her delving fingers. She rode them, using them to heighten her pleasure, sucking them in, moaning as she enveloped them, gasping, panting, biting her lips. She rose slightly as she felt her orgasm approaching, and she opened her eyes, to take in just one last glimpse of the young girls. She watched them, their legs wide spread, licking each other, stroking each other's cunts with their tongues, and Sappho felt the urgency for release burning within her. As she bit harder onto her lips, and felt the muscles of her body tensing with an irresistible wave of joy, she saw someone standing in front of her. He had appeared from nowhere. He must have been watching her all the time.

She stopped suddenly, her orgasm held back, her hand frozen where it was, her fingers still deeply inside her open, fleshy cunt. She felt a dribble of spit in the corner of her mouth, but did not dare lick it away. Her face flushed uncontrollably.

'What are you doing here girl?' asked the man sternly.

'I ...' faltered Sappho, shaking nervously. 'I do not know sir.'

'If you do not know what you are doing, we should ask Pelador. I'm sure he will be able to give you an answer.'

The man laughed and grabbed Sappho by the hair.

'Please sir, no. I could not bear to be shown up like that. Surely there is something I could do to change your mind. Please sir, do not take me to Pelador. The shame would be too great. I will do anything.'

The man, himself young and handsome, looked down at the shamed Sappho. Slowly, she withdrew her fingers from her sopping crack. They glistened with wetness and she flushed even more as she saw the young man staring down between her legs.

'It looks to me as though you like the games which Pelador lays on for his young girls. Is that true?'

'It is, sir.'

'Would you like to be amongst them? Would you like to do what they are doing?'

'Oh no, sir. I only like to watch. It would be too embarrassing to take part. No, sir, I could never do that.'

'And what will you offer me to save you from Pelador's anger?'

'Anything sir. Anything you want.'

Sappho shivered when she heard herself saying this. She could hardly believe that she had spoken the words. But her fear of being taken before the priest Pelador drove her to it and she repeated, 'Anything, sir. Anything.'

The young man pulled Sappho to her feet. Her robe hung down over one shoulder, exposing her breast. Her pale pink nipple was hard and the young man took it between his thumb and forefinger. He pulled her forward on it. She drew her shoulders together slightly as the pain dug into her breast, but still she allowed herself to be led. He brought her out, in front of the statue. She looked around anxiously, in case anyone else could see. He brought her to the edge of the raised balcony on which they stood. From here, it was easy to see everything that was happening below and, if they chose, anyone below could look up and see Sappho.

'Here you can watch, but also may be watched. Now, squat down as you were before. That's right. Now open your knees, let me see that beautiful slit. I want to see its wetness.'

Sappho did as she was ordered. Trembling, she crouched at the edge of the raised balcony and opened her legs. Her cunt was still wet and, as she opened her knees to the scene below, she felt the warm wetness still on the swollen lips of her exposed slit.

'Now, continue what you were doing,' he said. 'Push your fingers in. Yes, like that, deeply.'

She slid her fingers into her cunt. They went in easily, she was so wet, so silky. Immediately she felt a wave of pleasure come over her. The penetration of her fingers unlocked the joy of watching the scene below, the exposure and the instructions of this unknown man. She was overwhelmed. She did not think she could hold her orgasm back. It was all too sudden. She threw her eyes up, her head went back and, as she tightened all over, she was shocked by the explosive convulsion which ran through her. It was as if she had been struck by a bolt of lightning. Her jaw dropped. She cried out — loudly, uncontrollably. She pushed her fingers into her cunt as far as they would go. She tipped forwards.

The young man grabbed her and stopped her falling. He held onto her as the shocks of her orgasm ran through her. She felt his hands against her skin as she let her ecstasy break over her and flow.

Sappho stared at the scene below. Pelador walked amongst the young girls, their bodies intertwined, blood streaking their pale skin, flowers sticking to them. As he stepped between them, they raised their hands towards him, clutching at the fleece that covered his back, reaching up to his thighs, rubbing themselves against him. He bent down to one and drew her up to her feet. He looked at her beautiful body then pushed her onto her knees.

The girl remained motionless as Pelador summoned three men. They stepped between the other girls and stood around the girl Pelador had selected. He motioned to the men. Two of them took her arms and bent her forward. The third raised a long cane and held it over the girl's back.

Sappho panted as she watched, aware of her own subjugation to the young man's will, her exposure, her overflowing pleasure. The young man gripped her tightly and she yielded to him without question as he bent her forward.

Pelador nodded to the man with the cane and slowly he drew it back. Still, the girl did not move. The girls around her became still. Everyone went silent. The man held the cane high and waited for Pelador's instruction.

Sappho bit her lips as she waited. She felt herself bending forward as more passion within her started to be released.

Pelador shouted loudly and, to gasps from the worshippers, the man brought the cane down across the young girl's buttocks. They cut across her skin and she fell forward with a piercing scream of agony.

'Again!' shouted Pelador and for a second time the cane was raised and brought it down cruelly onto the girl's taut skin.

As Sappho watched the punishment, she could not stop her fingers moving up and down her cunt. The action flowed like music within her. The crack of the cane as it came down against the young girl's skin, coincided with Sappho's fingers penetrating as far as they could. The relief as the man lifted the cane and the girl was saved for a moment from punishment came at the same time as Sappho withdrew her fingers almost completely. She rested them against her throbbing clitoris, allowing them to hold the fleshy mounds of her swollen, pulsating labia.

The cane came down repeatedly. Each time, the girl's legs bent and she fell forward. Each time she fell, the men propped her back again, forcing her legs straight and bending her at the waist. Sappho listened to the girl's screams and they fed the fire of her own desire. She wanted the young man who held her to grab her hair. She wanted him to throw her down and smack her across the breasts with the palms of his hands. She wanted him to bend her forward like the girl she was watching, and smack his hand across her buttocks as hard as he could. She wanted to scream out like the young girl. She wanted to fill the air with the sound of her suffering. She wanted to froth at the mouth with spit. She wanted to screech with pain until, finally, unable to stand any more, she would fall forward and, still with his hand smacking down across her buttocks, she would let her orgasm go.

Suddenly it was silent. Sappho lolled against the young man's grip, her eyes closed, her hand hanging loosely between her legs. She was dissipated, exhausted. Her ears buzzed in the silence. She heard her heart beating wildly. Her chest heaved as she gasped for breath as she struggled to regain control.

But her relief was short lived.

A sudden flurry of activity below brought shouts and the sound of running feet.

'Who is there?' men shouted. 'Who is watching our private ceremony?' 'Who has dared break the code of Pelador?'

Within seconds Sappho was surrounded by angry men. They pushed the young man aside, and grabbed Sappho roughly. She tried to struggle free, but it was hopeless. They ripped her robe from her, exposing her nakedness to the eyes of all and, holding onto her arms, they marched her between the staring congregation and down to Pelador.

Chapter 4

Pelador's anger

Sappho stood naked amidst the blood-smeared young girls. She trembled as Pelador approached. His mask was in the image of a ram's head. It had empty eyeholes and huge, rough-surfaced curling horns. The ram's fleece covered his back and was tied at his neck. Otherwise he was naked. His genitals were large, a pendulous penis hanging between two huge testicles supported in a stretched and venous scrotal sack. Sappho shivered when he stood closely before her.

He cocked his masked head from side to side, looking her up and down, sniffing at her like an animal, prodding her with a bloodstained, outstretched finger.

No one spoke. No one moved. Pelador stepped back and shook the glittering knife in the air angrily.

'You dare to defile our ceremony to Apollo,' he screamed. 'You have tainted our sacrifice. Our god, Apollo, will be angry. He will need something more to placate him for this sacrilege. What is your name?'

'I am ... ' she hesitated. She could not speak. She was too afraid. The men holding her tightened their grip and shook her insistently. She took a deep breath and tried again. 'I am, Sappho, sir. Daughter of Philoctetes. Sir, I meant no harm. I — '

'Meant no harm! Screeched Pelador. 'You have entered the sacred ceremony of Apollo! You have caused grave harm. And you will be punished. Here and now, you will discover what harming the god Apollo means! Bring her! Fetch the Chinese Master Wang. Prepare for the ceremony he learned from the Japanese of the east. Inform him that we wish the ceremony of Buk-ka-ke.'

Sappho was dragged to the centre of the sunken temple floor. The dead ram was removed from the altar block. Glistening pools of blood soaked the smooth marble surface, and shone in the twinkling light of the candles that surrounded it. Sappho trembled as she was led to the altar. She did not know what to expect, and the unexpected filled her with fear.

She struggled as they lifted her onto the altar block. She felt the now cold blood against her back as they forced her down. Her legs bent at the knees and hung over the end of the short altar. Her arms trailed at the sides. Her head hung backwards over the other end, stretching her throat and allowing her long hair to touch the ground. The men parted her knees, opening her legs to expose her slit. They tied ropes around each ankle, winding them methodically and carefully six times before knotting them, then pulling the free ends into iron rings that were bolted to the floor. They pulled her wrists down at the side of the massive marble block, wound ropes around them, this time eight times, and pulled them down into more iron rings at the side. They pulled her full auburn hair together and wound it tightly into a rope. They led it back and pulled the end securely into another iron ring. It held her head firmly in place, hanging down over the edge of the marble altar.

Everything she saw was upside down and the flickering lights, the scents, the chanting and the weaving naked bodies of the blood smeared girls all added to her confusion and fear.

A small man, dressed in an embroidered silk robe, came and stood at the head of the altar. His long, twisted moustache reached down onto his chest and his long, talon-like finger nails were as long again as his fingers. He reached his hands into the air and cried out in a shrill, high-pitched screech.

'Buk-ka-ke! Buk-ka-ke!'

Sappho sensed the air of excitement around her and she shuddered with fear. She saw the young men rushing around the altar, shouting wildly as they threw off their robes. The naked girls gathered around and, as the men formed a circle around the altar, the naked girls dropped to their knees behind them, waiting eagerly for what was about to happen.

'Buk-ka-ke! Buk-ka-ke!' the small Chinese man shouted again.

Each of the young girls, their faces now pressed against the young men's buttocks, circled their hands around the young men's hips and took hold of their cocks. Some were already hard, reaching out and throbbing, others needed coaxing and the young girls pulled them gently, stretching them, gripping them, stroking them, as they responded to their touch.

Sappho gasped. Her mouth fell wide open at the sight which surrounded her. She could not believe that this was happening, and yet she knew she could not doubt it.

The young men stepped closer to Sappho and the girls followed them, some now licking between the men's buttocks as they continued to massage their cocks. Sappho could see five of them, but she knew the circle of men surrounded her completely. Her nostrils filled with the scent of incense and, for a moment, she gagged as the acrid fumes filled her throat. She watched the cocks in the hands of the young girls. Their ends were swollen and hard and, each time the girls brought their hands up the shafts, the ends swelled more fully, reddened more deeply, and throbbed more heavily. The veins stood out on the stiff shafts as they stretched with excitement and desire. Sappho wanted to cry out, but her throat was too dry. Her eyes were wide and she could not close them. When she tried to lift her head, and she felt the tightness of her hair secured by the rope into the iron ring beneath her head, her terror only increased.

She had a sudden feeling of embarrassment, of fear of exposure. She felt freshly aware that everyone could see her nakedness. She tried to bring her knees a little closer together, but it was impossible, her ankles were tied too tightly. When she attempted to lift her hips in the hope she could twist herself sideways, it was impossible. She tried to swallow but that was impossible too — her neck was pulled back too severely. She gasped, let out a weak cry, and felt lost to the hopelessness of her despair.

The small Chinese man became increasingly urgent in his proclamation. 'Buk-ka-ke! Buk-ka-ke! Buk-ka-ke!' he screeched. 'Buk-ka-ke! Buk-ka-ke! Buk-ka-ke!'

Some of the young girls now forced their tongues between the men's buttocks. They licked at their anuses, delving the tips into the muscular rings dilated by excitement and need. The girls' blood-streaked bodies entwined the men, their eager hands holding onto the men's cocks, squeezing them, pulling them, wanting them. Sappho saw one of the girls draw back, resting for a moment, licking her tongue across her lips, tasting the man's anus, savouring it, relishing it. Sappho watched the girl closing her eyes again in ecstasy as she returned to the source of her joy.

Suddenly, Sappho felt heat on her face, and something was dripping across her cheek. A massive burst of semen had spurted onto her. She watched the man's pulsating cock, still in the young girl's hand, semen still streaming from it — copious, hot, sticky, white. She watched the glans beating, throbbing heavily as it spurted again, and she saw the young girl's hand tighten on the shaft, squeezing on it in time with its contractions, making it flow more eagerly, letting it run more plentifully.

Sappho tasted the semen as it ran down onto her lips. It was salty and thick. She licked at it, timidly at first, then she let it run inside her lips. She held it there, behind her upper lip, letting it run stickily and slowly into the side of her mouth. The taste changed as it went in further — it sweetened — and when it reached the inside of her cheek it was the sweetest liquid she had ever tasted.

Another burst hit her face, this time alongside her nose. She smelled it first — dry, almost bitter — then, as it ran down into the corner of her eye, she felt again its overpowering sweetness. Again she watched the girl's hand working on the stiff shaft, massaging it, tightening on it, holding the throbbing burst back for a second, then releasing it so that it squirted heavily and fast. Her vision blurred as it ran into her eye but, seeing through it, somehow only increased the capacity of her vision, made it more acute, more sharp.

Then she felt more. This time a drenching. She could not see where it came from but it covered her throat, heating her skin then cooling it as it ran up under her chin. She wondered if it would run as far as her lips but her attention changed as a full, soaking burst came right into her open mouth. It hit the roof of her mouth first, then her tongue. It poured in, filling her mouth, covering her tongue, sticking to her distended lips. It ran across the roof of her mouth to the back of her throat and, as more came into her mouth from another, it dribbled down her throat. She breathed heavily as it ran in. She felt her throat tightening, then closing as she gagged, but the tightness passed, and she relaxed and let it run freely into her.

Another burst splashed into her other eye. Another one on her forehead then one right into one of her nostrils. She choked as she sniffed at it. It burned her slightly as it ran up. The scent was so intense, beautiful, and she inhaled it deeply, sniffing it in, drawing it inside. More came onto her neck and face and when she breathed out, even with her mouth wide open, bubbles and frothing semen covered her lips. She was drenched in it. It ran down her throat and back into her nose. It flowed up her nose and back into her throat. It ran from her nostrils and from her mouth. She was covered in semen. She felt it on her breasts and on her stomach. She felt it running between the crack of her cunt and on the insides of her open thighs. She heard the Chinese man screeching 'Buk-ka-ke! Buk-ka-ke! Buk-ka-ke!' She saw more men congregating around her, and more young girls lining up behind them on their knees. Sappho was overwhelmed, covered in it, drowned by it.

Semen ran down her body, along her arms, across her knees and down her legs. She was covered in it. In some places it was thicker than others, but all her skin was covered in the translucent sheen of warm and sticky semen.

Finally, they released the ropes from the iron rings and she curled forward as the tension eased. She went to wipe her face, to clear her eyes and mouth and nose, but they did not allow her. They dragged her from the altar, flung her to the floor and made her kneel.

She let her head drop as she knelt, her arms by her sides and her wrists, still trailing the ropes which had bound them to the iron rings, against the sides of her hips. Semen ran from her nipples, dripping stickily in white glutenous strands down onto the tops of her thighs. She felt deeply shamed and humiliated. She opened her mouth and licked the semen from her lips. It was warm and its salty tang made her draw in breath. She licked some more and let it run onto her tongue. It sat in the hollow of her tongue and, as more ran in, it flowed over the sides, around her teeth and inside her cheeks. She raised her head and let it run to the back of her throat. Its scent filled her and she inhaled more through her nostrils. The semen ran down her throat and she swallowed on it, pulling it down, eating it, inhaling it, devouring it. She licked more, wiping the tip of her tongue as far as she could around her mouth, onto her chin and up into her nostrils. The odour absorbed her, the texture enraptured her and she wanted more. She looked through her bleary eyes and hoped the men that surrounded her would start again, would cover her again, would drown her in their semen so that she could satisfy her appetite for it.

One of the men raised her head; another offered her a silver goblet. He pressed it against her lips and she parted them as he tipped it. She felt the syrup of semen tipping into her mouth and she took it in and drank it deeply. It was an elixir to her, bringing her back to life, filling her with joy. She gulped at it, wishing her hands were free so that she could hold it herself and tip it back faster. It was a delectable sauce, sweet yet salty, thick and pure. Her throat gulped heavily as she took it in, and she drank deeply and eagerly until the goblet was empty.

The goblet was taken away. Sappho looked at the men around her. They stood in a circle, naked, the enfolding arms of the young girls wrapped around their hips. Their cocks, now limper and more fleshy, still held in the tight grasp of the naked girls that knelt behind them.

Then something different splattered on her face, something more liquid, less sticky, hotter, more drenching. Then some more, across her cheek, and, as some entered her mouth, she tasted the astringent tang of urine. The men were all urinating over her. It soaked her hair and ran down her face. It splashed on her shoulders and flowed down her arms and onto her bound wrists. It streamed across her breasts and stomach, wanting more, and opened her mouth and caught as much as she could. The semen was washed from her and her body sparkled brightly with the pale lemon sheen of the crystalline urine.

As she was cleaned, as she felt the full force of her degradation, she also felt a strange heat boiling inside her. It started in her throat, blocking it at first, tightening it, constricting it. It went into her stomach and she tensed as it gripped her. She felt it on the insides of her thighs, building quickly from a dull ache to a screaming pain. Finally, she felt it against the swollen edges of her cunt as it probed inside and gripped her very being. She could not keep her eyes open. She could only think of what was happening, what she was being put through, how she was a humiliated victim, how she was merely an object for the humbling abasement of the men who surrounded her. As their urine flowed over her she was filled with a sense of joy she would never have thought possible. Her skin was inflamed by their drenching liquid, setting it on fire at every point. Their eagerness to humiliate her filled her with pleasure. It was a fever that could only dissipate with the release of her ecstasy. And she could not hold it back. She opened her mouth as wide as she could. She slurped up their splashing urine. She cried out, screeching as loud as she could, yelling to them for more, beseeching them to allow her orgasm to flow.

She fell forward jerking, twitching, convulsing with its power. They continued to urinate on her and, with every drop that fell on her, she twitched again with joy.

Again she was lifted and this time tied face down onto the cold slab of the altar. She dropped her head forward as they retied her. Tighter this time, stretching her arms and legs around the corners of the marble slab, exposing her back and buttocks, displaying her perfect, dark anus and her swollen, soft and moisture-covered cunt.

The men and young girls stood aside as a beautiful young woman walked between them. She walked erect, her chin held high and her square shoulders draped with a white embossed robe. It was split at the front and parted provocatively with each assured step she took. Her breasts were full and rounded and her hard, compact nipples pushed out against the thin material of her robe. The sheeny material of her robe pressed hard against her hips and dipped tightly against her flat stomach.

Pelador stood back and slowly removed the ceremonial mask from his face.

'Ah, my daughter,' he said calmly. 'You are so beautiful, so elegant, so chaste. You are indeed the glittering prize of Troy. Even Helen cannot compete with you for beauty. And your purity is a tribute to Apollo. All marvel at how you resist the temptations of the flesh that others are so easily victim to. Daughter, Chryseis, how can I honour you? What can I give to you? How can I honour your beauty?'

Chryseis walked over to the altar and looked down at the captive Sappho. One of the naked men rushed forward and, grabbing Sappho's hair, lifted her head to show to his priest's daughter.

'She is so beautiful,' said Chryseis bending her head to look into Sappho's face. 'And she has no slave mark. She must be free. I want her as a friend. Yes, that is what you can give me father. I will take this beauty as my friend.'

'She is yours, my virtuous darling,' Pelador said, and turning to the young men that still surrounded Sappho. 'Release her! We are done with her!'

Chapter 5

Chryseis' game

'Bring her in here,' commanded Chryseis.

The young men carried Sappho's limp body into the opulent room, its high, brightly decorated ceiling a panoply to fine furnishings, vivid and expensive drapes and a deep, marble-edged bath. She was unconscious from exhaustion.

'Put her near the bath and send my girls in to bathe her. Now go! I will call you again in a while. I think there are services you will need to provide before the night is out.'

The young men bowed and backed away, never for a moment, daring to turn their back on the beautiful daughter of their revered priest of Apollo, Pelador. Chryseis giggled at their subservience, threw her mass of dark hair back and turned away.

Sappho lay on her side on the edge of the marble bath. Her arms trailed into the water and the ropes which were still attached to her wrists floated on its milk-coloured surface. Her long red-brown hair spread around her face in wet tangles. It highlighted the paleness of her skin and accentuated its smooth clarity. Ropes still hung from her ankles and harsh red marks on the insides of her thighs showed where she had been pulled down forcibly against the cold, sharp-edged altar.

Her closed eyes portrayed a chaste sweetness hard to attribute to a mortal.

Chryseis knelt down beside her and stroked Sappho's forehead.

'You are truly beautiful, Sappho, my new friend. I think Apollo himself must have sent you for me.'

Chryseis clapped her hands and six naked girls ran up beside her. Their hair had been cropped short and their pubic hair shaved. Each wore a golden necklace. One, Calliope, had a shiny ring piercing her clitoris. Another two had golden rings through their pert, dark pink nipples. All the girls knelt down beside Sappho, giggling and looking to their mistress for instructions. With their knees together their slits could not be seen, but the flats of their stomachs, descending to the beautiful disguising vee made by its union with the tops of their thighs, told more of the hidden delights in their absence than could ever be told by their obviousness.

'This is my new friend Sappho,' said Chryseis. 'When she wakes, you must do anything she wishes. You must take her instructions as if they were mine. But first, you must bathe her, shave her pubic hair and anoint her body with scent and oil. When you have done that, you can plait her beautiful russet hair, and file and paint the nails on her toes and fingers.'

The girls set straight to their task. Carefully they released the ropes on Sappho's wrists and ankles, first untying the knots then slowly unwinding the encircling rope until it was free. Sappho's wrists and ankles bore bracelets of red marks where the ropes had been. One of the girls with rings in her nipples, massaged Sappho's wrists while one of the other massaged her ankles.

They lifted Sappho carefully into the marble bath. The water, milky with oil and scent, enveloped her body and its warmth flushed the paleness of her skin with a rosy sheen. They held her face out of the water while they took large sponges and gently rubbed her whole body. Her coppery hair floated on its surface reaching out in lazy talons and twisting like a mermaid's in the fragrant water.

Two of the girls put their arms beneath Sappho and lifted her up in the water until her breasts, stomach and the fronts of her thighs were above the surface. Water lapped around the sweet slit of her cunt, sometimes obscuring it, sometimes exposing it. When it was above the water, droplets ran between the pink labia on each side of it, mixing with the glistening of Sappho's own moisture which shone on the delectable fleshy edges.

A tall girl mixed some sudsy soap and spread it around Sappho's cunt. She rubbed it all over her pubic hair and between her legs. As it foamed, some of it slid away into the water in tight bubbly masses. Calliope, the girl with the ring in her clitoris, fetched a shiny blade set in an oyster shell handle and waded into the bath. She stood alongside Sappho, naked, as they all were, the milky water lapping just above the top of her own shaven slit. She leant forward and moved the shiny blade along the top edge of Sappho's pubic hair. She worked slowly and carefully, lifting the blade away and cleaning it in a bowl held by another girl so that the cut hair did not go into the bath.

Calliope asked the girls holding Sappho to bring her a little higher and to part her legs. The girls raised Sappho in the water, opening her legs so that Calliope could work now on the outer edges of Sappho's beautiful crack. Calliope used the blade to cut all Sappho's pubic hair away. Finally, she checked carefully and saw that she had not missed any. Satisfied, she stood back and admired her handiwork. She nodded her satisfaction and the girls holding Sappho plunged her deep into the water to wash all the suds away. They lifted her out, her skin now perfectly naked, and laid her on the side of the bath. Two other girls came up straight away and massaged sweet-smelling oil into her skin. They rubbed eagerly where all the pubic hair had been cut from, lubricating the freshly shaved skin and the edges of Sappho's perfectly shaped and flawless, fleshy slit.

Chryseis bent down and looked at Sappho enquiringly. Sappho's hair was now tangled in long wet strands across her shoulders and the tops of her breasts. Chryseis lifted some of the strands away and laid them aside. She ran her hand down Sappho's stomach and across her hips. She let her hands rise up onto the taut skin that covered Sappho's hip bones, before sliding them down between her slightly open legs.

Chryseis drew the palm of her hand squarely against

Sappho's fleshy slit. Contact with the perfect skin made Chryseis close her eyes for a moment in a reverie of delight. She sighed and let out a slight moan. She probed her finger first into the centre of Sappho's flesh and then into the darkness that lay beyond the pink softness of the exterior. Chryseis' finger slid in easily, the edges of the outer flesh were moist and warm from the bath and the inner flesh, the channel of delight that led into the interior, was satiny with the natural moisture of desire.

Chryseis' little finger found a stray hair in the crack at the top of Sappho's thigh. It was short, had been cut once but had not been completely separated. Chryseis removed her fingers from Sappho's cunt. They glistened in the light of the flickering oil lamps. She held them up, sniffed at them, then licked them until all of Sappho's moisture had been removed. She swallowed deeply, inhaling the scent as it ran down her throat.

'Girl!' she shouted to Calliope. 'Come here. At once!'

Calliope ran over, expecting her mistress' congratulations. She dropped to her knees beside Chryseis, placed her flat palms on the tops of her thighs, opened her eyes wide and nodded willingly.

'Mistress?' she said. 'Have I done well?'

'Open your legs!' ordered Chryseis. 'Stay on your knees beside me, but open your legs wide.'

The girl did as she was instructed, still expecting a favour from her mistress.

Chryseis gave her fingers one last lick then thrust her hand forward between Calliope's legs. She grabbed the clitoral ring, twisted it and pulled it hard at the same time.

Calliope gasped, tried to close her legs and bent forward in pain. Chryseis stared hard at her and Calliope, fearful and surprised, bit her lips and held back her scream. Chryseis turned the ring further, twisting it a complete semicircle. Calliope's clitoris throbbed under the turn of the ring, but still she did not give way to her need to scream.

'Your job was not done properly,' said Chryseis, leaning forward and looking deeply into Calliope's tear-filled eyes. 'I will allow you to correct your mistake. But any further error and ... ' She twisted the ring even further and Calliope dropped her bottom lip and exhaled in a final bid to hold back her agony. ' ... and this,' said Chryseis pulling hard at the ring. ' ... will seem like the softest kiss.'

Calliope took up the blade again and, still with Chryseis holding firmly onto the ring, she bent over Sappho and put it close to the single, missed hair. Her hand trembled and the blade would not stay still. Tears began rolling down her cheeks and Chryseis, seeing her fear, twisted harder on the ring, now turning it three quarters of a full revolution. Calliope tried again to close her knees together, hoping that she could trap Chryseis' hand and stop it inflicting further pain, but her action only increased Chryseis' anger. Chryseis called two of the girls over. She made them sit on each side of Calliope and hold her legs wide.

The girls did as they were told, enthusiastic to carry out their mistress' orders as well as to maintain the distraction the attention on Calliope provided from their mistress' anger. Calliope struggled against them but, when she did, Chryseis only tightened the twist on the ring further. She twisted it now a full circle from its starting point and the pain was so intense that Calliope submitted completely to the girls.

Calliope sat on the upturned soles of her feet, her knees widespread, and her cunt exposed and open. Chryseis' finger held tightly onto the fully turned clitoral ring.

'Now get to work, or my kindness will run out,' exhorted Chryseis.

Calliope tried again. Her hand still quaked with fear, and she could not place the blade smoothly on Sappho's skin, but she did not dare hold back. The sharp edge of the blade came against the single hair. She drew it forward, hardly knowing what would happen. The blade sliced the hair and Calliope drooped her head in relief.

Chryseis smirked. She drew her finger out of the ring, but still held it in place, twisted as it was, with her other hand.

'And for doing such a bad job to begin with ... ' Chryseis licked out her wet tongue and re-inserted her finger into the ring, already tightening the hard bud of Calliope's clitoris by a full turn. ' ... I will give you an extra reward.'

Chryseis held the ring there for a moment, savouring what had not yet happened, enjoying the fragrant moment of potential. Suddenly, she lurched forward and twisted the ring as far as the flexibility in her wrist would allow.

Calliope threw her head back and shrieked. Spit ran from the sides of her lips and sprayed in showers from her gaping mouth. She shrieked again and Chryseis laughed. She squirmed down onto her shoulders, lying between the tortured girl's legs as she attempted to twist her body over so that she could apply even more rotation to the ring.

Without warning, Sappho's eyes opened wide as she regained consciousness. She did not know where she was, she could not imagine. As her head was filled with the screeching cries of Calliope, she drew her hands up over her exposed breasts in an instinctive act of self-protection.

Chryseis, distracted, let go her grip on her victim who fell back, choking on her scream, clutching her hands between her legs.

'Take her away,' ordered Chryseis. 'I will decide tomorrow if I still want her to serve me.' Chryseis pulled herself close to the still confused Sappho. 'You are truly so beautiful,' she said as straight away she began playing with Sappho's wet hair. 'And hungry with desires, I think.'

'I do not know what you mean, mistress. You embarrass me,' said Sappho, slowly coming to her senses.

'First, you do not call me "mistress",' said Chryseis. 'I am your friend. You call me "Chryseis". And your embarrassment is well placed for I know what I say is true. I have seen it in you. I have watched your pleasure.'

'Mis ... Chryseis,' Sappho said nervously. 'Chryseis. I am sure you are mistaken. I have not been with a man. I am too chaste for desires.'

'No woman is ever too chaste for desire,' shrugged Chryseis. Sappho relaxed back on the heavy satin throws, a little more at ease but still confused. 'My dearest Sappho,' continued Chryseis. 'I watched as you enjoyed the 'buk-ka-ke'. I watched you revelling in the streaming semen, bathing in it, washing yourself in it. And I saw your pleasure when they urinated on you. I watched you drink your fill. I know your desires. If you want more, I can arrange it any time you wish. I can have more men brought, men specially selected by Master Wang for their copious semen, and for how far and how hard they can eject it. Would you like that Sappho? Would you like that?'

'Yes ... Well ... Yes ... ' said Sappho, embarrassed that Chryseis had seen her and embarrassed that her joy had been so obvious. At the same time, she could not escape the knowledge that she had been excited by the delights of being watched. 'Yes, I would,' she affirmed. 'Could you truly arrange it?'

'Of course. There is nothing I cannot do. My father is the priest of Apollo. His worshippers cater to my every need. They are so afraid of Pelador, and so afraid of Apollo, there is nothing they will not do. If you want buk-ka-ke you can have it. If you want thrashing, there are many experts here who will oblige. They can thrash you for hours and only leave the faintest red marks on your buttocks, your breasts or the soles of your feet. Or, if you prefer, they can create red, ridged weals wherever you want, angry and sore and impossible to bathe because of the pain. Or whipping. In any way you can imagine and in ways you could never imagine. I have had girls whipped with flails and belts, with wooden paddles, and tightly bound braids. I have had them whipped for hours or even days and they have begged for more. So exquisite has been the pain, my dear Sappho, they have begged for more. You can be suspended by your wrists or ankles or both. You can be hung up as long as you want, and perhaps take a thrashing or a whipping while you hang there, incapable of protecting yourself, at the mercy of your torturer. Just think of that, Sappho! Watching the flail cut into your nipples or seeing its ragged talons biting the insides of your legs and the soft outer edges of your cunt. Or perhaps you like your mouth plugged? It can be filled with any sort of gag imaginable, large balls, serrated devices made from precious metals, iron bars, and, of course, cocks! You can have as many cocks as you wish. There are so many men available in this city. Master Wang can arrange anything. He does things all the time for me. I wanted to see a girl squeezed into a tiny iron cage and he brought me one. I kept her there all day as she urinated and cried and begged to be released. I had water thrown over her for an hour afterwards. I like that in particular — drenching — sometimes I have it done to me. It is delectable. Sappho, especially if the water is ice-cold. It is the most delightful pleasure imaginable. That is something you must try.'

Sappho smiled but she was mesmerized. She had not even thought of such things. She did not know what to say.

'You look mystified, my dear new friend Sappho. Perhaps you do not believe me. Watch. I will show you.'

Chryseis recalled the naked men and had them line up.

'As you seem so uncertain, I think I will choose something for you. Something simple but something that will encourage you. Yes, I have it!'

One of the girls with rings in her nipples was told to bend down on all fours. Chryseis helped position Sappho, first kneeling her behind the girl then bending her forward over her back. Chryseis made Sappho wrap her arms around the girl and push her fingers through the rings in her nipples. The girl winced as the rings pulled and stretched out her flesh.

Sappho felt nervous — excited and filled with anticipation. But she was afraid of what might happen — worried in case she could not bear it.

The girls made sure Sappho's buttocks were high, and that they were squeezed open so that the swollen shape of her delectable crack poked between them. Two of the girls knelt beside Sappho's head and cradled her chin on their joined hands. She felt the centre of attention, as though everything was happening because of her. There was no sense of the excitement of being discovered — she was fully exposed — but that exposure thrilled her deeply. She gulped in expectation, and swallowed hard against the strain that the girl's cradling hands caused on her extended throat.

One of the naked men was sent for a thin, flat leather strap. He brought it and stood behind Sappho's raised buttocks. He waited. Another man was told to kneel in front of Sappho's face. She looked at his bulging cock as he held it before her and she could not stop herself licking her lips which were dried by the tension of the building excitement and the unreleased anticipation.

The first blow across her buttocks surprised her and she gasped loudly in shock. She waited for the second, and the third, and tightened herself in ecstatic expectation. Each smacking sting increased her pleasure. The first few strokes only made contact with her buttocks but, as she welcomed more, she opened them enough for the edges of her cunt to receive the same punishment. That was where she found the greatest pleasure. The rhythmic strokes against her tender flesh caused her to drool and roll up her eyes. She was overtaken by it, enveloped by it, and as the beating got harder, fiercer, she welcomed it more. As the thrashing continued, and her joy brimmed higher to the surface, she felt the throbbing glans of the cock in front of her against her gaping lips. She opened her mouth as wide as she could and, as she took it in, and sucked hard and swallowed it as deep as she could, she rose against the beating strap and collapsed forward in a surge of uncontrollable joy. She sucked and gasped and gagged and swallowed and burned all over and only wanted more.

When the cock was finally drawn from her mouth there was no semen, she had drained it completely. She dropped her jaw for more.

Each man took his turn to continue the thrashing, each one harder than the one before. And each one took his turn to fill her mouth and drive his cock deeply into her throat as he finished copiously and she sucked it all.

Chryseis sat on cushions watching. A young girl masturbated her. She was distracted only for a few moments when Master Wang appeared behind a curtain. Chryseis pointed towards the girl who had the ring though her clitoris and nodded.

Master Wang, the Chinese who organised buk-ka-ke throughout the city, slipped away from the temple of Apollo. He held a leather leash which was firmly attached to a collar around the neck of Calliope. He crept through a labyrinth of passageways and alleys, pulling the girl behind him, until he arrived at a narrow iron grating door in a thick bricked wall. He reached up and rang a bell on a heavy iron chain.

'Who is it that seeks entry?' a deep forbidding voice asked from within.

'Praxis. It is me, Wang. I have a little something for you. A pretty little something, I can assure you. She is from the best of places too. From the temple of Apollo.'

A large bald head appeared behind the grating. Two copper rings dangled loosely from tattooed ears and another ring hung from a pulpy, reddened nose. The head leant forward into the dim light in the alley and revealed two roughly sewn sockets where eyes had once been.

'Bring her in,' said Praxis gruffly as slowly he opened the grating and let the Chinese in. 'I hope she is strong enough, Wang. I have found many new ways of torturing the slaves who find their way into my emporium. And some fail me before I am done with them'

'If this one does, Praxis, I know of another who certainly will not.'

51

Chapter 6

The raid on Troy

As Achilles and Ajax set out for a surprise raid on Troy, Eva was left to suffer. After their humiliation on the beach, she and the other women had been rounded up and driven into a compound made from animal hides stretched on stakes. The compound was encircled by dogs, all straining on taut leather leashes tied to iron rings driven on spikes into the ground. The women were forced to kneel most of the day then, at night, they were made to crawl on all fours and do the bidding of their masters, the cruel Greeks. Each night they were beaten, sometimes with long canes, sometimes with whips or flails. They all screamed as they were punished, but Eva less than the rest. She felt it honourable to be strong in her suffering, to show the others she was of royal heritage — brave and forbearing. But her silent suffering brought its own perverse penalty. The more she trapped it in — the longer she suppressed her screams and torment — the more it inflamed her senses, her passion, her need. The longer she trapped her passion, the wilder were her screeching exclamations as ultimately they exploded in a turmoil of ecstasy, pain and pent-up desire.

One night, two of the dogs were removed from their leashes and Eva and another woman were collared and tied up in their place. By the morning the other woman was howling like all the other dogs. She was crawling around on her hands and knees, sniffing the others, drooling spit, licking at them, growling. Eva, though, was still where she had been left, never having moved, never having given in to the animal instincts which could have so easily been aroused. They released the other woman, but even though Eva was left there for two more nights, still she remained in control of herself, her body and her desires.

Achilles came to see her sometimes. He admired her

strength but she was also a challenge to him. There was not a woman yet he had failed to conquer, and he did not intend that Eva should be the first.

Eva watched the raiding party depart. She remained pinioned well off the ground against the side of a ship. A large ball was bound tightly into her mouth, her arms and legs were spread wide and tied by ropes into heavy iron rings fixed into the ship's boards. The large smooth ball was crafted from stone. A hole was drilled in it through which was passed an iron rod with a ring on each end. Black leather straps looped through each ring. They led up on each side of Eva's nose then, on the bridge, were twisted together before pulling tightly across her forehead. The twisted straps were stretched along the middle of her long red hair, then twisted again in a knot at the back of her neck before returning along her jawline and back into the rings on the iron rod.

Eva flared her nostrils and breathed in deeply. She knew that Achilles and Ajax would soon be back and that when they returned they would have new ways of increasing her seemingly unending suffering. Some dogs sniffed around her. She glared down at them with her piercing green eyes and they ran away.

Two sailors, bored by their absence from home, and tired of the never-ending encampment on the beach, stopped to look up at her.

'She is a rare beauty Crios,' said the first as he poked a stick he was carrying into Eva's foot. 'A German princess some say. And with an appetite for pain and suffering that is impossible to satisfy. While others whine, she bears all, they say.'

'Perhaps she has not had enough of a test yet, Abas,' said the second.

'Perhaps not,' said Abas smirking. 'Perhaps she has met her match today though. Perhaps Crios and Abas can bring her to her knees.'

A shudder passed through Eva. She fixed her stare ahead. She did not know how much more she could take.

'I think we might just do that,' laughed Crios, running the point of the stick along the base of Eva's foot.

Eva licked the back of the stone ball on her mouth. It was cold from the chill of the night. Her mouth was stretched as wide as possible and her face felt strained and tight. Her teeth pressed against the stone, top and bottom, and even though it was perfectly smooth, they grated loudly if there was any movement between them. She smelled the leather strap that held it in place, and its tightness against the back of her neck. She squirmed her head from side to side in a vain attempt to ease it.

'I think she is trying to ask us something,' said Crios, still pulling the point of the stick along the sensitive soles of her foot.

'Yes, she wants the same done to the other foot I think.'

Abas laughed, picked up a stick and started doing the same to her other foot.

Her ankles had been bound tightly — twelve revolutions of the rope before they were fixed into the iron rings. She could hardly move her feet at all but, as Crios and Abas drew the points of the sticks along her delicate soles, she could not stop herself from flexing them in a pointless effort to prevent the irritation. Bending the skin gave a moment's relief, but as soon as the points came in contact again the movement that had brought some respite had now made them even more sensitive. If she kept her feet still, the irritation was lessened, but so was her ability to keep them still. The irritation, the tickle, the glancing sense of almost unmade contact, shivered up her calves and into her knees. It travelled like a stream of fast flowing water, seeking out every place where there was sensitivity, every place where she could feel contact with sensation. It ran up her thighs and joined together, doubling in its force before, like a clasping claw, it grasped her fleshy cunt. First it went into the swollen flesh of her outer labia, enriching it with a slight burning. Then it ran along the crack between them — fizzing, tingling, setting her on fire. Before entering her, before penetrating her body fully, it ran around her anus causing it to contract then dilate in a quick regular rhythm, uncontrolled, of its own accord.

Eva licked the back of the ball. It was warming now. She wished she could bite down onto it, to relive some of the tension, but she could not, did not dare. Then, like a tantalising tentacle of fire, the sensation that arose on the soles of her feet, entered her cunt. It burned her clitoris. It was as if it had been grasped by fiery fingers. It boiled the moisture that clung to the inner flesh of her crack. It burned as deeply into the warm darkness as possible, then, with nowhere else to go, it exploded into her whole body. It filled her completely and, with a sudden jerk of passion, she submitted to the overwhelming storm of ecstasy.

Spit ran on the inside of the ball in her mouth, but it was too tightly fixed to allow any to run out. She gulped and swallowed hard and her teeth involuntarily ground against the stone ball. She could not swallow and tried again. This time it made her choke and, as she coughed, she bit harder, more painfully, onto the unforgiving ball.

The sensation from her feet burst in her head. She saw sparkles in front of her eyes and they ran out in glittering showers, erupting in a wild tempest of light. She gasped again, and coughed, and she was overcome by the light of her joy as it filled her mind completely.

She heard herself groaning with pleasure. She tried to stop it. She licked her tongue flatly against the now hot stone in her mouth. She allowed the spit to build up behind her stretched lips and on the inside of her cheeks. She squeezed her eyes up tightly. But nothing could stop it. She groaned again and gave up trying to hold it back.

She was not aware of it stopping but, when she saw Crios

beside her, on a ladder, untying the ropes at her wrists, she knew it must be over. At last, she was being released. Her suffering had come to an end. She was being saved.

She turned her head and looked at him, young, vigorous and handsome. He did not return her glance. Her arm came free but it had been kept stretched wide for so long it stayed there, sticking out rigidly as if she was nailed to a crucifix. Crios moved to the other side and undid her other wrist.

Eva stayed against the side of the boat, balancing now on her ankles, in place only because of her stiffness. She dropped her head forward, relieved by what she thought was happening and she toppled forward. She arched out against the fulcrum of her ankles, falling stiffly away from the boat side then, as she described a semicircle, coming back to the lowest point at the bottom of her fall. The curvature of the boat's hull allowed her to swing beneath it before rocking back to the perpendicular. She hung, now upside down, by her ankles, her arms stretched down but just off the ground, her long red hair trailing down in a rich, fiery tangle of shining curls.

The sudden shock of falling, of stopping at the bottom of the fall, made Eva bite hard onto the stone ball. Pains shot through her as her teeth ground against the inflexible surface. Her nostrils opened wide as her heaving lungs demanded breath. Her rapidly beating heart throbbed in her constricted chest. She swung for a few moments, looking down to the ground, reaching with outstretched fingers in a vain attempt to reach it. She needed to swallow but could not, and again she coughed as the spit that filled her mouth ran into the back of her emptily gulping throat.

She did not have time to realise her situation. She felt heat between her legs — sudden, penetrating, overcoming. Abas had his face against her spread cunt, his chin against her anus, his hands against the insides of her thighs. He delved his long hot tongue inside, searching out the fleshiness of her crack, its moisture, its fragrance. Eva felt it probing deep, lapping up her own moisture, depositing its own. How could she wish for him to stop when she wanted more? How could she deny the pain of her humiliation when it was her very dishonour, her disgrace, which was causing her to want it.

Even against the weight of her body and the pressure on her ankles which supported it, she allowed her hips to rise. She needed him to know that she wanted more, that she wanted it deeper, wetter, hotter. She wanted him to chew on her flesh, as if he was consuming her.

He buried his face against her cunt. She allowed her anus to widen against his chin, hoping to pull it close against the pulsating muscle — it too wanted filling. He pressed down against her and she felt his chin against the inner edges of the dilated muscular ring. His tongue went into her cunt as far as it could, and she rose higher and allowed her orgasm to flow. She wanted to grasp his head between her legs, to hold him there while she convulsed against his lips. But her bonds constrained her from doing it, made her convulsion that much more potent. She felt her anus throbbing against his chin and her cunt tightening around his tongue. The wetness of his spit mixed with the moisture of her cunt. It ran between her spread buttocks and into the small of her back. She bit hard onto the stone in her mouth and heaved rhythmically with the beats of her ecstatic dissipation.

As he pulled away, she felt the draught of coolness across her flesh. It calmed her for a moment and she relaxed. Her muscles lost their tension then, unexpected and unprepared for, she felt a cutting lash across her back.

The first one surprised her. She did not really know what it was. Her face was directed towards the side of the boat, and she could not see what was happening. The second allowed her to realise what was happening. The third simply hurt. And the pain increased with every blow as Crios stood back on the beach and thrashed her with his wide leather belt.

'Now we will see if she can stand the suffering of the belt!' he shouted excitedly as he drew the heavy belt back again. 'There is no woman yet who has!'

Time and again he drew back the belt and brought it down on Eva's taut skin. She twisted in agony as they fell. Her back and shoulders soon became sensitized so much that each new blow made her giddy with the penetration of its pain. Her buttocks took blows as well — hard and lashing blows, blows well aimed and blows that missed their mark. Crios raised the belt vertically as well, and brought it down squarely against her exposed cunt. It smacked against her flesh and sent shivering pains out into every part of her body. They culminated in stinging spasms of agony in the tips of her already hard and throbbing nipples.

She took it all. Holding the ball tightly in her mouth, breathing hard through her nostrils. Allowing the pain to feed her own desires. She took it all. For some reason, the worst was on the insides of her thighs. The pain there was so sharp, so brittle, and it made her squirm and the squirming made her dizzy and that made her feel like vomiting. She tasted it in her throat and was filled with terror that it would erupt from within her, and that it would have nowhere to go past the plugging stone in her mouth.

Crios finally tired. He licked her cunt and along some of the red lines his belt had left on her pale skin. She closed her eyes and allowed the pain to flow through her. She panted as, slowly, it began to dissipate.

'Abas. Wash her down!' shouted Crios. 'We will give her another taste another time. She will not forget us, I am sure of that. Yes, douse her and take the heat of my belt away from her. Let her cool before we leave her to the dogs.'

Eva hung there, staring though bleary eyes at the wooden planks of the boat. The salty moisture of her own sweat burned into the reddened stripes from the belt, and the stinging pain was heightened by the heat of the sun as it burned down on her exposed skin.

Her body twisted as a drenching bucket of water was emptied between her wide-open legs. It splashed against her sore, dilated cunt, flowing onto it and around it before rushing down her stomach and between her buttocks. Eva gasped in shock and held her breath. By the time she was breathing in again through her wide-open nostrils, the water was gurgling past her nose. She sniffed some of it in without realising, and she choked on it. Its acrid saltiness burned her throat. Another splash as another bucket of water was thrown against her already soaked cunt. Its flow took the same route, but this time quicker, reaching her nose in copious amounts and running straight into it without her breathing in. She twisted again and brought her hands up to her face — it was as if she had only just realised they were free.

She tried to shield her face but it was impossible. Each new deluge of water ran faster than the first — got to its goal quicker, was more of a deluge.

She felt the full force of it against her cunt and anus. The natural reaction of her body was to close itself against the torrent, but Eva did not want that. And, even had it been possible, she would not allow it to happen. The feeling of the warm salty water flowing inside her cunt and up into her anus, was something she did not want to avoid. Slowly she let her hands fall away from her face. She watched them trailing down towards the wet sand beneath her head. As they dangled loosely before her wide open eyes, she saw, with their surrender, her own yielding — her complete submission — to the controlling power of her cruel torturers.

Eva did not resist them as they took her down and stretched her out on her back. She was too exhausted — too used to do anything to save herself. She lay on the hot sand limp and soaking, her skin glistening in the bright light of the sun, her hair as radiant as its fiery rays. She dropped her head to one side and pressed her tongue hard against the back of the hot, stone ball that still gagged her mouth tightly. She was not exhausted by the men's humiliation of her, nor of the pain they had inflicted on her. No, if it was only so simple she would not be so confused. She was exhausted by her own delight. The shocks of her ecstatic convulsions had filled her body until it overflowed. She was exhausted by her own passion. Worn out by her own uncontrollable ecstasy.

Crios and Abas pulled Eva's arms and legs wide using the ropes which still dangled from them. They drove some long spikes deeply into the sand and fixed her onto them by the ropes. They kicked sand over her before leaving, laughing and pushing at each other. The gritty sand stuck to her wet body. It darkened for a few seconds as it soaked up the moisture, but quickly returned to its bright, silvery colour as the heat from the sun dried it out again. Some dogs came around, sniffing at her, licking her, whining their attention, growling possession of their new found prize. She tightened her muscles and stared up into the wide blue sky. She thought of home, of freedom and a life without pain — and she thought of her pleasures and how they had been born of captivity and suffering.

Chapter 7

The ill-treatment of Praxis' slaves

Chryseis and Sappho crouched behind the iron grill let into the wall of the disused prison cell above the training area of Praxis' slave house. It was here he kept his slaves, and here he trained them to provide pleasure to anyone who would pay enough. Anyone searching for the most beautiful women or men, trained in the most extraordinary sexual practices, knew that Praxis could oblige. He would provide slaves that were disobedient or obedient, young or old, versed in every technique, or chaste and unknowing. He would make sure that whatever was wanted could be fulfilled, whatever was imagined could be had.

Although Praxis' eyes had been put out by Ajax years ago, he was no less aware of everything that went on. He prowled around his training camp with a brass-ended rod in his fist, the ever-present Master Wang acting as his eyes and his informant. If anything displeased Praxis, he struck out at it with his rod, punishing anyone who acted against him or who, for whatever reason, he did not consider warranted his continuing patronage. Instead of his sense of sight, Praxis used his sense of smell. He smelled things wherever he went. Sometimes it was objects, sometimes it was simply suspicion. He would hold out his rod and stop, then, sniffing the air until he was satisfied it was in order to move on, bring his rod down and continue. Sometimes he reached out, grabbed people and sniffed them, deeply inhaling their scent as he ran his nose across their faces, their hands and feet, or their genitals. If he could not get what he wanted from scent, he touched things, mauled them with his large sinewy hands, and licked them — there was nothing that escaped the unseeing Praxis. His slaves lived in fear of his knowledge and his vicious temper, knowing that if they crossed him or displeased him their future was both dark and short.

Chryseis came here frequently, to this small cell with the iron grill. She usually masturbated as she watched the suffering slaves. Sometimes she brought one of the men in her service so that she could use him as well. There were old bits of rope, thongs and unrepaired whips littering the tiny room. Sometimes, she would get the man to masturbate her, instructing him carefully on the method first. She liked him to rest his finger at the top of her crack, just inside the slit, and move it up and down so that he squeezed the flesh of her cunt which put pressure on the tip of her clitoris. Sometimes she would masturbate him. She liked to hold a cock when it was stiff, she revelled in its venous texture, its heat, its hardness. She liked to watch it thicken and deepen in colour when it was about to eject its semen, and she liked to suck in the semen when finally, as she held the shaft tightly, it was spurted from the pulsating cock. Usually, when she did this, she kept one of her fingers in the man's anus and did not take it out until it had stopped contracting with delight. Once she kept it there for an hour and the man's cock hardened again so, after holding it and massaging it in the way she liked, she sucked more semen from it and still had not removed her finger. Sometimes she would tell the man to tie her as he wished and as tight as he wanted. Sometimes, and against her protestations, he would leave her there, bound and unable to escape, until the next day.

Chryseis smiled at Sappho and pulled her face down close to the grill.

'Look! It is Praxis. How evil he looks,' said Chryseis, barely able to control her excitement. 'Look at the ugly scars where his sockets were sewn up by Master Wang after Ajax put his eyes out. They say he never made a sound as it was done.'

Praxis marched into the courtyard with Master Wang at his side.

He stopped and held up his brass-ended rod.

'Wang! Bring me the new girl! And the others you have

been collecting. I must find out what we have. We have clients to satisfy!'

Master Wang waved to some men carrying short, double tailed leather quirts. They ran forward and took his instructions.

At the far end of the courtyard were two heavy wooden doors to the outside. In front of them were three iron braziers, alive with sparking red flames. Along the one wall was a row of small cages stacked three high. On the opposite wall was a timber scaffolding with a water tank at the top of it. On the wall directly below where Chryseis and Sappho huddled behind the grill, was a row of beautiful, naked girls all chained together through rings in tight leather collars around their necks. In the centre of the courtyard was a large timber cylinder, an axle through its centre resting on a crossed timber mounting on each side.

'Sappho,' whispered Chryseis. 'Have you ever seen anything so exciting?'

Sappho, her eyes wide with amazement, shook her head, but could not answer.

Chryseis grabbed Sappho's shoulders and pulled her down closer against the grill. Sappho felt the cold of the rough iron grating on her face. Its metallic smell excited her and she inhaled it deeply.

Sappho peered down into the courtyard. The men Master Wang had instructed went to the cages stacked against the wall. Sappho could hardly believe it. Each one had a young woman inside. There was barely enough room to accommodate their bodies. Each of them was crouched down tightly, their arms between their legs and their faces pressed down against their knees. One of the cage doors on the top tier was opened and the woman was pulled out. She fell to the ground and shouted out in pain. Two of the men struck out at her with their quirts. She screamed, but could not stand up. She remained huddled in the same position she had been forced into in the cage. They struck her again and slowly she stretched herself until, with more kicking and beating, she managed to stand up straight. Her tear-stained face was expressionless and her mouth gaped open in despair.

Master Wang kicked out at her and she scuttled into the centre by the timber cylinder. One by one, each cage was opened and all the women were brought out. Some were so stiff they had to be beaten hard before they stood up straight. Some squirmed on the dusty ground in fear, crying and wailing. One urinated as she managed to get to her knees, and one of the men lay beneath the stream and drank it. All the women were naked and all had their hair cropped short. They huddled together, some holding their forearms and hands over their breasts. Others pushed their hands down between their legs, in a pitiful effort to reduce their exposure or protect some hoped for scrap of dignity that may still be left to them. Master Wang instructed the men with the quirts to thrash the women's legs until they dropped their hands by their sides. The men followed his orders enthusiastically until, in the end, all the women stood upright, to attention, with the palms of their hands at the sides of their thighs.

Their exposure excited Sappho. She imagined herself in their place, being driven around the courtyard where there was no hiding place. Being unable to cover herself or turn away. Being the victim of anonymous and cruel men. Being thrashed and beaten, and ordered to humiliate herself. Being forced to submit herself to the peering eyes and mockery of others. She felt a moistness between the crack of her cunt and pushed her hand down between her legs. As soon as her fingers touched the crack it opened. Her fingertips slid inside the satiny valley. She licked her lips as her flesh responded with a gentle throbbing and an increased warmth. She pressed the palm of her hand against her tingling, hardening clitoris.

Chryseis saw what Sappho was doing and, pulling Sappho's hand away, replaced it with her own. The shock of difference sent an anxious thrill through Sappho's body. She felt the heat of Chryseis' fingers against the soft, moist flesh of her cunt, pressing herself against them, welcoming them, inviting them to enter. Chryseis did not have to press, the merest touch allowed her fingers to slip between the swollen edges of Sappho's cunt. Sappho licked back a drop of spit that ran from the corner of her mouth and swallowed it with a gulp. She stared down hard into the courtyard.

Sappho watched the women being bent over — each one in turn forced down onto her knees. If one looked up, she received a keenly delivered stroke from a cutting leather quirt. Every time these double ended strips of leather smacked across one of the women's backs, or her buttocks, or breasts, Sappho tensed herself and breathed in sharply. It was as if it was happening to her. It was as if seeing the women punished allowed Sappho herself to feel their punishment. As the slapping, flattened end of the quirt hit down on the women's skin, Sappho felt it against her own. It felt so real. It made her jump with the shock, recoil from the pain and sting with the heat of hurt as it penetrated her. And each time this happened she tensed her thighs, rose up a little and drew Chryseis' fingers further into her own delectable, wet cunt. The image of pain and suffering that met her eyes, mixed with the ever-deepening penetration of Chryseis' fingers to form a delectable blend of anguish and pleasure.

Praxis paraded amongst the women. He touched one with his brass-ended rod. He dug it forcefully into one of her breasts, and made her stand. He held his face close to hers and sniffed around her mouth and nostrils. She whimpered and he grabbed her cheeks, as quickly and accurately as if he could see.

'I'll give you reason to whine, my smooth skinned beauty,' he said laughing. 'You will whine louder than ever you could have imagined.'

He squeezed her cheeks hard and sniffed inquiringly at

her panting breath. He let her go and ran his free hand down across her breasts and onto the flat of her smooth stomach. He cocked his head to one side and rested his hand at the base of her stomach. He attended to the feel of her skin, sensing its warmth, its smoothness, its pliability. Then, with a suddenness that made her jump, he continued with his hand until it reached the top of her naked crack. He prised the soft flesh open and wedged his fingertip beneath the curved entrance the pressure of his fingertip caused. He pulled it upwards, stretching it, and she raised herself on it, unwilling to show him her distress yet unable to stand any more mistreatment.

'A fine one, Wang!' he shouted. 'She has the flesh of youth. And the moisture to go with it! And she responds nervously, afraid of what might happen to her. Yes, she is perfect for a client who needs a frightened fawn. Wash her down. We will keep her for training.'

Master Wang grabbed the girl from behind. He pulled her elbows together and marched her to the side of the courtyard. He pushed her hard against the timber gantry and she cried out as she thumped against it. He leant against her — his body pushed between her shoulder blades — and held her in place. She struggled but her breasts were pressed hard against the timber upright of the gantry, and Master Wang had pinned her so tight from behind, it was impossible. She looked up appealingly toward the grill where Sappho and Chryseis crouched.

They both ducked down in case the young woman saw them. Sappho tensed her muscles and Chryseis fingers were suddenly enclosed more tightly by her succulent flesh. Straight away, Sappho pushed herself down hard on Chryseis' fingers. She lifted herself up then pushed down again, opening her thighs and spreading the entrance of her cunt to let in more.

'How deep do you want it?' asked Chryseis. 'How deep?'

'As deep as I can have it,' replied Sappho, staring again

at the woman below, sensing her fear, picking up her vulnerability, and feeding on her exposure. 'As this woman's suffering increases, so I want your fingers to go deeper. When she is screaming for mercy, I want you to release my joy. Only then do I want to feel the flow of my ecstasy.'

'How will I do that, dear Sappho?'

'By going faster. As she screams more, by going faster. And by going deeper as her terror increases. And, when you are certain, by entering my anus. Yes, that is what I will need. When it is time, when I am ready, I want you to thrust your fingers in me there as well. They must go in hard. You must force them deep. You must have no mercy. I want to feel them against my innards. Oh, yes. Up in my bowels. I do that to myself. I squat down and it opens it. It is easy to enter then. I use two fingers and I keep my cunt full while I enter my anus from the back. My fingers slip in so deep when I am ready. It is as though I am full to brimming. Am I bad for asking you this? Chryseis, am I bad? Can you do that? Can you do that for me? Oh Chryseis, tell me I am not bad. Tell me.'

'My beautiful Sappho. You could never be bad. Your sweetness overflows. I will do that for you. I promise. When the moment is right. I will bring you all the pleasure you need. I will not hold back. Do not fear.'

Sappho smiled and pressed her soft wet cunt against Chryseis' hand. Trustingly, she tightened her muscles and drew Chryseis' fingers in further, now knowing that her pleasure was assured.

She looked down again at the woman pinned against the timber gantry. Wang beckoned two men who tied leather thongs tightly around the woman's wrists and ankles. They forced a large leather ball into her mouth and secured its trailing leather ties tightly behind her head. She looked terrified. She shrank back against the gantry as if, somehow, there was escape to be found in retreat.

Sappho drank in the woman's fear. She looked deeply

into the pathetic woman's eyes and felt only Chryseis'
fingers in her cunt. She saw the woman's shaking body,
and she drooled spit from the corners of her mouth. She
watched as the men tied their victim back against the rough
timber gantry, her legs spread wide and her arms extended
as wide as they would go. Sappho lapped at the spit that
bubbled from the edges of her mouth as if it were ambrosia.
She inhaled deeply and her body filled with the heady aroma
of joy. The scent of her pleasure was the misfortune of
another, and it smelled delectably sweet.

A long, flat leather rope, knotted together from many
separate thongs, was wrapped around the woman's waist.
It was taken around the post at her back twelve times until,
holding her as tight as possible against the post, it was tied
off securely. She gasped against the confining gag, and tried
to squirm against her bonds, but the only movement she
could make was to bend her head forward in sorry
submission. Tears filled her eyes as she awaited her
unknown punishment.

One of the men scrambled up the gantry and leant over
the edge awaiting instructions. Another unwrapped a long,
loose hose made of animal skin that led up to the water butt
at the top of the gantry.

There was a moment of silence. The line of naked women
stood still. Sappho could not pull herself closer to the grill
so instead pushed her hands through the grating. She lifted
herself slightly and, sitting back fully on Chryseis' fingers,
she pushed her feet through as well. The feeling of her hands
and feet hanging out over the courtyard — there to be seen
if anyone looked — sent new thrills of joy through her body.
She shivered and shook with excitement. She sat back
heavily onto Chryseis' fingers, now pushed even further
into the welcoming, eager flesh of her sopping, wet cunt.

Praxis held the brass-ended rod high. The man holding
the end of the wide, leather hose held it above the woman's
head. Master Wang screeched an instruction to the man on

the gantry. He bent down and turned a large wheel until a sudden and massive flow of water poured from the end of the hose. It hit the woman full in the face, knocking her head back against the timber beam. She flared her nostrils and fought for breath. The man holding the hose brought it close to her face, directing its full force at her. She screwed up her eyes and shook her head from side to side. A spray of droplets surrounded her in a massive halo. The man kept the hose directed at her and it splashed heavily into her ears and up her nostrils. Her eyes were the only testament to her screams, now silenced by the plug of the gag, the frantic array of rainbow-coloured rain around her head, the only clue to her desperation. The bubbles foaming around her nostrils, the evidence of her grip on life so easily quenched and silenced by the sound of the fierce, splashing water.

Sappho pushed her arms and feet further through the grill. She wanted someone to look up at her, to see her exposure, her pleasure. She wanted to scream out. She wanted to be caught, dragged down into the courtyard and treated like the woman. She stretched her arms further out. She wanted everything she could see.

The man with the hose directed it on the woman's breasts. She threw her head back with the shock when it hit her. The fingers of her hands, spread wide against the bonds that held her wrists, tensed and released in quick succession. She bit onto the ball in her mouth as hard as she could. Her nipples rose up hard and stiff against the cold flow of water. The paleness of her breasts flushed with the chill of the cold, and her stomach tensed as she tried somehow to hold in the pain.

Sappho started moving on Chryseis' fingers, heralding the quickening speed she needed. Chryseis responded, pressing deeper into her cunt then slipping back before thrusting in again. And she delved her fingers deeper into Sappho's anus, now dilated wide and throbbing with the excitement of the sensitising thrust.

When the man with the hose directed it straight at the woman's exposed cunt, her eyes widened and she went stiff. The water ran into her slit, filling it, bubbling between its soft folds, flowing inside it, running out of it. Only her eyes told of the shocking pain of the cold water, the violation of the splashing flow and the degrading humiliation of shame that accompanied it.

Sappho was absorbed in it. She felt every harsh splash, every brutal smack of the water. She imagined it inside her, chilling her innards, shrinking her flesh, freezing her, stealing her warmth. In her mind, she felt the glossy ice cold water, hard and sharp against her skin. She reached out with her fingers and sat back. Chryseis increased the speed of her fingers, thrusting them hard, poking them deeply, eager to bring Sappho to the point of joy she wanted.

Suddenly all eyes turned from the woman. From a side door in the wall by the cages, a beautiful, naked woman with a small ring glistening at the front of her crack was marched into the centre of the courtyard. Calliope stood erect and stared around fearfully.

Chapter 8

Calliope's suffering

They left the woman tied to the gantry. She hung there on her bonds, dissipated and used. Water poured back down her nostrils, stickily running away across the ball in her mouth and off the end of her chin. Strands of spit that squeezed out from the side of the ball joined it and streamed down to her breasts. It stuck to her hard nipples and crisscrossed her skin with a mask of white, bubbly strips.

Praxis walked menacingly up to Calliope. She did not move. She was frozen with fear. He sniffed at her face. She held herself stiffly, not moving at all as he ran his hand across her breasts, her flat stomach and down between her legs. He curled his huge rough fingers into the entrance to her cunt and pulled sharply upwards. She rose onto her toes to try and reduce the pressure.

'You have found a fine one indeed, Master Wang. Does she have any skills? Or do we have to train her from the beginning?' he asked, still holding her up on her toes with his fingers.

'She is a gift from the temple of Apollo, my lord. The girls from there always need complete training. They have desires but no skills. They spend too much time in worship. And not enough time on their knees!'

'Then we shall begin straight away. Bind her to the cylinder. That is the best place to begin her course in obedience.' He pulled his fingers up hard and Calliope rose until she was on the very tips of her toes. Her muscles were taut and defined, her teeth biting together in concentration and terror. She was terrified.

Sappho stared down from behind the grill. Calliope's predicament made her ache with desire. She imagined Praxis hand against her own cunt, pulling upwards, stretching her tender flesh, holding her, controlling her. She was consumed by what she saw and sensitised by what she felt. She felt herself taken over by Chryseis' probing fingers, filled by them, heated by them, drawn on by their quickening pace towards the reward of her ultimate pleasure. She dribbled copiously from her mouth and could not lick it away — there was too much. The feeling of it running out of her mouth and onto her chin — the feeling of her lapping tongue unable to suck it back — caused her whole body to pine with yearning. Her eyes were wet with tears of joy. They ran down her cheeks and mixed with the spit that streamed for her gaping mouth.

She pushed back and then lifted away. Chryseis' fingers were tight in the encircling ring of her anus — treating it to the pleasure of pressure, forcing it open on entry, tightening it on withdrawal.

'Faster,' Sappho whispered to Chryseis. 'Faster.'

Sappho clawed her hands through the bars of the grill, stretching her fingers towards Calliope, wanting to touch her, wanting to feel her fear. Calliope was truly beautiful. Her tall elegance, square shoulders and black, short-cropped hair gave her a proud bearing befitting nobility more than slavery. Her breasts were firm, her nipples dark, hard and erect. The slit of her shaved cunt puckered slightly where the shiny golden ring emerged from its resting place. Chryseis could not take her eyes off her. She filled her mind.

'Strap her down tightly Master Wang!' ordered Praxis, finally removing his fingers from Calliope's cunt. She dropped back from her toes and stood squarely on her feet. Sappho could almost feel the release as Praxis' hand came away. She saw the relief on Calliope's face, and she saw the fear that came over it straight away as she realised she was not being freed.

Sappho watched closely as two men dragged Calliope to the large wooden cylinder in the centre of the courtyard. Master Wang spun it on its axle to test how easily it rotated. He smiled and ordered the men to bend Calliope backwards over the wooden cylinder. She struggled and another man came to help.

Sappho saw the tension in Calliope's muscles as she fought against the men — the tightness of her thighs, the strain on the edges of her well-defined slit. Sappho's eyes fixed on that most of all. The slit of Calliope's cunt was delectable. It was so fine, so precise, its edges raised only slightly, its colour only slightly pinker than the surrounding skin. When she lifted a leg to get away for her captors, the flesh that surrounded it was pulled sideways, the crack opened a little and the flesh on the one side pulled against the flesh on the other. The symmetry was broken and a delightful new shape was formed, in its pliability somehow more available, more tantalizing, more captivating. The golden ring raised and twisted and hinted at the pressure caused on the unseen, pierced clitoris. Calliope lifted her leg higher and the shape of her cunt changed again, this time exposing a glistering sliver of its inner flesh and, for a moment, the place of entry of the golden ring. Sappho wondered when it had been pierced, how it had been done, who had done it? She imagined it being inserted and she dribbled more spit from her gaping mouth. She squirmed herself back harder onto Chryseis' fingers. Chryseis pulled herself closer, breathing against Sappho's neck, increasing her heat, firing her passion, setting her ablaze.

They pulled Calliope backwards against the massive wooden cylinder. Praxis came forward and prodded at her with his bass-ended rod. The men held her legs apart and Praxis pushed the brass end of the rod between them. He guided it to their tops and let its bulbous end rest against Calliope's crack. The brass end made contact with the golden ring and he probed at it inquisitively.

'You have a ring, my beauty, now, who gave you that I wonder?'

He pressed the brass end a little harder, squeezing the fleshy edges of her cunt aside, opening them a little, exposing the pinkness that lay within.

'What does she look like Wang?' asked Praxis, turning. 'Is she beautiful as you promised?'

'Oh yes, my lord. No one could be more beautiful. Her skin has the satiny gloss of youth. She is like a ripe peach.'

Praxis laughed.

'Then let us feed on her!'

He pulled the brass-ended rod away and Calliope slumped back into the men's arms. The brass end glistened with her moisture.

Sappho pulled herself up and down Chryseis' fingers as they dragged Calliope to the wooden cylinder. They stood her against it and bent her over backwards. Her body curved across it, stretching to its curve, bending to its shape. She could barely stretch back enough to conform to its arc, but they forced her back until she could. Her arms were pulled back, continuing the circular line of the cylinder, and her legs were stretched around it as well. She lay against it, pulled back to the extreme, her breasts almost flattened by the strain, her hip bones prominent on either side of her stretched flat stomach. The crack of her cunt was pulled so tight that only the faintest slit could be discerned between the stretched out flesh of its edges. Her smooth skin gleamed.

The men wound leather straps through holes in the cylinder. They tied them around her wrists and ankles, binding them twelve times before securing them with firmly pulled knots. They left her head free and did not plug her mouth but, at the position the cylinder was at, her head hung backwards towards the ground and she could not raise it. When one of the men tried to pull a heavy ball into her mouth Master Wang knocked it away. She would, he said, need her mouth open for her training to take full effect.

'Faster,' said Sappho not thinking about anything else except what she was watching and what she was feeling. 'Faster. I need it as deep as you can. Can you get another finger in my anus? Three. I need three. I need the tightness. The tension. The pain. I need filling. And faster. Faster!'

Sappho dropped hard on Chryseis' fingers. Now she wanted more in her anus than her cunt. She flexed her feet, stretching her legs forward as far as she could through the grill. She bounced herself back hard on Chryseis' fingers. The unforgiving iron grating dug into the back of her ankles, but the heavy penetrating pain only caused her to do it more. Chryseis responded, quickening the pace, driving her three fingers in and out of Sappho's pulsating anal ring as forcibly as possible.

Master Wang pushed at the edge of the cylinder. It revolved easily and Calliope was spun around, turning upside down and returning twice to the place she started before Master Wang grabbed the cylinder and stopped it. Calliope looked terrified. Her eyes flitted from side to side, unsure where to look, not knowing from where the threat was coming, only apprehensive of its unknown form. She gasped, panting uncomfortably against the straining position she was in, desperate for breath.

Master Wang pushed the cylinder slowly until Calliope's head hung backwards and her taut, strained slit was uppermost. He stroked her nipples — so hard against her squeezed flat breasts — then ran his hand across her stomach. He inserted his finger into her cunt. She looked around frantically, not knowing who was violating her, not knowing what was going to happen next. He pulled his finger out slightly and took hold of the golden ring. He yanked at it and Calliope yelled out. He wrenched it again and she yelled louder. He twisted it and she screeched. He twisted it more and she screamed and would not stop.

Her screams reverberated around the courtyard and Sappho drank them in. Her spit-smeared mouth gulped at the air and drew Calliope's suffering in, eating it, feeding on it, nourishing herself with it.

Master Wang released the ring and Calliope's scream turned into a relieved bleat. Master Wang ordered one of the men to kneel in front of Calliope's face and insert his cock into her mouth. Sappho watched the cock go in, slowly at first, finding its way, pushing against Calliope's bleating cries, then more forcibly, and finally, when it was secure and Calliope could not hold it back, it went in completely, right to the hilt. There was nothing to be seen of it. Calliope's lips were pressed firmly against the base. Sappho pictured its lengths inside Calliope, the bulbous end down her throat, plugging it, the thick shaft impressed against its sides. She imagined the sensation of its throbbing bulk, its venous surface, squeezed in so tightly and she felt her own pleasure increasing and her own need demanding more. She did not know how to get it and so abandoned herself to movement, dribbling, clawing, reaching, and imagining. She had lost control of herself.

One after another the men thrust their cocks into Calliope's mouth. Each one went in completely — never into her cheeks, always down her throat — each one emerging covered in bubbling spit and oozing semen. The spit and semen dripped up into Calliope's nostrils and into her eyes, sticking to her eyelids, forming white pools in the corners of her eyes, pulling down her eyelashes with heavy, sticky globs.

When they had all spurted their semen into her throat, and when her face was covered in it, they spun her on the cylinder, winding it around until she was too confused to sense the ground. Disorientated and giddy, her head reeled with the sickening dizziness of her confused senses. Sappho watched Calliope's eyes turning upwards, thickly smeared with spit and semen, straining to tell up from down. She watched her mouth gaping and her tongue hanging forward, but she did not feel sorry for her — Calliope's pitiful state only drove Sappho's ecstasy higher.

Master Wang ordered the hose brought and, when they released the full flow of water from the high tank, it was directed squarely at Calliope. They kept her spinning giddily and the force of the water was aimed at her revolving body. First it smacked her face, filling her mouth and nostrils, washing the spit and semen from her eyes, making her choke and cough. It found her breasts, hitting them harshly, causing her already hard nipples to tighten even more. Then, as she spun relentlessly, the force of the water streamed between her legs, opening her crack, spraying harshly between the fleshy sides, squirting forcibly into her anus, and running away in a torrent between her taut buttocks. Then it was directed at the soles of her feet — a cold, brutal stream sloshing across their tender skin. Then the cylinder went full circle and, still gasping and choking from the first dousing, and still with water and semen streaming from her mouth, she took it again in her face.

'I can stand it no longer,' gasped Sappho. 'I cannot wait. Are you ready for me?'

Chryseis held her fingers stiffly inside Sappho, holding her back, keeping her on the brink for a few more seconds. She looked back at the thick handle of an old whip cast aside and left in the cell. She licked her own lips in fresh expectation.

'Yes, I am ready, my dear Sappho.'

Chryseis pulled her fingers out of Sappho's anus, grabbed the handle of the bull whip and thrust it in their place. Sappho screeched out as it went inside, gulping for breath, her eyes wide with shock. Her mind filled with new sensations: surprise, the coldness of the thick leather handle, the hardness of it, its length, its penetration. She felt the bulbous end deeply in her rectum, forcing higher, reaching into her bowels, entering high into her body. She was afraid. She held her breath, unsure what was going to happen, unsure if she could take it. Suddenly, as if a dam had burst, she found herself riding it, crouching back and riding it, drawing it up higher, burying it inside her as deeply as she could. Now she only wanted it to penetrate her, only needed it high within her. She just wanted to feel stuffed with it, filled to the brim, impaled on it. She screamed out loud — a shrill spasm of a scream, high-pitched, endless — and her orgasm began to flow.

Sappho watched Calliope spinning on the cylinder as the men brought out whips and flailed her breasts. The ragged-ended whips caught her nipples sharply and, as she revolved, they bit into the tender flesh of her cunt. Sappho was overcome — filled with it all. Her rectum was stuffed full — she could feel the whip handle in her bowels. She was filled with what she saw, breathing in extra flashes of it sharply whenever she could gasp. The pains in her arms and legs where they poked through the grill only fed her joy. The biting sting of the metal edges had overcome her too. And she felt drowned in her own spit-smeared face and the speed of the Chryseis' penetrating fingers in her sopping cunt. She could no longer hold her ecstasy in. It was built up fully inside her, choking her, spewing out of her, making her head reel, turning her inside out. She coughed and choked then, unable to resist its pressure anymore, she submitted to it and it was released. She screamed loudly — long and shrill — a plume of spit frothing from her mouth and running down her chin. She could not lick the spit away from her mouth. She tried but her tongue flopped flaccidly against her lips — out of control, fleshy, dissipated. Her spit ran in long trickles, thinning out into a gossamer thread, stretching down and, finally, breaking before splattering on the dusty ground below. Her screaming would not stop, it was continuous, a flow of high-pitched sound that spoke only of her ecstatic submission to pleasure. Her privacy was in tatters. She was completely exposed. She had relinquished all control of herself and had become her own vulnerability.

Praxis swung around, not knowing what he was hearing, but somehow directed by everyone else's glare. Master Wang looked up and saw Sappho, her arms and legs forced through the grill, her face pressed against it, spit dribbling from her gaping mouth. She saw his gaze and, spitting and frothing with her interminable scream, she convulsed with a jerking orgasm that, once started, would not release her.

She bucked and shook and, as she saw all eyes below turn onto her, it began anew, taking on a different form, drawing on fresh sensations, fresh resources. Now her orgasm was coming from her exposure to all the eyes that watched her, to the vulnerability of it, the embarrassment, the dread that came with their staring, intruding eyes. She shook faster — in a fit. She gasped for breath then, her eyes bulging, her face flushed, she started screaming again.

Suddenly there was a loud crash at the huge wooden entrance doors to the courtyard. Praxis looked around blindly. He held up his brass-ended rod with one hand and grasped desperately for Master Wang with the other. Another crash against the doors and they both fell forward into the braziers in an explosion of fiery ashes, dust and smoke.

Achilles and Ajax stood at the entrance, their legs wide, their shields up and their gleaming swords piercing the air.

They spotted Chryseis and Sappho straight away. Now, they were both pressed against the grill, their squirming legs wrapped around each other's heads as their tongues delved into each other's splayed wide cunts. They had hardly heard the Greeks breaking down the doors. They were too absorbed in their own mutual pleasures. When they realised something was happening, it was too late to hide themselves or escape.

One of Achilles' men dragged them down into the courtyard. They were both flushed with shame and hung their heads as they were pulled before Achilles. Sappho still had her robe on but it was pulled up around her shoulders. Spit ran down her breasts and the insides of her thighs glistened with Chryseis' spit and her own silky moisture. Chryseis was naked, breathless and soaked with sweat and spit.

Achilles looked only at Sappho. She captivated him. He strode up to her. Chryseis tried to stand in front of her — a faint act of protection — but Achilles brushed her aside. Chryseis tried again but this time Achilles smacked her hard across the cheek and she fell silent to the floor.

'You are truly beautiful,' he said to Sappho, shaking his head in disbelief. 'Are you a god or a mortal? What is your name?'

'Sappho,' she replied nervously.

'Sappho, you belong to me,' he said with assured certainty. Turning to his men, he shouted. 'I claim her as my prize!'

Achilles turned and walked back to the broken doors. Ajax ran up to him.

'And the other one my lord?' Ajax looked back at Chryseis. 'What will you have done with her? Should she be shared amongst the men?'

'Send her as a gift to Agamemnon. He did not join us in battle today. Perhaps this woman will help make sure his muscles do not ache too much from fatigue!'

Ajax looked around the courtyard. His eyes fell on Praxis, now cowering behind the gantry and holding onto Master Wang's shiny green robe. Ajax strutted over to him, recognising him immediately.

'And here, I see we have an old friend from the past. Praxis, I see you have fared well since we last met. Do you not recognise me?' he said mockingly. 'Can you not see it is I, your lord Ajax?'

'My lord Ajax? Is that truly you?'

'It is indeed, Praxis. And I have decided, this moment, to take you back with me. You will be far more use in the Greek encampment than you are here. Come, gather your flock together. I look forward to benefiting from your skills.' He pointed to Calliope. 'And do not forget that one. She seems spirited. I am sure she will be no match for Ajax, even though she may have defeated the mighty Praxis.'

All the slaves were collected. Sappho had a tight leather collar, with Achilles' emblem on it, clipped around her neck. Chryseis had the same, but with the mark of Agamemnon blazed along its edges. Naked or clothed, they were all paraded out of the courtyard and into the streets outside. It had only been a raid, and the Greeks were keen to escape before the Trojans mustered their resources and came in force to meet them.

Together with the others, Sappho and Chryseis were bundled through an opening broken into the massive wall of Troy. They looked around amazed as they found themselves in the open. Neither of them had ever seen the world outside the city before. The great plain of Troy stretched before them. Bodies of fallen soldiers lay in the sun waiting for the evening when they would be collected by their comrades. Sappho and Chryseis were not allowed to pause as they were driven out across the wide field between the high walls and the Greek encampment of ships. They gasped for breath as they were hurried across the exposed area of ground and Sappho, glancing back only quickly, wondered if either of them would ever see their home in Troy again.

Chapter 9

Dividing up the spoils of war

The women were marched into the Greek encampment. They all had their wrists tied tightly behind their backs with leather thongs. Some walked upright, their breasts thrust forward, proud and disdainful. Others hung their heads, fearful of their futures, shamed by the humiliation of their nakedness, degraded by their captivity. Short chains were clipped to their collars and they were strung together in a long row. They were so close together that it was difficult for them to walk and some of them tripped on the heels of the one's in front. They were all dirty from their journey across the dusty plain. It clung to them in muddy smears. The dust mingled with their sweat and stained the smooth skin of their breasts and buttocks. It was as if they had been roughly daubed by a defiling hand.

The Greek soldiers stood around their boats and jeered and shouted as the women shuffled and stumbled past. Some of the men prodded at them, some spat on them, one lashed out at them with a thin cane. The cane caught Sappho on her bare buttocks and she winced as the sharp pain penetrated her. The man laughed and struck her again. This time she did not react, hoping he would leave her alone.

'A dirty bitch indeed!' he shouted and struck her again. 'We cannot allow such unclean women into our camp.'

Sappho hung her head in shame. Chryseis walked in front of her and looked up but, when one of the soldiers spat on her, she dropped her head again and fixed her eyes to the ground.

They were driven into a clear area of smooth yellow sand. It reflected the heat of the sun from its surface. Massive wooden boats towered above them on each side. Banners, flags and armour hung from their heavy, black sides and soldiers lined up in four rows to form a gigantic square.

Sappho felt the heat of the sand on the soles of her feet. She screwed up her toes to try and reduce the burning but, as she was pushed forward, she lost her balance and fell. She dropped heavily on the collar around her neck, hanging on the short chains which led in front and behind her. She gasped and fought to get back to her feet but, as she was dragged along by the other women, it was impossible to stand up. She heard the soldiers laughing at her, and she felt a sharp stick poking in her side. She twisted on the collar, coughing and choking, falling backwards and being hauled along by the neck with her heels trailing in the sand. She looked up at the hot sun as, with her mouth wide open, but unable to breathe, she felt her eyes rolling upwards and the warmth of unconsciousness sweeping over her. The men's laughter turned into distant echoes. The collar around her neck felt so heavy she thought she would be dragged beneath the earth. She felt hands around her ankles, lifting them, suspending her by the neck on her collar. She felt herself swaying from side to side. The sun flickered in front of her eyes. Her mouth felt so wide she thought she could swallow it. Suddenly she was back on her feet, running, struggling to keep up, as the women were driven inside the square of men.

They were all made to run. Sappho, barely conscious found it impossible to keep up. The collar grabbed painfully at her neck. She was pulled forward and backwards — jerking with every snatch, her mind filled with terror, her stomach churning with anxiety, her body reeling with pain. She tried to look around but it was a flashing blur. All she could see was jeering men — some holding their stiff cocks in their hands, some urinating, some scooping up dust in their hands and throwing it at the captive, frightened women.

Suddenly, the movement stopped. The women were lined up in the square. Several men ran behind them, flicking captives with canes, making them stand straight. Sappho felt the sharp sting of a cane across her buttocks. It made her rear back. Her nipples were achingly hard and, as she looked down she could see them sticking out more than she had ever seen them before. They throbbed with pain, with uncontrollable, hidden, ridiculous excitement. She breathed deeply, hoping that her nipples would soften, would stop throbbing, but her concentration on them only made them worse. She looked around in fear at the men. Her robe was wrapped around her waist and hung to her side across one of her hips. She felt so vulnerable, so defenceless. Men pointed at her, threw dust at her, spat at her. She felt her nipples hardening even more as she realised her helpless exposure to the men's mockery and taunting.

'Look at that one there,' shouted one. 'Her nipples are so hard I could hang off them.'

'And that one,' shouted another pointing at Chryseis. 'Her rosy cunt could take us all. And she's a temple maiden too. Dark haired and lusty, like them all. I could bite her nipples forever!'

Sappho glanced at Chryseis. Her face was covered with dirt. Her pale skin daubed with the sweat-drenched dust, her naked body, striped with the harsh marks of the searching cane. She looked fearful and cowed — as if she could not suffer any more.

'I wonder how long she could stand that!' a soldier shouted back and they all joined in, chanting, shouting and laughing at their powerless victims.

'Let's put them to the test!' another shouted, running forward from the line and standing in front of Chryseis. 'Here, I will take the first turn. We will see how these Trojan women can stand the passion of Greek men! I need two assistants!' Two men ran to his side. 'Lift this one. Just enough for her to feel the collar at her neck. High enough for me to reach her nipples with my mouth!'

The two men grabbed Chryseis under her arms and lifted her off her feet. The short, tangled chains that led from her collar pulled tight and the leather collar squeezed tightly around her neck. Sappho bit her lips as she saw the look of fear on Chryseis' face and before she knew it, the extra tension on the chains fed through to her. The collar pulled tightly around Sappho's neck as well, and she rocked from side to side to try and ease it.

The two men held Chryseis. She squirmed but it was useless. Sappho watched as the man in front of her leant forward. He stopped, his open mouth in front of Chryseis' erect, throbbing nipple. Mud was smeared across it and he licked his tongue out and pressed it against the dirty smear. He licked it away and swallowed heavily. The soldiers in the square cheered loudly and the man bared his teeth and set them eagerly around the throbbing, erect flesh. Chryseis pulled back, trying to avoid his bite, but the men holding her tightened their grip and kept her fast.

Sappho bit harder on her lips. She sagged against her collar, feeling the tension around her neck, enjoying the feeling of captivity. She watched the man's teeth tightening around Chryseis' nipple and she dropped back more heavily. The man breathed in deeply and bit down, slowly at first, increasing the pressure gradually, then he bit harder. Chryseis opened her mouth at first and Sappho looked at it, wide, ready to scream. Sappho felt a heat between her legs and she squeezed her thighs together. The heat increased and, as she tightened the insides of her thighs again, she felt the moisture of desire oozing across the swelling labia at the entrance to her cunt. She could not believe her excitement. She lolled back further as the man bit down harder. Suddenly, Chryseis screamed out — loud, penetrating, shrill. Sappho, felt the surge of heat in her cunt and squeezed her thighs even tighter. She held them together, confining her cunt, pressing the flesh until it hurt — it was like sharing Chryseis' pain. Chryseis screamed louder as the man bit harder, and the louder she screamed the more Sappho squeezed her legs.

Sappho felt the throbbing of her flesh, tightly confined,

pressed hard by her squeezing legs. Each pulsation thrilled her. Chryseis' screams filled her mind. Sappho felt a trickle of spit on her bottom lip. She licked it back, but it was relaced by another, She licked that as well, sucking it back and swallowing it, but another came, and another, until a stream of spit ran from her gulping mouth,

Chryseis dropped her head forward when the man stopped. She gasped and panted, trying to get her breath back, trying to recover. But the men holding her did not let her down. They kept her off the ground, the collar pulling at her neck, her other nipple exposed. The man took that one quickly, biting hard onto it, not waiting, not restraining his hunger. Chryseis screamed again as the man's teeth bit hard into her tender flesh. She threw her head back, but it only served to tighten the collar already straining at her neck.

Sappho tightened the muscles in her stomach — it helped her bear down on the tightness at the top of her legs. She felt an ever-building sensation, a welling up inside her, and she bit her spit-covered lips hard, hoping to encourage it, hoping the pain inflicted by her own teeth would reward her with a release of joy. But it would not. She bit harder, and listened to the screaming product of Chryseis' pain. But still it would not come. She could not stand it. She was bursting with frustration. She opened her mouth wide and she too started screaming.

Sappho's scream joined Chryseis' — two voices in a harmony of agony: Chryseis' from the biting pain or her suffering, Sappho's from the frustration born of the absence of what Chryseis could not endure. More men ran forward. Sappho felt hands beneath her armpits, lifting her up. She felt the strain of her collar, pulling at her, holding her fast. Then a man was in front of her and she looked down at her nipples. They were so hard — stretched, throbbing, pulsating — she could hardly stand it. Her breasts ached with the pain of the pounding in her extended nipples. The man opened his mouth and bared his teeth again. She watched him bring them close to her right nipple. She felt herself stretching it out to him, not pulling away, not shrinking back in fear, but pushing it towards his teeth, wanting him to take it between them, wanting him to bite down hard.

The pain went deep when he did. It shot through her breast and penetrated her body. She shrieked out, abandoned to her agony, unable to stop it, incapable of holding it back. The pain went into her stomach and down into the hot, throbbing flesh of her cunt. She rocked against the bite, pulling herself away when she knew his grip was tight, extending her nipple against his locked teeth — pulling it, extending it, torturing it. She yelped like a dog and dribbled frothing spit as she was seized by a pent-up pleasure that, for the moment, only wanted feeding with pain.

Another man took her left nipple between his teeth and pulled at it, biting deeply into it, stretching it, drawing it out. Sappho screeched again, as loud as she could. Bubbles of spit burst from her gaping mouth. She clasped her hands tightly together and pulled against the bonds around her wrists, increasing the tension, bringing herself closer to the moment of release. Suddenly, she felt it flow and she jerked wildly, spinning sideways, pulling herself against the men's clasping teeth, descending into the fathomless depths of rapture, into the exhilarating joy of complete, overcoming ecstasy.

They threw her to the floor, still jerking, still frothing at the mouth, still squeezing her thighs against the throbbing flesh of her swollen, wet cunt. The two women on either side of her fell as well, pulled over by the chain that joined them. A man with a cane thrashed at the three of them. The stinging pain cut into Sappho and she opened her legs. She hoped the cane would find its mark against the soft, wet flesh of her slit. But she was pulled up and driven forward again.

Between the two gigantic boats, the men assembled a corral from spears forced into the sand. The women were driven into it like cattle. They crowed together, the chains that joined them, tangled and wound in knots. Sappho struggled to stand, not knowing which way to move to get relief from the tightness of her collar. Her face was pushed against the face of another woman. Sappho saw the fear in the woman's eyes, and watched in terror as spit ran freely from the woman's gaping, terrified mouth.

'Unchain them!' someone shouted.

Men ran between them unclipping the chains from the women's collars. They pulled at them roughly and Sappho was tugged sideways then knocked over. The loose chains rattled around her, filling her head with noise, her mind with apprehension.

First they were forced close together in the centre of the spear-lined corral. Their wrists were still tied tightly behind their backs but, with their chains removed, they could turn at will. They were forced together in a cowering knot on the edge of the corral. Sappho tried to dodge the sharp cane as it was brought down repeatedly. But she could not avoid its cutting slices and could not pull against the chain enough to gain protection behind the others. The cane slashed at the ones on the outside, cutting into their buttocks, or if they twisted away, their backs, and if they did not, their breasts. Sappho, unable to turn quickly enough as it slashed down towards her, felt its penetrating sting across both her breasts. She gasped as it struck and elbowed two other women aside so that she could get some shelter behind them. She pressed her stinging nipples against the naked back of another woman, hoping the woman's sweat-cooled skin would ease her pain.

The man with the cane thrashed at one of the women and drove her out of the cluster which they now all formed. He separated her, caning her viciously all the time, and drove her to the centre of the spear-lined corral. He forced her onto her knees and thrashed her several times across the back. He returned to the rest of the women and drove out another. Sappho cowered in the centre of the bunched up women, hoping she would not be chosen, hoping to remain unseen, unexposed. Another woman was driven out, this time shrieking loudly as the cane found its mark across her nipples. She too was made to kneel alongside the others. One by one they were all separated, Sappho was the last. She found herself isolated — the only one left — exposed to the jeers of all the soldiers that stood around the corral, and to the cutting slashes of the viciously wielded cane. She turned her back against the cane, running to the edge of the square of soldiers and cowering against the spears. She held onto a spear as the whip cut across her back then slashed angrily across her buttocks. She tried to save herself by turning sideways, but the thrashing continued, this time against the sides of her thighs. One of the men reached over the spears and pushed her forwards. She fell to the ground, her legs splaying wide as she fell on her back. She clawed at the ground with her tied hands but could not get up. The cane came down between her legs, slicing across her open slit, cutting into her soft, swollen labia. She shrieked with pain, but it came down again and her second scream drowned out the first.

The man with the cane drove her to the end of the line of kneeling women. She scrabbled in the sand, fighting her way forward, scratching at the ground, kicking her legs, trying to protect herself. Sand filled her eyes and tears streamed from them. She coughed and choked, and still the cane thrashed her, flailing relentlessly, stinging the insides of her legs, her nipples, her cunt, her buttocks. The more she fought to get away, the more she was thrashed. The less able she was to get to her feet, the more the cutting cane punished her for her failure. Finally, gasping for breath, panting loudly, and striped all over with the marks of the furious cane, she managed to take her place at the end of the row of kneeling women.

Sappho hung her head. She pulled her legs tightly together, hoping the tension in her muscles might stave off the throbbing pains that the cane had set in place throughout her body. She bit onto her lips and tensed herself. She could not stop shaking — she was filled with fear and dread. She looked down and she saw her nipples — hard, proud, throbbing. They pulled at the ends of her breasts — aching, smarting, pulsating.

The men chanted, banging their shields with their swords. The clamour filled Sappho's ears. The spears were parted and two men came into the corral. They struggled as they carried a large skin of water between them. They went to the opposite end of the line from Sappho and stood in front of the first woman there. They raised the skin, held it above the woman then suddenly tipped the heavy contents over her. It was a massive deluge, knocking her forward as it hit the back of her head. Her long hair flattened against her face. The water sluiced down across her back, onto the tops of her thighs and splashed into a sandy pool around her legs.

They fetched more and washed down the second woman. She fell face forward into the wet sand. Most of the weight of the water splashed heavily on her back. It sloshed between her arms that were fixed so tightly at her wrists in the small of her back. She choked in the water as it slopped around her face and, when she managed to lift her head, her mouth was filled with wet, choking sand.

The two men worked their way along the line, more men fetching replenishments of water, more helping to lift and sluice it down over the defenceless women. The woman next to Sappho screamed out for mercy, begging her torturers to spare her, to end her suffering. But, after they threw a first skin of water down over her and knocked her forward with its weight, they fetched another and threw it down onto her as she lay face forward in the wet, sticky sand. She coughed loudly, but did not stop yelling for mercy.

They held her head down into the wet sand and it bubbled up around her face as still she screamed and pleaded to be set free.

Sappho tensed herself, knowing that the weight of water would probably knock her down. She had heard the screams of the others, and seen their suffering, and she knew what to expect. She tightened the muscles in her legs, pulling her knees against each other, squeezing her thighs close together. She hung her head low, hoping to take the force of water on her back. She waited, her heart beating fast, her neck throbbing with her pulsating veins. She saw the shadow of the men holding the skin of water above her head, and she closed her eyes in anticipation. Suddenly she felt herself knocked sideways, then onto her back. She struggled with her bound wrists but as she did, her legs were forced apart and her cunt completely exposed. Immediately the water came flooding down. It hit her exposed cunt, shocking the soft flesh at its sides, entering her, sluicing inside her, washing her from within. Then another, in her face, and she choked and coughed and could not get her breath. And a third, again between her legs, forcing itself against the soft flesh, flattening it, deluging it. Sappho could not breathe. She lay there, open and exposed, now not wanting to draw her legs together. She only wanted more. She wanted them all to see her. She wanted them all to wash her down, to soak her, to sluice her, to drown her. She dropped her knees wider, inviting them, tempting them to give her more, enticing them to fill her, pleading with them to bring on her joy, begging them to release her pent-up pleasure.

Several men came into the corral with brushes used for scrubbing the decks of the ships. They dipped them into the sandy mud that surrounded the women and scrubbed the women roughly. The women wriggled and squirmed under the harsh treatment. If they fell on their front, the brushes were pushed up between their buttocks. If they fell on their back, their legs were pushed wide and the rough bristles of the brushes were forced against the tender flesh of their exposed cunts. Sappho fell on her back — and not because she could have avoided doing so. It was because the coarse bristles of the brush that was forced against the tender flesh of her slit, served to bring out the heat that had been stored for too long within her. The sharp, bristly contact of the brush let it out — allowed it finally to burst, like a torrent from a broken dam.

Agamemnon entered the camp with Achilles at his side. Their burnished armour gleamed and the crowns of their helmets shone in the late evening sun. Achilles strolled along the line of women, pointing out their beauty and regaling Agamemnon with tales of the adventure which had led to their capture.

Achilles stopped at Sappho.

'This one, my lord Agamemnon, I have chosen for myself. She is delightfully youthful and filled with desires for the pleasures of man. I have watched her throbbing with the heat of ecstasy. Look, even now, after beating and mistreatment, her nipples remain hard and erect.'

Agamemnon looked at Sappho, pinched her nipples between his thumbs and fingers and smiled.

'Achilles, you tell me of this prize as though she is the prize of a king. I wonder why you have not selected her for me. I can see in her flashing eyes the pleasure she could bring to me. Am I to suspect you have chosen the best for yourself, and forsaken the needs of your king?'

'My lord, how could you think such a thing,' Achilles laughed as he moved on to Chryseis. 'This is your prize, sire. A temple maiden. Daughter of the priest, Pelador. Herself already trained in the arts of pleasure — a necessity for the worship of Apollo, I am told. This is your prize, my lord Agamemnon. The greatest prize of all. I have picked her for you, and now I present her to you as a tribute of my devotion as your faithful servant and general.'

Agamemnon ruled because he was the strongest, the most vicious, the most powerful — and he took Chryseis eagerly as a prize worthy of his status. His guards marched her away, her robe in tatters, her face tear-stained and dirty, her hands still bound tightly behind her back. The soldiers pulled her viciously by her short dark hair and, as Sappho dropped her head to the side in helpless sympathy, her friend was dragged away.

Chapter 10

Calliope's Grudge

Sappho felt empty and alone. Ever since Chryseis had been dragged away, she had imagined what might happen to her at the hands of Agamemnon. She thought of her suffering and pain, and hoped she could stand it. She hoped she could bear the cruelty and humiliation that would surely be the reward for her beauty and youth. She thought of her in Agamemnon's control, bound and gagged, thrashed endlessly, humiliated and degraded, broken by punishment. She pictured Chryseis' beauty, her dark hair and pale, smooth skin. She saw the look on her face as, every time she was unchained from another night of captivity, she was subjected to a new selection of cheapening debasements.

Sappho's reverie was broken by the sudden silence that came with the entrance of Achilles, leader of the Myrmidons, the greatest fighters in the whole of the Greek army. Achilles was moody and fiery. His outbursts of temper were only tolerated by his king because of his unerring courage on the battlefield, and his inspiring and unmatchable skill as a fighter. Everyone stood transfixed, awestruck by the magnificent hero that came amongst them. Achilles eyes blazed with vitality, his smooth, tanned skin glowed, his armour — created by the Gods themselves and burnished and polished to a dazzlingly high sheen — fitted his muscular body as if it were a second skin. Behind him, Ajax followed closely and behind Ajax, the blind Praxis and an entourage of women, one of whom was the tall, slim Calliope. Calliope was naked, a thin gold chain attached to her clitoral ring ran up to a thin leather collar at her neck.

Achilles' eyes fell immediately on Sappho. She shivered as he approached and shrank back nervously as he stretched his hand towards her. He turned to Ajax.

'Ajax, I have not seen my delectable prize since we

returned from Troy. I hope she has been looked after well.'

'Praxis! You blind dog!' shouted Ajax. 'Tell my lord Achilles how his prize has been prepared. And be prepared yourself to give a good account, or it will be the worse for you. Remember, I am your master now. You do my bidding as if you were one of these women.'

Praxis moved forward unsteadily, holding out his hands and feeling his way towards Sappho. He grasped her face and felt around her mouth and eyes. He opened her mouth wide and probed the insides of her cheeks and the sides and tip of her tongue. He sniffed at his fingers, then rubbed his hands across her breasts. He squeezed them tightly before pinching her nipples viciously between his thumbs and forefingers. Again he sniffed at her, this time her neck and tawny hair. Suddenly, he thrust his fingers between her legs.

'Yes, a fine prize indeed,' he said, leering as he squeezed his fingers roughly between the wet flesh of Sappho's cunt. 'And she has responded well to training, my lord Achilles. She has exposed her particular talents keenly. I will show you.'

'Leave her!' boomed Achilles angrily. 'Demonstrate on that one. The woman with the chain through the ring in her slit. Show me how my prize has been tutored to please me. But do not handle her yourself!'

Praxis moved away slowly. Begrudgingly, he removed his fingers from Sappho's delectable cunt. He paused to sniff them, then beckoned Master Wang to bring Calliope.

Sappho moved back, squeezing her shoulders up as she tried to relieve some strain on her wrists which, every day since she had been captured, had been bound fast behind her back. She wriggled them as much as she could, but the wet leather thongs — which were freshly secured each morning after the women were fed — had already begun to dry out and tighten against her smooth skin. She dreaded the heat of the midday sun — then her hands would be throbbing with the pain of ever increasing constriction, and there would be no relief until the coolness of the evening.

With a single finger, Achilles beckoned Sappho. She was unsure at first, worried that he might be tricking her, fearful of his wrath. She looked sideways, pretending she had not seen his gesture, yet knowing at the same time that such pretence was pointless. He walked over to her, put his hand beneath her chin and lifted her head. He squeezed her cheeks together, pursing her lips and forcing down her jaw. He probed between her lips with his fingers, taking the tip of her tongue between them and pulling it forward. She felt the back of her throat tighten and the sides of her tongue tingle as it was elongated. Her eyes widened, appealing to him to stop the pain, to let her rest for a while from the torture and humiliation she had been facing everyday. He pinched the end of her tongue and released it.

'What a beautiful mouth you have. And a soft, wide and delectable tongue. I am intrigued by it.' He turned away. 'So, Praxis, show me how you have trained my little prize. Let us see the ringed beauty demonstrate my treasure's skills. And keep my prize secure so that she is reminded of what she has been taught. The day will not finish before she has to pleasure me, that is for sure.'

Master Wang, the incongruous oriental amongst these muscular, tanned Greeks, stood Sappho against a post used to secure women until they took their turn for training. He wound a thin cord around each of her nipples, knotted them in place, then wound them around the post. He drew her up against it so that she was held firm. He checked that Sappho could not move and nodded to the blind Praxis, as if he could see and approve.

He dragged Calliope by the arm. Her tall slim figure, pale in the morning sun, contrasted absurdly with the decorative embroidery of Master Wang's silken green robe and the shiny red of his hard, four cornered box hat. He pushed at her insistently until she stood exactly where he wanted her.

All the time, she kept her head lowered so that the chain leading up to her neck retained some free play and did not tug painfully against the ring in her clitoris.

'First, my lord, she is obedient to the whip,' announced Praxis.

Master Wang lightly pushed the back of Calliope's head. She understood the instruction straight away and dropped onto all fours. He placed his foot so that she could see it, and tapped his toes on the sand. She hung her head in response and waited obediently. Master Wang held out his hand and the stubby handle of a short, single tailed leather whip was placed into it.

Sappho watched closely what was happening. She allowed her legs to fall either side of the thick timber post. She squeezed her knees inwards against it. The cord around her hard, erect nipples tightened and pulled.

Praxis moved forward and spoke.

'See how she obeys instructions, never hesitating, always ready, always obedient. This is how your own prize has been trained. This, my lord, is what Praxis can provide like no other.'

He looked around vacantly, not sure where Achilles was standing.

'You are right,' said Achilles nodding in agreement. 'Your skill at the training of slaves is almost as great as mine is as a warrior.'

Ajax laughed at this and stamped his foot by Calliope, demanding her attention, as Master Wang had done. Uncertain, she did nothing.

'Then why does she not respond to me?' Ajax asked angrily.

'There is skill in being a master, my lord,' said Praxis unthinkingly.

Ajax strutted over to the blind Praxis angrily and pushed him backwards viciously.

'You should be careful of your opinions, Praxis, or your benefactor may quickly turn into your enemy.

Praxis realised he had spoken thoughtlessly. He quickly regained his balance and looked at where he thought Ajax was standing.

'But it is not a skill you lack, my lord. No. No. It is the girl. She has forgotten some of her training. I can hardly believe it. I will correct it immediately.'

He stumbled over to Master Wang, who took his arm and steered him behind Calliope. The golden chain looped up from the ring in her clitoris, between her well-rounded breasts and into the clip on the thin collar around her neck. It glinted as it swung slightly in a shallow curve between its two points of attachment. She bit on her lips nervously and stared hard at the ground.

Sappho pressed her breasts closer to the timber post and it eased the pressure on her nipples. She kept her stomach against the post though, and her legs either side of it, then leant back slowly, just enough to restore a bearable tension from the thin cord. The tugging ache on her nipples caused her mouth to gape. She felt the heat of her breath coming back into her face from the timber post.

Praxis placed the whip carefully against Calliope's buttocks. Master Wang leant forward and moved it higher, to make sure it was in exactly the right place.

'Now,' announced Praxis. 'When the lord Ajax gives you an order, make sure you follow it!'

He drew the whip back slowly, took it behind his head and held it in the air.

Sappho felt a wave of pleasure surging over her as she anticipated the stroke of the whip. She pulled her legs tighter against the post, feeling the soft flesh at the top of her crack opening slightly with the increased pressure.

Praxis brought the whip down quicky, without any warning, and it cracked across Calliope's taut buttocks. A single red stripe appeared immediately. She sank forward, gasping loudly with the stinging pain and shock. She was unable to stay where she had been placed. Praxis sensed she had dropped forward and reached the whip to place it against her buttocks again. Calliope had not had time to get herself back up onto her hands and knees and the whip did not come against her buttocks when Praxis expected it. The blind slave trainer looked around angrily, waiting for Master Wang to correct things. His head turned this way and that, hopeless without his aid, unable to act without his assistance.

Sappho thrilled as she saw Calliope sprawling on the ground. She pulled herself upwards against the post. Her slit opened enough for her clitoris to press against the ungiving timber, its surface rough — cleaved with a long splinter-edged split, and harsh with knots and eruptions. She pressed her clitoral bud against it. Heat ran through her like a fire. She bit hard onto her bottom lip, suppressing a dribble of spit than ran from the corner of her mouth. She felt a surge of joyous warmth running between the swollen flesh on each side of her cunt. She squeezed her legs harder against the post. The hot surge of pleasure ran into the dark recesses between her taut buttocks and into her dilating anus.

Aware of Praxis' distress, Master Wang slipped his arm beneath Calliope's stomach and quickly pulled her back into place. The thin golden chain pulled tight as he grasped her, and she pressed the base of her stomach forward to ease the painful strain on her clitoris.

'Get her straight, Wang!' shouted Praxis, anxious not to further inflame Ajax' anger. 'Bring her into position! I must teach her a lesson!'

Master Wang hoisted Calliope's buttocks high and Sappho saw the oval split of her cunt squeezed between them. Sappho pressed her throbbing clitoris harder against the post and licked spit back from her lips.

Praxis, brought the whip back again and swung it down even more aggressively towards Calliope's taut skin. The single leather tail swished loudly through the hot air then landed hard against Calliope's upturned buttocks. It cracked loudly and another red stripe appeared on Calliope's pale skin. Again she fell forward but this time her elbows bent and she dropped onto her forearms. Her buttocks raised up and, before she could do anything else, Praxis brought the whip down again, Calliope sprawled forward. She fell fully into the sand — her arms stretched out, her legs wide apart.

Ajax ran up and kicked the sand into Calliope's face.

'And still she does not get up!' he shouted seething with anger. 'Get up! Get up!'

Sappho moved herself rhythmically against the timber post, feeling its roughness, the nicks of splinters, the splits and knots. None of its pitted indentation escaped her — she revelled in it all. The heat in her cunt increased and, as she watched Ajax grasp Calliope by the hair and pulled back her head, she felt an overpowering wave of delight deep in the pit of her stomach.

Calliope screamed loudly as, with her head pulled back, the chain at her neck tightened in the ring through her clitoris. It pulled hard and stretched the throbbing bud of flesh more than she could bear. When Ajax saw her pain, he pulled her head back even more and stared at her fear-filled face. Praxis stepped forward and stretched his arms out. Ajax thought he was protecting the girl and flew into a rage. He struck out at Praxis and knocked him down. He kicked out viciously at Calliope as she struggled to get away.

Sappho could not stop herself. Her excitement had control of her. She massaged herself rhythmically against the rough post. She let every sharp splinter, every tight crack, every raised knot, stick into, and pull against, her throbbing clitoris. She pressed hard, opening her labia, exposing her cunt, revealing her clitoris to the roughness that was controlling its joy. She stretched her shoulders back, increasing the strain on her nipples and, as the stinging hurt at the tips of her breasts penetrated deeply, she felt her body jerking with the onset of a convulsion of ecstasy.

'Get up! Get up!' shouted Ajax, as Calliope crawled away in the confusion.

Achilles stepped forward and held Ajax back.

'Now, my lord Ajax, you expend too much energy on a mere girl.' Ajax nodded. 'Even though she has got the better of you!' exclaimed Achilles playfully.

Achilles laughed loudly but Ajax, infuriated by the embarrassment, broke from his grasp and kicked out wildly at Calliope. She rolled sideways and gasped for breath. He kicked her again. Achilles held him back and, this time, he would not let him go.

'My dearest comrade, Ajax. Leave the girl. She is nothing. Look. I will show you the sort of joy I expect from the real thing. My prize!'

Calliope crawled away, her head hung low, her dark eyes filled with hatred and anger. Ajax kicked out at her again but this time she did not shrink away, she turned towards him like a wild animal, trapped and with nowhere further to run. She stared up at him, prepared to fight until the end. He kicked again and she spat at him. She waited, filling her mouth again, hoping he would return her offence so that she could attack again. He looked at her and realised she was his enemy. He was a warrior and had seen that look before. He was used to enemies, and to vanquishing them, but this time, something in this woman's eyes told him that, for all his strength, she posed a threat. He turned, threw his hands up, laughed with difficulty, and embraced Achilles.

'And look,' said Achilles laughingly. 'She is making herself ready!'

They turned and saw Sappho jerking with ecstasy against the rough timber post. She stopped moving when she saw them looking at her. But her orgasm still flowed. She stood helplessly, her arms stretched tightly behind her back, her hard nipples firmly fixed around the post by the cord, jerking uncontrollably with the heavy convulsions of unstoppable pleasure.

Chapter 11

Sappho's Suffering

Achilles ordered Master Wang to untie Sappho from the timber post. He unwound the cords from it and tried to pull her away but, still moving herself rhythmically against it, she resisted. She clasped her knees tightly around it as he pulled at her. Achilles laughed. He grabbed the ends of the thin cords that hung from her nipples and gave them a sharp tug. Sappho's eyes widened with surprise, as though she had woken from a dream. Achilles pulled again, this time sharper and more forcefully. She realised she could not resist him. She dropped her head and moved at his insistence.

Achilles led Sappho by the cords, pulling her hard nipples, extending them further, yanking on them if she showed any signs of holding back. He led her across the shore to his tent — a massive low structure regaled with banners and surrounded by fine shields and magnificent weapons. Inside the tent it was quiet and cool — its heavy dark cloth protecting it from the noise outside and obscuring the glare and the heat of the punishing sun.

Achilles placed Sappho at the centre of the tent. She stood naked, her hands still tied tightly behind her back, the two thin cords tied tightly to her nipples, their loose ends trailing onto the fronts of her slender hips.

Ajax came in and, without invitation, sat at a chair covered in heavy throws.

'What is it like to be bettered by a woman?' teased Achilles, thinking again of how Calliope had managed to avoid Ajax' instructions. 'She must be a warrior-queen disguised as a humble slave to have the advantage over the mighty Ajax!'

Ajax shrugged resentfully and told a woman slave to bring wine.

'That is not the end of it, I assure you,' he said, producing a leather bag and opening it. 'But there will be time enough for that.' He removed a shiny silver object from the bag. 'Look, my lord, another of Praxis' inventions. I had him have one made for me. Perhaps your prize would enjoy its discipline. It was created by a jeweller to a precise pattern dictated by Praxis. It is an invention born of his years of experience at training slaves.'

'Quite so,' said Achilles smiling generously.

Achilles leant forward and looked at the object. It was like a horse's bit, with two silver rings at each side. From each of these extended a long silver strip about two hands in lengths. Between the rings were silver pieces, one bending upwards before returning to the other side, one bending downwards. At the centre of the upper piece a further strip extended for about the same length as the two at each side. Near to its joint with the upper bar it split before reforming again into a single piece. Between the upper and lower bent pieces, and stretching again between the metallic rings on each side, was a clamp with a screw attached on each side. The beautifully crafted creation jingled as he handled it.

'This should suit your little prize well. Should I fit it, my lord?'

'Certainly, Ajax,' said Achilles dropping down onto a huge sofa and taking wine from a naked slave girl. She bent to serve him. Her firm young breasts were conical and topped with hard pink nipples. The line of her taut buttocks were picked out in the soft yellow lamplight. She trembled, nervous at being so close to the god-like Achilles. 'I will be interested to see it in operation,' he said thoughtfully. 'And to see what pleasures it brings. Yes, fit it.'

The young girl backed away, still bowing, still trembling, her nipples even harder than when she first approached her terrifying master.

Ajax lifted the cords attached to Sappho's nipples, stretched them up to the roof of the tent and bound them into a pole that spanned the sidewalls. As he tied them onto the pole, Sappho had to lift herself up on her toes. Even so, stretching up as much as she could, the cords still pulled tightly and her breasts were stretched out by the tugging leads that ran from her hard nipples. She found it impossible to keep her balance for more than a few moments at a time. Whenever she lost her footing and fell sideways, the cords pulled painfully at her nipples and she had to fight quickly to get back into position and relieve the strain. Her heart fluttered with anxiety as she realised her predicament.

'Now, my beauty,' said Ajax, squeezing Sappho's cheeks between his thumb and forefinger. 'Let me and your lord see how you take to Praxis' little jewel.'

He lifted the glinting contraption up in front of her. Sappho's eyes widened. She tried to pull away but she could not. The pain in her nipples stung too deeply to be able to move from her precarious position on tip toes. Her heart beat fast and she breathed heavily.

Ajax released her and she dropped back. Her captured nipples injected searing pain into her body and she rose again on her toes. She was filled with anxiety and shivered, but even that caused the tension in the cords to heighten, and the pain in her breasts to increase. She did not know what was going to happen. Her fate was in another's hands and she felt overcome with fear and despair.

He poked his fingers into her mouth. She tried to resist, biting her teeth together, fixing her jaw. But he was far too strong for her to resist him. He probed harder and got her mouth open enough to get the tips of his fingers in. He pressed his thumb against her upper teeth and forced her jaw down. He held her mouth wide. She gaped, fearful, breathing hard, gasping emptily.

Sappho looked over to Achilles, sprawled on the heavy throws — smiling, amused, intrigued. For a moment, she wondered if he would intercede, save her, but she could tell from his expectant gaze that he was only interested in her humiliation. She wanted to beg for mercy but she could not speak. She felt herself dropping back on the cords again. She strained up onto her toes as much as she could in an effort to relieve the pain. Her legs quivered as she struggled to keep her balance.

Ajax took the silver contraption, Praxis' jewel, and held it in front of Sappho's gawping mouth. She could smell the sterile metal, sense the shininess, the coldness. She looked down at it, glinting in the lamplight, shining like the blade of a dagger. And she looked at Ajax' face as, quizzically, he turned the jewel this way and that until he had it the right way round. Satisfied he had it right, he pressed it towards her mouth and again she backed away as much as she dared. This time she slipped off her toes completely and gasped loudly with a deep shock of pain. The pole onto which the cords were tied, sagged under the strain — her nipples stretched agonisingly, her breasts filled with pain. In desperation, she struggled back up onto her toes.

She felt the metal edges of the jewel touch her wide-stretched lips. It was cold, smooth, unforgiving. For a moment she wanted to lick it. She moved the tip of her tongue towards it, but she drew it back as she felt herself toppling again. Ajax pressed the jewel in and it stretched her mouth even wider. The rings on its sides pressed against her taut cheeks as the upper bent piece covered her upper teeth and the lower bent piece covered her bottom teeth. She breathed in deeply, gagging as she did, struggling to swallow, feeling her mouth drying up, her throat constricting, her nostrils flaring.

She fell back again and struggled frantically to get back up. Her nipples seared with pain, her breasts stretched and pulled. She fought desperately to get back onto her toes and flushed with fear as she thought she might not. Ajax stood back and leered at her. She laboured to stand, still breathing hard, wondering what was going to happen — filled with apprehension, shaking with terror.

'She likes it, my lord,' Ajax announced. 'See, she jumps for joy at the pleasure it brings.'

Sappho's eyes filled with tears. She regained her balance again and stood quaking with fright. She did not know what to expect. She was overcome with suffering and pain. She felt so alone, so abandoned, so misused. She could only stare as Ajax stretched his hand forward and reached his fingers inside her mouth. She felt so deeply violated. She breathed hard. She heard her breath hissing against his hand. He grasped the tip of her tongue, squeezed it in his tight grip and pulled it forward. She caught her breath as he drew it outwards. She gagged again and the heaving movement that came with it caused her to drop again on the cords from which she hung. She felt the sting of vomit in her throat and swallowed to suppress it. But it was only a reflex action, she had no spit in her mouth, it was dried out with fear, there was nothing to take down. She tried to wriggle free, tried to scream, but her effort to move, constrained as she was in her precarious position, brought barely a movement of her head, and her attempt to cry out resulted in nothing more than a whimper.

Ajax drew the tip of Sappho's tongue between the two straight pieces of silver that stretched across the centre of the upper and lower bent pieces which now, like gumshields, covered her teeth. He held its fleshy pinkness between them. He turned, first the screw on one side, and then the screw on the other. The clamp tightened down onto her tongue and held it firmly in place. Sappho knew her tongue was fixed, knew she could not move it, but it did not stop her from trying to wriggle free. An involuntary action made her try to withdraw her tongue, to pull it back into her mouth so that she could swallow. But the pointless action only caused her more anguish. It made her swallow dryly and that made her gag again, and the sting of vomit returned into her throat. She choked but, as she did, she realised she could no longer control her choking. She breathed in and out heavily, a rhythm set in train only by her desperate need and her complete inability to carry out the action she intended.

Ajax laughed, leant forwards and licked across Sappho's wide, staring eyes. His tongue was hot and wet and the pressure of it dragged at her eyelids and stung her eyes. She wanted to cry but could not. His spit served as tears.

'And now, my lord,' Ajax pronounced. 'The jewel's secret.'

Achilles' eyes widened with increased interest as Ajax opened the three long metal pieces of the jewel. The one leading up from the upper bent piece that covered Sappho's upper teeth, he pulled up the front of her face and back against the top of her head. The other two, leading from the rings that were pulled firmly against the fronts of her cheeks, he took around the sides of her head. The slit in the one at the centre, fitted around her nose, passed over her forehead and the top of her head before joining the other two at the back of her head. The three clipped together at the back of her head with a special spring plate.

Sappho stood motionless, the shiny silver jewel stretching her mouth, covering her teeth, clamping her tongue and encasing her head in its intricately worked metal.

'There, my lord,' announced Ajax. 'That is the jewel fixed. Now I will show you how it works. Crios! Abas!'

It was only a few seconds before Crios and Abas appeared at the entrance to the tent.

'My lord?' enquired Crios. 'You need our service?'

'I do indeed,' said Ajax. 'Look, we have a maiden waiting. And she is willing for your attentions.'

'Shall I bring a cane lord? Does she need the disciplining sting of a rod? Or the slap of a belt perhaps? Or the deep bite of a whip? Maybe she needs to feel the flat of a hand? Or the slap of a hide or — '

'No, Crios. See, she has Praxis' jewel fitted. Her mouth is dry and it needs wetting! Unhitch her from the tent pole. It is too kind. The jewel cannot operate unless we place her against something less forgiving.'

Achilles pulled himself up on his elbows and looked on

with inquisitive interest. The naked slave girl returned with more wine. She bent to serve him and he pressed her hips down across his lap. She draped his knees, hanging her head down on the one side and widening her thighs slightly on the other. Her pert buttocks stood up in a smooth curve and he rubbed his hand across them carelessly.

Sappho felt relief as Crios and Abas undid the cords from the pole. She dropped onto the floor, hitting it hard, taking her breath away. She tried to cough as dust went into her mouth but, with the jewel holding her mouth so open, and her tongue fixed so painfully, it was only a hopeless, barking sigh that resulted. She dropped her head back against the ground and for some reason the tension on her tongue was relieved. She pressed her head back again, and again she felt the squeezing pressure of the clamp across her tongue ease. She sighed with relief, and lay there gasping heavily. But her relief was short-lived.

Crios took one of the cords and Abas the other. They each pressed a foot against one of Sappho's shoulders to pin her down. They held her fast, then pulled the cord tight. She raised her stomach, trying to arch her back to relieve some of the tension, but they held her down too tightly. She gasped for breath and tried again unsuccessfully to swallow. Her throat tightened as she gagged and the taste of vomit spread into the back of her mouth.

'Bring her here!' shouted Ajax. 'Against this post!'

They pulled her up, teasing her forward with the cords, pulling at her nipples, jerking them, then easing them, then snatching them sharply. They placed her against an upright tent post so that the jewel's clasp at the back of her head was forced against it. As it was pressed, she felt the pressure on her tongue decrease. She sighed with relief as her throat relaxed and some moisture slipped against its sides. Leaving her wrists bound, they secured her to the post with leather thongs wrapped tightly around her ankles and knees.

Crios and Abas pulled again on the cords attached to her

nipples. She moved forward to ease the pain but, as she did, the clasp at the back of her head relaxed against the post and the pressure increased on her tongue. Surprised and confused, she coughed, gasped for breath and pulled back. Even thought the burning pain penetrated her nipples like fire, the pain in her tongue was so great she had to pull back to relieve the constriction the jewel caused on it.

'Now you see the magic of Praxis' jewel, my lord,' said Ajax. 'The tightness on her tongue can only be relieved by her pressing back against the clasp. But when there are so many good reasons to come forward — like relieving a little pain — it is so hard to stay back!' He laughed loudly and reached out to snatch at the cords himself. 'The jewel is both the bringer and the taker-away of pain. It is a miraculous invention. Worthy of the gods themselves, my lord.' He turned back to Sappho. 'Here, little prize. Let me see which pain you prefer: the pain that Ajax offers you, or the pain of Praxis' jewel?' He pulled hard on the cords. Sappho fell forward, unable to do anything except try to reduce the pressure but, as soon as she did, she felt the dreadful constriction of the clamp on her tongue. She did not know what to do, which way to go. Each pain opposed the other. It was an unsolvable dilemma. She moved forward again as Ajax once more snatched at the cords, but the constriction on her tongue was too much, she could not stand it. She stopped moving forward, stood against the pain the cords were inflicting on her nipples, and gradually, stealing herself, hoping that she could stand it, moved back against the post. Bit by bit she edged back. Each small movement increased the pain in her nipples, each small step brought her closer to relief of the pain in her tongue. Finally, she stood against the post. Her nipples were stretched out on the cords. Her body was filled with the fiery pain that scorched through her breasts. At last, she was able to gasp with some relief — the agony in her tongue was at least held at bay.

Sappho's mouth was so dry, it felt as if it was coated with dust. It spread into her throat and along its sides with an unbearable, rasping harshness. She could hardly breathe she was so dry. She kept thinking she was going to vomit, but somehow the dryness of her throat held it back. Whenever the acid moistness rose in her throat, she held her breath and hoped it would pass. Time and again Ajax or the others pulled on the cords. Each time she lurched forward, only to drag herself back again, all the time fighting with the pain in her nipples in order to get relief from the clasp on her tongue. Despair welled up within her in an unstoppable tide. It filled her until she was overflowing with it. She could only choose one pain against another. She could not stop her suffering. She could not escape. She could only suffer. She was suffocating in a deluge of unresolvable conflict, unquenchable pain.

Ajax tired of the game. He told Crios and Abas to amuse themselves as long as they wished. Ajax sat with Achilles who still petted the young slave girl's buttocks. They both watched as Sappho struggled repeatedly to reduce her pain every time she was dragged forward on the cords. Achilles opened the slave girl's thighs more and exposed the delightful shape of her moist, pink slit. He ran his finger around its edges and its silky flesh glistened in the lamplight.

'Her mouth is dry!' shouted Ajax. 'She needs something to wet it!'

Crios and Abas pulled Sappho forward. This time they did not allow her to go back against the post. They held the cords low, encouraging her with pain to bend forward at the hips. She could hardly stand the pain in her tongue, but she could not stand the pain in her nipples. They kept her there, bowed before them, her mouth pinned open by the jewel, excruciated with pain.

Crios was the first, delving his cock into her widespread mouth, pushing the swollen tip between the metal shields that covered her teeth and over the clamp that held her tongue fast.

Sappho felt the throbbing glans against the back of her throat and gagged on it, involuntarily tightening her throat around it, holding it fast. For a moment, she forgot the pain in her tongue and held herself on it, plugged by it, filled with it. She felt the throbbing end expanding, beating heavily, and she felt the swell of semen flowing up to it. Suddenly, her throat was filled with it — creamy and wet, sticky and salty. It ran into her, flowing down her throat in a massive gurgling tide. She pulled back, she could not stand it, the pain in her tongue was too much. She pressed her head back against the post and found some relief. She swallowed hard and tasted the massive flood of semen that had filled her. She gulped again but it was impossible to swallow now without something to swallow with.

Again she was pulled forward and this time Abas filled her mouth. His cock was throbbing and stiff, venous and swollen and, when its tip pressed against the back of her throat, she felt a surge of vomit running up into her mouth. She coughed but it was suppressed by a sudden burst of semen. The flood choked her, filled her, inundated her, drowned her. She could not gulp it, there was too much. She simply allowed it to fill her mouth until, covering her tongue completely and spilling over the bar that covered her bottom teeth, it poured, overflowing, from her wide stretched lips.

She threw herself back again and forced the clasp against the post. This time, she did not sense the relief from pain, she could not feel any pain, she just let the massive flood of semen run down her chin. She pressed her head back more. She lifted her chin so that any semen that was left poured into her throat.

When they had finished with her, Ajax ordered her released. Crios cut the thongs from her wrists. Her arms fell to her sides and she dropped her head. Ajax unclipped the clasp at the back of the jewel and removed it from her mouth. Her mouth stayed open, unable to close for a moment, and, despite the pains that racked her body, she sighed with pleasure at the alleviation the jewel's removal brought. Her lips felt stretched. As she let her mouth close slightly, they felt swollen. She drew back her tongue and, straight away, tasted the semen that lay upon it. She did not hesitate. She closed her mouth and swallowed deeply. The semen ran down her throat like nectar, and she looked back at Crios and Abas in the hope that they could provide her with more.

Abas cut away the thongs at her ankles and knees. He clipped a heavy ring to one of her ankles, secured it, and fixed a chain to it. He led her outside and locked the other end of the chain to a heavy post driven into the ground as an anchor. Sappho crouched down on the sand and rested her hands between her thighs. She breathed heavily, recovering from her ordeal. She felt her heart calming, and her breathing becoming regular again, she also felt her searching fingers slipping between the soft, wet flesh of her cunt. They probed around the edges of her swollen, slit, searching out the delights that lay within its delectable darkness. The images of her suffering came back into her mind. She thought of herself pressed against the post, holding back the pain in her tongue as her nipples burned with the deepest pain she could imagine. She sensed again the moisture of her cunt, wetting her flesh and covering her fingers with delectable silkiness. She thought of her mouth held wide, her tongue clamped and the men's semen flowing into her mouth and down her throat. She was overcome. She could do nothing except rise on her fingers and allow her ecstasy to take its irresistible course through her already jerking, throbbing body.

Achilles walked amongst his men on the beach, it was his way, asking about their lives, showing his knowledge of them, encouraging them. He leant on his spear, his golden skin glowing in the flickering light of the fire, as he listened to a soldier's story of battle and bravery. His attention was caught by a whimpering groan and he looked behind a nearby tent.

Sappho was crouched by the side of the tent, naked, drooling, her fingers deeply inside her slit. She panted as she worked her fingers inside the soft flesh of her cunt, breathing harder as they went deeper, sighing louder as they came back out to the pink, fleshy entrance. She was thinking of Chryseis. She was imagining her watching, imagining the worshippers at the temple staring at her. She was imagining herself crying out as she was filled with pleasure. She was imagining being thrown on her back as she was discovered. She was imagining herself filled with semen — drenched with it. She was imagining herself being whipped, caned, and thrashed until she could not longer stand it. And as she thought of these things, she thought of having them again, and again, and she moaned with the ecstasy of her pleasure, the joy of her plunging fingers, and the anticipation of more to come.

Achilles stared down at her. As soon as she saw him, she rose on her fingers for a last time and screamed out with a massive and overpowering convulsion of pleasure. Spit ran freely from her mouth and dripped down onto the sand between her feet.

'Take her away and chain her with the others,' said Achilles. 'I will keep her. She is my prize. But she needs more restraint. Yes, chain her with the others.'

Soldiers dragged Sappho away roughly. She was still shivering with the throbbing of her ecstasy when they strung her up — her arms and legs spread wide, bound in chains on the side of one of the massive boats.

They left her there and she hung on the chains in despair — now she felt hopeless and alone. Painfully, she turned to her side. Another captive hung beside her, her head bent forward, her flame red hair falling in a tousled mass, her naked body — taut and athletic — stretched tight on the imprisoning chains. Even in her pitiful humiliation, this woman looked beautiful and proud.

Sappho was unable to speak.

The woman lifted her head.

'My name is Eva,' she said, licking spit from her lips and swallowing it hungrily. 'I have been here since the Greeks pulled their ships up on this accursed shore. I do not think I will ever be free. I will never tread on the soil of my homeland again. Surely, it is all over for us both.'

Chapter 12

An Escape Plan

Agamemnon strutted through the Greek encampment. Chryseis was led by a heavy chain locked into an iron collar clamped tightly around her neck. She had been hard to control, and Agamemnon had her whipped every night. Still, she remained disobedient, resentful and hard to subdue. The collar had been fitted so that at any time, day or night, she could be taken easily to her lord Agamemnon for further punishment or discipline. When he went somewhere, he took her with him, having her led behind him on her chain, stopping sometimes to have her whipped or thrashed with a cane.

Chryseis spent her nights thinking of Troy, the temple, the naked girls and the young men. She lay on the hard ground which was her bed, her eyes filled with tears, and the flat of her hand across the flesh of her cunt, as she imagined her old home and all she had been forced to leave.

Everyone went silent as Agamemnon entered Achilles' tent. Achilles stood to greet him. They clasped hands and stared unyieldingly into each other's eyes. Agamemnon needed Achilles and his army of Myrmidons if he was to be victorious at Troy. Achilles needed the cause, the war which Agamemnon provided, to show his great skills and live the life of an indomitable warrior. The two great men were mutually dependant, mutually fearless.

Sappho and Eva had been put to work as serving girls. They had been dressed in light silk smocks which reached below their knees and were open at each side. As they bent to pour wine for the guests, their robes opened wide and their nakedness was revealed. Some of the high-ranking chieftains who were Achilles' company grabbed at them as the women leant over with their wine jugs. Eva pulled away from them, but they easily dragged her back. Sappho had more guile. She slipped their grasp and, pretending to be needed by someone else, she ran to another guest, her wine jug held high. This allowed her to escape more often than Eva but still, sometimes, she was caught.

Sappho stopped, wide-eyed and shocked, as Chryseis came in. She could not believe it. She smiled nervously and, without thinking, went to towards her. She was stopped by Agamemnon's brother Menelaus. He ran his powerful hand up inside her smock and drove it between her thighs. She tried to turn away, lifting her wine jug as if someone had ordered her over, but Menelaus would not let her go. He pushed his hand up the insides of her thighs and rubbed his fingers around the soft flesh of her cunt. It was moist and warm and, as he applied pressure to it, the lips opened and the silky pink edges folded around his fingertips. He smiled and thrust his fingers in. She rose on them to reduce the depth of his penetration but, as she did, she also tightened herself around them. She bit down hard on her lips and looked around anxiously.

'This is a fine prize you have found yourself, Achilles. Perhaps you would be interested in trading her?' said Menelaus, using his other hand to restrain the now struggling Sappho.

'Menelaus. You are the brother of my king, and very wealthy, and very powerful. But, even though this prize of mine does not please me at the moment, I will not let her go. You have nothing to trade that would be compensation for her loss.'

'Why does she not please you, lord Achilles?' asked Menelaus.

'She is wilful, Menelaus. But I will tame her eventually. In the end, I am sure, she will provide all the pleasure I would wish.'

Menelaus laughed and pushed his fingers even deeper into Sappho's cunt. She gasped as they stretched her flesh at the opening and she looked around frantically, hoping that someone would help her. She caught sight of Chryseis standing behind Agamemnon. They stared at each other. Chryseis, pitiful as she was — naked and chained to the heavy iron collar at her neck — smiled uncomfortably. Sappho opened her mouth, as if she wanted to speak, but she was snatched away from Chryseis' gaze as Menelaus flung her down across his knees.

'Perhaps you have not taken a strong enough hand in her punishment, Achilles,' he shouted. 'Perhaps the hand of a king's brother will make her obedient.'

Sappho draped Menelaus' knees. Her head hung forward almost to the ground, her toes clawed vainly to get a grip in the sand. He pressed his strong left hand in the small of her back and held her down. She felt captive to his power. His huge hand controlled her easily and, when she tried to raise herself against its pressure, it did not move at all.

'Yes, show us the skill of Menelaus. Show us how he brings slave girls under his control!' shouted Achilles, leaning forward, propping his chin in his hands and his elbows on his knees.

Sappho wriggled beneath the weight of Menelaus' hand but her pathetic efforts only made him laugh. The back of her smock had fallen to one side and one hip and leg were completely exposed. Menelaus reached down and took hold of the hem. He lifted it slowly, peeling it up so that Sappho's buttocks were fully bared. He dropped the light material so that it fell forwards over her head.

Sappho reached up and tried to pull it away. It trailed around her neck and got tangled so she could not free herself from it. Menelaus lifted his knees, forcing Sappho's buttocks higher, exposing the perfect shape of her slit, its pink crack, its soft swollen edges, the nub of her red, throbbing clitoris. He smoothed his right hand across the graceful curve, stroking her satiny skin: taut and welcoming, cool and enticing, perfect and unblemished. He rubbed her buttocks again, firmly, feeling their flexibility, their tension. The muscles of her buttocks responded with reactive tension, tightening, fixing their sumptuous curve, inviting more attention. Starting below the small of her back, he trailed his finger between them, letting it slip into the delightful crack, and onto the slit of her exposed fleshy cunt.

She closed her eyes as he touched her. The heat from his fingers caught her unawares, unprepared. Suddenly, she realised her exposure, lying across his lap, her buttocks bare, everyone looking at her, everyone expecting something from her shame. He stroked her again, and again she closed her eyes. This time fully realising her situation, fully knowing her position. This time fully aware of the delight it promised. Again he stroked his fingers between her upturned buttocks. This time he pressed in deeper. He found her anus and touched it with his fingertip, pressing it only lightly, letting her know he knew of its existence, its potential. She tightened as he touched it, she felt it closing against the tip of his finger, reacting to the contact, welcoming it, expecting more from it, hoping for something deeper, something more penetrating.Menelaus stopped with his right hand on her buttocks. He pressed them slightly, feeling their responsive tension. Sappho felt the strain of his holding back, the anxiety of not knowing what was about to happen. She was suffocating in the potential of the moment. She looked sideways, as though she was going to see something which gave her a clue to her future. But there was no answer. All she could see was the mighty Greek chieftains lying back on the heavy chairs and sofas, pointing, leering, waiting.

Menelaus' lifted his hand away. Her buttocks were cooled by its absence: exposed, naked, bare. She squirmed against his other restraining hand and breathed in deeply. Her throat throbbed with the pulsating beats of her pounding heart. He held his hand high above her, looking at it to ensure its correct position before bringing it down suddenly, with dramatic force, onto her beautiful curved, taut buttocks.

Sappho gulped as, with a loud smack, his open hand struck her squarely. The noise filled her ears. The sharpness of the contact spread into her body. The sting did not come straight away, it was not until he lifted his hand away that it arrived. When she felt it, she shrieked and tried to pull away, but it was hopeless, he had her fast. His hand came down again, a forceful smack, perfectly aimed, perfectly positioned. She was no more prepared than the first time. The sharp noise of the contact shocked her before she felt the biting sting that followed quickly in its wake. It stung her skin like a fiery brand, and the burning fire ignited on her buttocks spread in a wave of searing pain throughout her body.

Sappho struggled with the robe again, trying to untangle it from her neck. But her hands and arms seemed out of her control, she could not find which way to grab it nor hold onto anything even when she touched it. Another spanking smack came down, this time louder, more fierce. Sappho exhaled forcibly as the breath was knocked from her. The stinging pain filled her completely, she could not think straight. She knew her buttocks were reddened — she knew the shape of his hand was inscribed on her skin with the crimson mark of pain — but she could do nothing to stop it, nothing to help herself withstand it. Her mind reeled in confusion.

The smacks came down one after another. There was hardly a pause between them. She tensed her buttocks, and tightened her thighs until she felt the muscles in the backs of them hard and cramped. She had screeched to start with, but now she did not have the strength. She started yelping, regularly, weakly, in time with the smacks as they landed. Each yelp took her breath, and she struggled to inhale again ready for the next. But she could not stop. It was her only expression of the agony she felt. Spit ran freely from her gaping mouth and her tongue licked out, loosely reaching down as if there was some salvation to be had from its painful extension. She could hear nothing but the sounds of the incessant smacks. They filled her head and, as each separate pain gradually blended into the next, so each separate smack merged with all the others.

She was overtaken by it and, with the heat, the pain, and the continuous sound of his smacking hand, she felt a warm blurring sensation overcoming her. It started in the crack between her buttocks, where the redness from his hand had not spread. It flowed around her anus, prickling her with its heat, before entering it and heating up the inner surface of her rectum. It travelled around the soft edges of her cunt, warming the delicate flesh, causing it to swell and throb and moisten. It went inside her, between the wet lips of her slit, filling her to the brim, overpowering her. She felt it in her nipples, already painful, hard and throbbing, and she felt it biting into her breasts. It filled her stomach, and her head, and her tongue licked out for more as if the air itself could provide it. Finally, the heat overcame her and she felt herself jerking in time with the continuous smacking of the hand.

Each time it came down she jerked — filled with pleasure, filled with pain, unable to control herself. She could not see through her eyes — they were overflowing with tears. She could not breathe through her nostrils — they were blocked with streaming mucous. She could only cough out her pitiful breaths as the blows stung repeatedly on her tightened, crimson-red skin.

She opened her legs wider, hoping his hand would find the soft swollen flesh of her cunt. She needed the extra pain, the extra humiliation. One smacking blow caught this soft flesh and the sting sent fresh shocks through her. It inflamed her anew. She felt her passion, her joy, her pain, her suffering, all mingling with the agony and the degradation of her exposure. She reared back, hoping to capture it in a screeching moment of complete ecstasy. She tensed herself and opened her mouth wide.

'That is enough!' shouted Achilles. 'Look, she enjoys it

too much. Menelaus, you have not disciplined her. You have brought her nothing but pleasure! Here!' Achilles jumped to his feet. 'I will cool her down. Perhaps that will reduce the ease with which she finds joy in everything which is done to her.'

Menelaus released her and pulled her to her feet. Sappho did not know which way to look, what to do. She stood there gasping, panting, confused. Her robe was still tangled around her neck. She made no effort to remove it. Her naked body glistened with sweat. Her buttocks were reddened all over by the punishing spanking she had received from Menelaus. She licked her wet lips and felt herself still shuddering with the unreleased tension of her frustrated and pent-up passion. She had been stopped just as she was prepared for joyous release. She was caught on the edge of her potential ecstasy, and her head spun giddily as she tried to absorb it.

Agamemnon grabbed a jug of wine and threw it over Sappho's face. She shrank back but did not dare move from where she was. It splashed into her eyes and filled her gaping mouth. Menelaus did the same, and Ajax and others joined in, each emptying a jug of wine over her. It ran through her hair and down her nose and cheeks and dripped from her chin. It flowed between her breasts and fell in drops from her hard nipples. It ran down the front of her smooth stomach and into the precisely defined crack of her shaved cunt. It streamed down the insides of her thighs, over her knees, her calves and onto her feet. The robe tied around her neck was soaked and dripping and hung limply from her shoulders.

'Now push her, and all the others aside,' said Achilles. 'We have important matters to discuss. Agamemnon, my king, we have a war to plan.'

Soldiers pulled the girls away and pushed them together into the back of the tent where Chryseis stood, still chained by the neck. Sappho, drenched and pitiful, stood beside her.

'Chryseis,' she said panting and exhausted and still filled with an unliberated excitement. 'I thought I would never see you again. But to see you like this! Collared and captive on a chain. I cannot stand it.'

'Sappho,' said Chryseis, knowing each moment together was valuable. 'We must escape. We must get back to Troy, to my father, to the temple. We must escape from these terrible, cruel Greeks.'

Sappho took Chryseis' hand and, on feeling its warmth, her suppressed excitement bubbled again to the surface. She felt the warmth of her cunt wetted by the moisture of her again growing joyous anticipation. She squeezed Chryseis' hand tight.

Eva heard what they said and pushed her way up to them both.

'I know a way of escaping,' she said. 'If you take me with you. If you provide safety for me in Troy, I will show you.'

'Of course,' said Chryseis eagerly. 'Of course. I am the daughter of Pelador, the high priest of Apollo. We will welcome you to our temple in Troy. If you help us, you will never have to fear again.'

'Could you help me find my way home to my own country?'

'Yes, we have traders who will transport you. Now tell us how we can escape.'

'I have been mistreated since I was brought here,' she started. 'I have suffered every indignity. I could never have imagined the things which have been done to me. I have been bound and chained, whipped and thrashed with straps and canes. Men have taken me in every way, in every part of me. And I have taken their semen everywhere. They have covered me in it, and made me drink it. I have been tied out on the sides of ships and bound on stakes in the water. I have been suspended on ropes and thongs of leather. I have been bent over and beaten until I have been sent unconscious. Each night, I am taken by a group of soldiers to a place on the edge of the Greek encampment. No matter what suffering I have been put to during the day, they still take me, still use me, still defile me further.'

Sappho crouched down and started to untangle her robe. Its wetness made it difficult but she managed to free it. She stayed where she was looking up at Eva and Chryseis, listening to Eva's story. Her hand drifted between her legs and straight away found the softness of her cunt. She felt its swollen edges and inserted two fingers into its moist, welcoming darkness. The ecstasy which had evaded her was still there, still waiting, still needing to erupt.

'They make a crucifix from spears,' Eva continued as Sappho looked up and began moving her fingers in and out of her soft, dewy slit. 'And hang me on it. Bound by the wrists to the cross piece. Pinioned by the ankles to the upright. All the soldiers visit and look at me, limp and hopeless, victim for anything they care to do. Most of them urinate over me. Some spit at me. Most use their cocks on me, releasing the flow of their semen over me, or into me, or into something that I have to drink from. They eject their semen into bowls and, as I hang on the crucifix, I have to drink it all. Sometimes I gag on the amount I have to drink. They never let me stop until it is all gone.'

Sappho increased the rhythm of her movements and opened her legs wider so that her hand was free to delve deeply.

'When they have finished with me, they go off drinking,' continued Eva. 'They cut me off the crucifix. Several of them drag me off and throw me down by the deserted outer picket of the camp. Some stay and make me suck their cocks or perhaps they thrash me. But, in the end, they always go and join the others. They just leave me on the ground and do not bind me or secure me. I can walk free from there if I want. I know I can. I have seen soldiers crossing out of the camp to meet prostitutes. I have seen the route they take to avoid being seen by their commanders. I have been afraid of approaching the great city for fear of what would happen to me there. But I know that, together, we could escape from there. I can lead us out of here. And you can take me into your wonderful city. There I will be safe.'

Sappho, the image of Eva on the crucifix of spears fixed in her mind, felt spit running from her mouth and now, unable and unwilling to check herself, she shouted out loud as her pleasure claimed its freedom. She knew she was being too loud, she knew she would be heard, but she was not prepared to suppress it. She cried out again as, with a final deep thrust of her fingers, her joyful ecstasy was, at last, liberated.

Achilles, annoyed by the intrusion of Sappho's screams, had her dragged back into the centre of the tent. She stood, depleted and ashamed. Male slaves were ordered to wash her down with basins of water. She stood there until they had completely soaked her. But Achilles would not let her go. He ordered his men to remain on guard all night while she was forced to stand in the pool of water and wine that lay at her feet.

In Troy, the temple of Apollo glowed with the eerie yellow light of a thousand candles. The naked girls of the temple moved slowly in a circle, hand in hand, around the massive marble altar. Pelador stood before it, the heavy ram's fleece on his back, the ram's mask covering his face, his arms held high. He called to Apollo, invoking a plague upon the Greeks. A plague, he hoped, which would only end when his beautiful daughter, Chryseis, was returned to her rightful place beside him. A flash of lightning heralded a mighty boom of thunder, and a gust of wind running through the temple, and setting the candles flickering, gave notice that Apollo had responded to the appeal.

Chapter 13

The plague continues

There was no standing against the terrible plague that Apollo sent. In the Greek encampment the food turned rancid and the water sour. The soldiers were afraid and wanted to return home. Their spirit for fighting disappeared. The chieftains did not know where to look for a resolution. Achilles said that the plague had been sent by a Trojan ritual to the gods. It would, he said, only be dispelled by a more powerful Greek sacrament. Calchas, the Greeks' chief prophet, was summoned and ordered to drive the plague from the beach and save the army of Agamemnon.

Four huge boats were hauled up the beach and levered into a massive square. A great rounded boulder was dragged into its centre as an altar. Lanterns and burning torches were erected on pikes all around the area. By the evening, thousands of soldiers packed into the arena, scrambled onto the boats or gathered beyond them in the rising dunes above the beach. They beat their shields with their swords and screamed war cries as if going into battle. The whole beach was a turmoil of clamour, colour, noise and flickering light.

Calchas appeared between the ships. Just like Pelador, he wore a heavy ram's fleece on his back and his face was covered with a horned ram's mask. He held his arms high and walked slowly towards the massive boulder. A procession followed him. At its head, six naked girls, their hair shaved and in its place a crown of yellow flowers. They sprinkled water from small jars as they danced behind Calchas with light, sweeping steps. The nearest soldiers threw coins down to them and when they bent to pick them up, their taut, youthful buttocks exposed the shape of their naked, tight cracks. Behind them came four men dressed only in loose robes. One carried a many-stranded leather flogger, its ten strands, about the length of a man's arm, attached by intricate plaiting to the rigid leather handle. Another wielded a single-tailed whip, woven from fine strands of leather. Its length was the height of a man and it tapered to a split end burned by the heat of its cracking snap. Its handle was weighted and bulged out into a heavy ball at its end. The next held a double tailed quirt that he flexed between his hands to show its unforgiving harshness. The last man carried a bamboo cane from Egypt. Knotted with joints along its length, it extended to half the height of a man. Every few paces, the man swished it downwards, cutting it through the air in a frightening, hissing sweep.

Behind them came a collection of enslaved women surrounded by guards. Some were manacled at the wrists with heavy iron cuffs. Some walked anxiously in a train held by a chain attached to iron collars at their necks. Some were gagged with hard, leather-covered balls secured behind their heads with tight thongs. Some were blindfolded with leather straps pulled so tight that their eyeballs showed through the close-pulled hide. One was dragged in by a rope wrapped tightly at her ankles. Her short dark hair was filled with wet sand and her face was dirty with smears of mud. Her arms were tied folded across her breasts. A leather strap was pulled tightly across her mouth. It was Sappho.

Last in the procession was the blind Praxis and his assistant, the Chinaman, Wang. Master Wang held onto Praxis' arm as he helped him into the arena. Praxis stared around unseeing, cocking his head from side to side, listening, raising his chin and smelling the air.

Calchas stood at the altar still with his hands high. The naked young girls gathered around him, kneeling first, then bowing slowly one by one. The four men stood around them in a square.

Everything went quiet as Calchas started chanting. He turned and pointed to one of the captive women — the dark-haired Calliope. The chain was unclipped from the collar at her neck and she was led forward to the altar. She looked around anxiously, pulling against her captors, filled with fear.

They pulled the leather strap from Sappho's mouth and unbound her ankles. Her arms were left bound tightly across her breasts. She struggled up onto her knees. She could not move her arms at all. They were so tightly bound to her chest that she found it hard to breathe. She watched the frightened Calliope held before the altar. She could hear her own heart beating in the eerie quietness. She licked her dry lips. She tasted the mud on her lips, smeared over them when she had been humiliated in puddles of urine before she was brought in.

The men pushed Calliope face forward against the massive boulder, draping her over it, bending her body to its curved shape. Master Wang ran forward with two soldiers. He instructed them to drive long iron stakes, with rings at the top, into the sand around the boulder. He tied Calliope's ankles with ropes to two of the ringed stakes and her wrists to two more. He pulled them tight, leaning back as far as he could and pulling with all his weight until he was satisfied. He led Praxis forward to check his work. Praxis pulled on the bonds and smoothed his hands across Calliope's taut, well-shaped buttocks. He nodded his approval. Calchas ordered one of the girls forward. She brought a jug of oil. He commanded her to pour it over Calliope's upturned buttocks. The young girl did as she was told, lifting the jug high and tipping out its contents slowly. It ran in a glistening, golden stream across Calliope's taut skin. It ran between the crack of her tight buttocks, around her dark anus and across the shapely flesh of her slit. It dribbled down the moist centre of her crack, running onto the insides of her thighs and then down behind her knees and onto her calves. Finally, it ran onto her feet and soaked into the sand around them.

Calliope tried to move against her bonds — Sappho saw her muscles tensing with the effort — but it was pointless, she was so tightly pulled against the boulder that she could barely breathe. Sappho licked her lips again. She thought of Calliope's exposure — bent forward, naked in front of the eyes of thousands of expectant men. Sappho found herself panting with expectation.

Master Wang stood back and again took the blind Praxis' arm Calchas motioned to one of the men who stood in the square around the naked girls. The man stepped forward and swished the ten stranded flogger at shoulder height. The separate strands curled in unison, slipping through the air with ease, then flexing in a biting snap when he stopped the downward action.

Sappho breathed faster.

Calchas chanted, holding his hands high, imploring Apollo to release the Greeks from the terrible plague he had placed upon them. He dropped his arms and immediately the man with the flogger stepped behind the bound Calliope. The silence was intense.

Sappho's heart pounded in her chest. She bit her dry lips and waited.

The naked girls, still on their knees, slowly leant back. They placed their hands behind them on the ground, widening their legs, and exposing their tight slits. They lifted their hips, rising on bent legs until they held their cunts as high as they could. The flogger was raised and dropped in practise.

Sappho panted, her eyes wide, her mouth gaping.

The flogger was raised again and this time it was brought down forcefully on the bound Calliope's buttocks. It hit with a thud. The only signs of its inflicted pain were the slight sign of increased muscular tension in Calliope's buttocks, and the spray of oil that was driven off her skin by the impact. It came down again, another thud, other twinge of increased tightness, another spray of oil. And again, and again.

The thrashing continued. Sappho saw spit dripping from

Calliope's gaping mouth. Each time the flogger struck, a glob of spit ran down from her lips and ran down the side of the boulder. Sappho imagined running forward and licking the spit away. It made her swallow hard. She looked around at the quiet audience of soldiers and wished that their eyes were on her.

The next man was ordered forward. He flexed the double tailed quirt. Master Wang ran up and smoothed his hand across Calliope's buttocks, wiping the oil around them, ensuring they were covered completely. He nodded and, without any preparation, the man brought the crop down fiercely. Its two tails snatched through the air and, hard and unbending, they fell on Calliope's buttocks with two quickly snapping smacks. Calliope tightened all over. Sappho could see her agony. She could tell the pain was great, was hard to bear, was filling Calliope with fear of more. The quirt came down again, and again. The spray of oil this time sharper, penetrating the air in a fine fan of golden glitter. The dribble of spit increased and now flowed copiously from either side of the gasping Calliope's mouth.

The naked girls pushed their hips high, gyrating them. They balanced back on one hand, using the other to massage the flesh of their cunts. With their stretched out fingers, they opened the soft flesh, exposing themselves, giving themselves to the eyes of all those that watched — absorbing the men's stares, feeding on their delight.

The man with the quirt stepped back and was replaced by the one with the cane. He lifted his knee and flexed the cane over it, showing how it bent, how it would snap against its victim, how it would deliver its pain. Again Master Wang came forward and ran his hand across Calliope's buttocks. This time he called for more oil and a whole jug full had to be emptied until he was satisfied. It poured between her reddened buttocks, down the insides of her legs and settled in golden pools around her feet.

The crowd was still silent but now, Calliope's panting

could be heard: short, repetitive, fearful, unending. The cane came down for the first time in a long, swishing slash. It cut across Calliope's buttocks and instantly she screamed out loudly. It was a shrill piercing scream. It cut the silence as sharply as the cane cut her taut skin. Then, as suddenly as it had begun, it stopped and her panting continued. The cane came down again and she screamed again. This time a loud penetrating screech that spoke only of agony and suffering. The thrashing continued, each cutting blow accompanied by an increasingly shrill screech of pain.

Sappho listened to Calliope's fearful cries as the cane thrashed her red striped buttocks. She listened to the panting interludes that informed her of Calliope's all consuming fear — her terror at what action must unerringly follow each pause.

Sappho opened her knees some more. She looked around and saw the mass of faces staring down at the spectacle before them. She imagined all those eyes were on her, and her alone, and she opened her knees wider. A draught of cool air spread across the soft flesh of her cunt and, as it moistened under the sensation of exposure, she felt the throbbing flesh swelling with excitement. She wanted to place the palms of her hands against the insides of her thighs and she widened her knees even more, but, with her arms bound across her chest, she could not. She stretched her knees as wide as she could. She looked down and a dribble of spit ran from her mouth and dripped into the parted slit of her cunt. It ran between the pink fleshy petals, glistening in the flickering light. She squirmed to help it move further. She watched with delight as it ran down her crack and onto the sensitive, slightly dilated muscular ring of her anus.

The man with the heavy single tailed whip stepped forward and took the other's place. Sappho looked up as he swished it around in a massive, slow circle above his head. Her stomach filled with anxiety at the sight of it, but she could not take her eyes from it. It threatened so much pain and the fear it generated only fed her increasing excitement. She struggled to free her arms but still it was impossible. The frustration only fed her desires more. She tightened her buttocks, one by one, so that she could feel the wet swollen edges of her cunt pulling around her throbbing clitoris.

The man with the whip paraded around Calliope, supine on the boulder. He pulled the whip handle back slowly to shoulder height then threw his hand forward. The long leather tail curled lazily in pursuit, stretching forward as the curl quickened. When it reached the end, it cracked with an ear-piercing, burning snap. A coil of smoke rose from its end as it settled to the ground. Each time he snapped it, each time it cracked, each time the coil of smoke rose from its burning end, Sappho grew more impatient, more in need. She did not know how to contain her mounting craving to release her pent-up desire. She was desperate to feel her fingers between the throbbing flesh of her cunt — desperate to feel her clitoris pinched between her finger and thumb. Spit ran freely from her mouth. She held her tongue out to direct it at her soaking, open cunt.

Calliope screeched when the whip cracked across her buttocks. Its end caught her precisely at the moment the looping curl unfolded on it. The suddenly released energy snapped the final shredded tassel of leather so ferociously that it burned. It cut Calliope's taut skin, inflicting a pain so deeply into her stretched out body that, when she opened her mouth to scream, no sound came out. She tried again, but it was impossible. The only sound to be heard was her incessant, rapid panting. The rhythm was broken by a second snap of the cracking whip. Again she could not scream or yell, she was too filled with pain. Her relentless panting became louder and, when a third cracking burn cut into her, her gasps blended into one long hiss.

Sappho was transfixed by the noise of the cracking whip and the sight of her own spit running in the pink flesh of her cunt. She could hear the cracking tip of the whip. She could see the flowing bubbles of sticky spit but she was unaware of anything else. She twisted from side to side, struggling to get her hands free, struggling to relieve the desires that centred in her soaking cunt. Still crouched, she rose on her toes, battling to squeeze her shoulders together so that her arms might come free. The tension of her unbreakable captivity only increased her need. She stretched her fingers pointlessly, flexing them out then crunching them back rhythmically — mirroring the throbs that pulsated in the swollen flesh of her cunt. She stretched her toes as far as she could and she squeezed her shoulders in as far as they would go. Without warning, she fell sideways. She hit the ground and her legs fell wide apart. She lay for a moment, her legs wide, the wet flesh of her cunt glistening in the flickering light of the massive arena.

Everything felt confused. She struggled to get herself up but, with her arms bound across her chest, it was impossible. Her feet kicked at the sand, trying to find a foothold, but there was none to be had. She closed her eyes tight, and rolled onto her back. She listened for the sound of the cracking whip, but it had stopped. Its absence exposed the total silence. All Sappho could hear was her own panting breath. Her mouth was wide open. She licked her lips, sucking some of her spit back and swallowing deeply. The silence filled her head. She froze, afraid to move then, as though she had been commanded, she opened her eyes wide. Master Wang was staring down at her.

Sappho looked around. Everyone was staring at her. She was completely exposed. The whipping had stopped. She had become the centre of everybody's attention. A wave of unsurpassable joy spread over her but, before she had taken another hurried breath, it was joined by a torrent of indescribable fear.

'Bring her here!' screamed Calchas. 'She will be the reason Apollo forgives us!'

Sappho was grabbed and dragged to the massive boulder. They flung her down on the sand. Her mouth was filled with it and she choked. They released the gasping Calliope from the altar where she had suffered so much. They undid her wrists and ankles and she fell to the side. Sappho looked into her face, it was tear stained and dirty. They hauled Calliope to her feet and Sappho stared at the red stripes and burn marks on her buttocks. The sight of them inflamed Sappho's passion. She felt the throbbing ache in the flesh of her cunt that warned her of its presence. She looked around. Within the square described by the boats, on the four boats themselves, and beyond them in the dunes, men were packed. They all stared hard at only her. She opened her legs slightly, testing out the feeling. She was rewarded with a surge of delight that streamed through her in a flood. She opened her legs wider and the flood became a deluge. She felt spit running from her mouth again and she licked out her tongue and leant forward. Her bubbling spit sparkled in the torchlight as it dripped down in strands onto her open slit.

They dragged Sappho to her feet and the dribbling spit spun down in long gluey filaments onto her breasts. They released her arms and straight away she drove her hands between her legs. She clawed at her cunt in a frenzy — filling it with her fingers, pinching her clitoris, squeezing at her flesh. They tried to pull her hands away, but she would to let them. She spat and screamed and kept driving her fingers into her flesh. She felt the rising tide of her ecstasy brimming nearer to the surface. She was on the brink of her rapture, burning all over with it, holding her breath, waiting to release it with a scream of joy, but they would not let her.

They dragged her hands away and flung her face down across the boulder. They held her pressed against it. She was shocked by the coolness of it. The pressure that they used to force her down took her breath away. They tied her by the wrists in the same way as Calliope. When they pulled the rope tightly at her wrists and pulled her down against the boulder, she felt the heavy pressure on her chest. When they secured her ankles and pulled them tight, she felt the exposure of her buttocks and her cunt to all that were gathered around to watch.

She lifted her buttocks as much as she could. She was making herself ready. She had watched the thrashing of Calliope, and expected the same. She knew that the first touch of the cane, or the whip or the flogger, would release her tension, would allow her the ecstasy her body was craving. She opened her mouth and felt herself panting like Calliope. She stopped and listened. There was absolute silence, just like before. She let herself pant again, and squirmed her buttocks. She felt the tension squeezing the moist flesh of her cunt. She did not know whether or not to close her eyes. She did not know how much she would have to suffer. She tensed her body and lay still, gasping quickly. The beating of her heart quickened as the silence filled her mind.

The naked girls lifted their hips higher as Calchas moved close behind Sappho. Their cunts glistened in the flickering light, their smooth stomachs forming a flat platform between their nubile, pointed hips. Their small breasts flattened against their chests as they bowed back their bodies. Their smooth-shaven heads, still ringed with crowns of yellow flowers, glittered in the shimmering light of the surrounding torches and lanterns. The look of yearning on their faces revealed their ecstasy.

Sappho waited for the first blow, but it did not come. She felt the presence of Calchas behind her. A darkness passed before her face. She opened her eyes wide. Something was being passed over her. It was a sheep's fleece. They carried it above her head then laid it over her back. The soft suede of the inside of the fleece made her shiver as it fell against her skin. Its length covered her buttocks and came up over her back as far as her shoulders. Immediately, she felt its warmth and tasted its animal smell on her wet, licking tongue.

Still she waited for the first blow to fall, but still it did not come. She felt someone pressing between her thighs. She could not see him, but she knew it was Calchas. She felt the edges of the long fleece that covered his back against the insides of her thighs. He pressed closer and she felt the warmth of his cock against her wet slit. There was no need for any pressure, the throbbing mass of his glans simply slipped between the wet petals of her fleshy cunt. He held it there for a moment, raising his hands and turning his ram's head mask up towards the starlit sky. Sappho clenched her teeth, feeling her own joy at last untethered. He pressed his cock in. Thick venous and throbbing, it drove inside her, deep and penetrating. She felt its pulsating surface and the massive throbbing glans, but that was all. Her orgasm flooded over her, her eyes rolled upwards and she started convulsing with a massive release of all that had been too long held in. Her head reeled giddily and everything around her spun out of control.

The silence was broken. A great roar went up as all the soldiers joined in a noisy chant. The beach throbbed with it. They beat their fists on their chests, or their swords against their shields. It was a monstrous cacophony. Sappho's head whirled with it and her body convulsed in time with Calchas thrusting and the huge throbbing cry from all who were gathered there.

She felt the burst of Calchas' hot semen inside her and she felt it dribbling away as he drew his cock out. She bit onto her lips as he drove it back straight away into her anus. She could not stop a fresh wave of jerking ecstasy overtaking her as again he filled her with his semen. She felt him again in her cunt, and again in her anus, she was not sure. As it continued, she realised less. The noise filled her head, but it drifted away, as though she was dreaming. In the end, she did not know how many took her, how many filled her, how many drenched her with their semen.

Later, the soldiers dispersed. They climbed down from the boats and walked away from the dunes. The captive women were led away. Calliope had her ankles bound by leather straps with a long lead attached. She was dragged out by the lead, her buttocks reddened and cut, her body covered in sand which stuck to her sweating body. The naked girls went out hand in hand, bending to pick up coins, exposing their delectable cunts between the tight curves of their taut buttocks. Sappho was left tied to the altar, the ram's fleece still covering her back, her buttocks upturned, semen running from her cunt and anus and down the insides of her thighs. Praxis bent to smooth his hand across her buttocks before Master Wang led him out. Calchas was the last to leave, walking silently between the boats. He nodded slowly as he assured himself that everything had been done to bring an end to the terrible pestilence bestowed on them by Apollo.

Chapter 14

Agamemnon claims Sappho

But all the efforts of the Greeks came to nothing. The plague continued: pangs of hunger turned to pains of starvation, apprehension turned to raw fear, confusion turned to desperation. Some of the soldiers banded together and sailed home, some deserted into the hills. Fourteen deserters were captured and hanged from ropes dangled from a ship's oars. One of them survived for two days before he finally died, still calling out for his home. The army of Agamemnon had lost its will to fight. The Greek expedition against Troy seemed doomed to failure.

A meeting of the chieftains was called. A space was cleared and large, heavy chairs laid out in the shadow of one of the great boats on the beach.

Agamemnon arrived with his retinue. Chryseis was still wearing the iron collar and was led on a chain pulled by a large-nosed dwarf. She hung her head low. She was fearful of incurring Agamemnon's displeasure, falling foul of which had already led to regular beating and humiliation. The day before, when she had glanced at him in a way he thought insolent, she had been made to suck the dwarf's cock and drink his semen. She stopped too soon and Agamemnon flew into a rage. She was beaten with a short thin cane across the flesh of her cunt, and forced to suck the last drops.

Achilles followed with Ajax. Sappho, wearing only a short skimpy vest, and with her hands bound behind her back, was made to kneel at Achilles feet. Praxis was led in by Master Wang and stood behind his protector, Ajax. Praxis brought a small group of slaves including Calliope and Eva. Calliope stood close to him and pawed at his cock as he stood looking blindly around him.

Agamemnon settled into a massive chair and spread his hands wide on the huge claw-shaped arms.

'Achilles, there has been never-ending trouble for us since your last raid on Troy. What is to be done?' he asked with a heavy sigh.

'I cannot control the work of the gods, my lord,' said Achilles sternly. 'It is the evil hand of Pelador — the Trojan priest of Apollo — that has brought this scourge upon us.'

'I grant that is at the root of it,' said Agamemnon sitting forward. 'But there is more. You have not been attentive to the rumours that fill the camp, Achilles. Some say that the ritual performed by Calchas was a mockery. That it was thwarted by the presence of the Trojan woman you captured. Some even say it is this woman herself who brought the plague.'

'Which woman is this, my lord?' asked Achilles tersely.

'The woman you call your "prize". It is said she has the better of you. It is said, she carries the plague with her. It is said, she works with the gods against us all, and that you cannot control her. It is said she plots behind your back, and you are powerless to defend yourself against her treachery. It is said you harbour the very evil which threatens to destroy us. What do you say, lord Achilles? Do you protect a viper?'

Sappho was filled with fear. She could not believe she was being talked about like this. That the great king, Agamemnon himself, was accusing her of such things. And, as she saw Achilles' anger boiling inside him, she could not believe that her lord's rage was because of her. She shivered all over, seized with anxiety and apprehension.

Achilles stood and looked around angrily at all those gathered. He could barely contain his fury.

'Who is it that says these things? Who speaks against Achilles like this? Let him show himself!'

He peered accusingly at everyone. No one spoke.

'Lord Achilles,' said Agamemnon still sprawling back in his seat. 'The answer is simple. You should show us that your prize is none of these things. That she is under your control. Even as I look at her now, I see the curse of betrayal in her eyes.'

Sappho dropped her head and stared at the ground. She knew all eyes were on her. She flushed with fear and shuffled her feet pointlessly as the terror of what was happening took hold of her.

Achilles furrowed his brow, unused to being challenged even by the king. He resented being put to the test like this. His natural conviction was to challenge and fight but, even consumed with rage, he steered the sensible course. He turned to Ajax, his trusted comrade.

'Ajax,' he barked. 'Have you heard these rumours? Let our king know he has been misinformed!'

Ajax looked to the king and nodded slowly. He turned back to Achilles.

'I have, my lord. I have heard these things spoken. They are worth heeding.'

'So even you, my friend Ajax, turn against me! Very well. I will show you all that this is nothing but the gossip of old women!'

Sappho shrank back as Achilles approached. She had never seen such anger. His teeth were set tightly together, his broad mouth snarled, his muscular frame was tense, his long hair flowed behind in as if he faced a terrible storm.

He grabbed Sappho's bound wrists and dragged her into the open forum at the centre of the cleared space. She stood, just beyond the shadow of the ship. She screwed up her eyes against the bright sun.

'I will show you who commands my prize!' Achilles shouted. He looked skywards. 'And I will show the gods that not even they can better the mighty Achilles!'

He pushed Sappho onto the ground. She rolled several times, unable to stop herself because of her bound hands.

'Look!' mocked Agamemnon. 'Already, she escapes your grasp! Achilles, this "prize" has you by the nose!'

Achilles' face flushed with fury.

He took a knife from his belt and held it above Sappho. He paused, then slashed the leather strap that held her wrists. He pulled her up by her hair and lifted her off the ground. He dangled her in front of Agamemnon and the chieftains.

'I will show you that my prize is nothing unless Achilles commands her!' he ranted.

Sappho wriggled in his grip, her feet well off the ground, her hands grasping hopelessly at his mighty hand. She realised she could do nothing against him. Fighting was pointless and ridiculous. She went slack, dropping her hands to her side and hanging limply from his fist.

'See, already she realises the great power of Achilles!' he shouted. 'I will show you, lord Agamemnon, that these rumours are a ridiculous fiction! No one controls Achilles!'

Agamemnon laughed and called for wine. A naked slave girl ran forward and served him.

Achilles dropped Sappho and she felt in a heap on the ground.

'Now kneel,' he ordered. 'Kneel before your lord, the great warrior Achilles.'

Sappho struggled to her knees. She wanted to jump to her feet and run away, to escape from his anger, but she knew that was impossible. She was a captive, his slave, and she had no will of her own.

Achilles called for his personal guard. Ten huge men ran into the area. They all looked from side to side as though they expected to protect their lord from danger. He told them to stand in a circle around his 'obedient prize'. They did as they were told. Sappho looked up at them, all massively build, all gleaming with armour, all ready to obey their lord Achilles and carry out his every whim.

She bent her head, not knowing what Achilles planned for her. She sensed the accusing stares of the men that surrounded her as she knelt before them. But even consumed with terror, petrified by their combined gaze, and exposed by her near nakedness, she felt something else — aroused by a sense of excitement. She felt it aching in the flesh of her cunt. It gnawed at her. But, for the moment, even though she was aware of it, it lay buried beneath the wave of fear that was threatening to engulf her.

As she looked up under her eyes, she saw Achilles' men opening their tunics, exposing their weighty cocks. Each one was stiff and venous. Each one throbbed with potency and desire. Each one was so close to her that she could feel its burning heat. She bit her lips with fear.

'Now, my little prize,' said Achilles. 'You will fill this with the semen of these mighty warriors. And do not waste a drop. It is the precious seed of the greatest men of Greece.'

He held before her a wide brimmed bowl with one side flattened and secured in a woven cradle of leather. He hung the straps attached to it around her neck so that the flatted side rested just above her breasts. She did not know what to do and stayed, kneeling, not moving, petrified.

'Already she disobeys you!' mocked Agamemnon, running his hand carelessly over the slave girl's taut buttocks.

Achilles grabbed hold of Sappho's short dark hair and pulled at it angrily.

'Fill it!' he shouted, taking her hand and stretching it out to the cock nearest her face. 'Here. I order you. Fill it!'

She wrapped her fingers around the throbbing shaft. She could hardly encircle it. The surface was heavily ribbed and the weighty glans was swollen and red. She lifted her other hand to it and used them both to hold it. She felt its heat and its need. She held its surface skin and pushed it down towards the root. She felt the strength of it as the loose skin slid along its massive hard body. She pressed the base of her palms against the man's heavy testicles, letting their heat soak into her hands. After a second, she drew back slowly, pulling back the skin as far as she could up the throbbing column. As she pulled it towards the end, the glans expanded and the orifice at its end, the meatus, dilated and widened. She gripped harder and repeated the action, now feeling the increasing firmness, the increasing heat. She looked up at the man's face, opening her eyes wide, fixing her stare on him as, repeatedly, she pulled her hands the length of his massive, pulsating cock.

She felt it swelling within her grip. Her fingers were forced apart by its distention, but she kept on: labouring, slaving, working for his pleasure. She went faster as she felt its throbbing increase. The base of it was pounding, surging with need, his heavy testicles swelling with desire. She held the soft underside near the glans, the fraenum, squeezing it tightly as her thumbs sensed the surge of semen within. Still she kept her stare fixed on the man's eyes. She watched him tense and stiffen as he realised his body's needs were inescapable. She held his pounding cock as tight as she could. The meatus opened and a flood of semen streamed from within. She directed it so that it flowed into the bowl at her neck. She kept her grip on it, helping it empty, until there was nothing left to come. She licked her lips, inhaling the scent, imagining the taste, wanting to drink.

Sappho shivered as she felt aware of her cunt, of its flesh, its heat, its moisture. She knew she had to turn to the next. She had been ordered by her lord and she could not fight against his will. Achilles did not have to instruct her this time. She shuffled on her knees, turning to the side and faced the next cock. She gripped it immediately and looked up into the eyes of the man that stood above her.

Again she brought out his semen, emptying it into the bowl, inhaling its scent as it flowed in front of her face, licking her lips as the last drops dripped from its end. And then the next, even larger than the first two, and copious in its deluge of semen. Then the next, massaging it slowly, emptying it fully, and watching the creamy stream of semen running into her filling bowl. The next poured out almost as she took hold of it, splashing into the semen already there. The next took longer. She became anxious with the delay.

She wanted so much to take it between her lips and suck at it, moisten it with her spit, and draw it out. But she did not dare; her lord Achilles had not commanded it.

Gradually, she moved around them all, staying on her knees, always looking up at their eyes, always holding their throbbing cocks until each one was completely empty. She inhaled the delectable scent of their semen, and felt the heat in the swollen flesh of her cunt. She suppressed the desire to suck on the cocks and draw the last drops out onto her tongue.

'Now, my prize,' ordered Achilles. 'Drink the product of your labours.'

It was the command she had been waiting for. A surge of pleasure ran through her in a massive wave.

Agamemnon sat forward on his chair as Sappho lifted the bowl away from her chest and raised it to her hungry lips. She placed her bottom lip against its edge and tipped the bowl back. She breathed in deeply though her flared nostrils as the sticky semen ran towards her open mouth. Her eyes rolled up in delight as she tasted the first drop. She stopped for a moment, not in hesitation but in delight. Even though she knew she had to carry out Achilles' instructions, she needed to savour this moment of potential, the seconds before completion of her act. The scent and salty taste of the flood of semen filled her completely. She wanted to take it down in one gulp. She tipped the bowl further and the semen touched above her top lip. She sucked at it — delicious, creamy, viscous — and drew it into her mouth. She let it run on the insides of her cheeks and into a pool on the back of her tongue. She opened her mouth more, taking another deep gulp at the same time that she swallowed the first. It went down her throat smoothly, a delectable emollient, and she felt its syrupy mass entering her stomach. It filled her with pleasure, warming her, setting her senses aflame. She lapped at the contents still in the bowl. She licked up every drop, every sticky smear. She drank it all eagerly, sucking it in, filling her mouth before swallowing ravenously. She had never felt so hungry for anything in her life. She could not get enough of it. As the bowl emptied, she tipped it back as far as she could to get the last glutinous beads. When she could get no more, she licked out her tongue and ran it around the bowl until it was completely clean.

She wiped her mouth, hoping to find some more of the glorious gluey semen. She licked her fingers, sucking at them eagerly, hoping for another taste of the delicious ambrosia. She stared ahead, her heart beating frantically, her head spinning, her eyes unable to focus. The dark shape of Agamemnon appeared before her. Her eyes widened as his massive, heavy cock pressed forward against her still wet lips. In one movement, the throbbing glans went between them and slid into her mouth. She took a hurried breath as it pressed over her tongue and against the back of her throat. She felt the venous shaft between her tightly stretched lips, then it went down, plugging her throat and expanding in it. It tightened against the insides of her throat, she could not breathe. She felt its burning heat as the glans expanded and she felt the veins along its length pulsating. Suddenly, a huge stream of hot semen burst from the throbbing end of his deeply fixed cock. It filled her throat, choking her, foaming into her. She could not pull back. He held her head fast. She just hung there, her face penetrated by his huge cock as it throbbed and emptied itself into her. She felt the creamy flow rising back up her throat, bubbling up between its sides and the throbbing venous shaft. It gurgled and foamed into the back of her nose and poured down her nostrils. It flowed out, over her top lip and onto the base of his still plugging cock.

He held it there until it was empty, until her had filled her with all his semen. When he pulled it out, she inhaled deeply, hoarsely. The bubbling semen that flowed from her nostrils was sucked back into her mouth. She drank it all, licking her tongue around her lips and up against her sticky nostrils.

He released her head and stood back.

'Your prize is truly ravenous, Achilles,' he shouted. 'But whether she is in your control is still a question I cannot answer. Here, Praxis, take her and teach her some obedience. And take this one called Chryseis as well. They are both from Troy, and both carry the same germ of disobedience in their blood. Yes, Praxis, see to it.'

Achilles looked down angrily. He resented Agamemnon's interference but, at the same time, knew it would be imprudent to contest his decision. He held back, but it was difficult, and he did not disguise his begrudging assent to Agamemnon's intervention.

Master Wang brought soldiers to drag Sappho and Chryseis to the side of the huge dark ship that towered above them. Small iron cages were fetched. They had hinges on one end which allowed that end to be opened. The cages were barely big enough, but first Chryseis and then Sappho was pushed inside their cramped confines. The hinged ends were locked. The cages were strung up against the side of the massive ship on heavy ropes led over the towering gunwales. They swung from their attachments, sometimes crashing into the wooden side of the boat, sometimes colliding with each other. Sappho could not move at all. She was crouched down, her knees pressed up against her breasts, her elbows alongside her thighs, her hands clasping her face. Chryseis' arms had been pulled behind her and she could just move her head, but still her face was pressed tightly against the unforgiving bars of the restricting iron coop.

Agamemnon ordered water thrown down from the ships.

'Perhaps we can cleanse their pride with a dousing,' he shouted.

Men hauled buckets onto the decks and, at their king's instruction, they poured it down in a deluge on the caged women. It splashed against them harshly, running all over their bodies, soaking them. Sappho braced herself as it ran across her back and between her buttocks. Its soaking wetness accentuated her exposure, her nakedness, her humiliation.

As the cages swung precariously high above the ground, Sappho became aware of the eyes that were on her: the soldiers staring up and pointing, the other slaves gawping, Agamemnon and his chieftains laughing and joking. Her thin, wet vest was pulled up around her neck and, the way she was crushed inside the cage, and the way her buttocks were exposed, meant she was unable to protect herself in any way against these prying stares. But, all the time, she knew that even if she could protect herself, she would not. The fear of the tight confinement filled her with anxiety but it was weaker than the surges of joy which now ran through her. The exposure of her humiliating confinement caused a seething heat of joy to flow through her in heavy, rolling waves. And this joy, this pent-up desire for release of all her ecstasy, was more powerful than any apprehension she felt.

Water dripped from her chin, her knees and her feet. She gazed down from the confines of her incarcerating iron pen. She watched the angered Agamemnon ordering Eva to be whipped. She saw the suffering woman crying out as they bound her to a stake and flogged her repeatedly. But Eva had suffered too much.

Even the pain of the flogging did not bring out the level of suffering Agamemnon expected. He shouted angrily and threw things in all directions. He lashed out, slapping many of the slaves and having some of them tied by the wrists and hung from oars on a nearby boat. He turned his rage on Calliope. He dragged her over his knee and thrashed her with a cane.

Sappho saw the look on Calliope's face: desperation, fear, suffering. She heard her screams, her anguish, and she wished he would let her go, throw her down and end her torment. But she did not wish this for the sake of Calliope. She wished it only in the hope that Agamemnon would bring her down from her cage and set her across his knee in Calliope's place.

But still the plague continued. Neither the ritual, the anger of the chieftains, nor their cruelty to their slaves, could turn it away. Three of the massive ships had been set alight by dissident Greeks. They burned like funeral pyres amid the moaning of the women and angry faces of the disenchanted soldiers. Agamemnon's chance of success at Troy looked in tatters. Calchas was summoned and told his own life was forfeit if he did not find a solution.

He stood before them all: Agamemnon, Achilles, Menelaus, Ajax and the great Odysseus.

'My lords. My king,' he said nervously. 'I have had a sign from Apollo himself. He has a favourite and she is amongst us.' Everyone turned to look, as though this woman would be revealed magically by their glance. 'And,' continued Calchas. 'Apollo has ordered her returned to the Trojans. He wants her to dedicate her life to his worship. Her name is Chryseis, my king. She is your prize from Troy. She must be given back to Troy. Only then will Apollo remove the terrible plague which is destroying us.'

'Then it is done,' said Agamemnon without a second thought. 'Have her taken immediately. I will not lose by it. My lord Achilles will surrender his little "prize" in her place. Chain this "prize" of his, the one they call Sappho, and bring her to my tent. She will stay there from now on. She will not have such an easy life with me, be assured.'

Achilles eyes blazed like fire. He wrinkled his brow deeply and stared hard at Agamemnon.

'My lord,' he protested. 'My — '

'It is done Achilles,' interrupted Agamemnon. 'I will have it no other way. The decision is made.'

Achilles turned on his heel and left, swearing to take no

further part in any battle led by Agamemnon. Ajax followed. The others looked at each other with troubling concern. Their hearts sank when they realised what had happened. They knew that without Achilles there would never be any victory for them here.

Chapter 15

Chryseis is returned to Troy

Sappho's heart sank as she watched Chryseis taken away. It was as if her last hope was being removed. She could not imagine how she could ever be free again. And, now that she was the captive prize of the king himself, she trembled at what might lie ahead.

Agamemnon kept Sappho in chains for many days after she was first taken. She hung, manacled in the dark hold of one of the ships, never seeing anyone or being fed. When she was released, it was only to be bathed and imprisoned again in a small cage suspended on a tripod of spears behind Agamemnon's tent. She clung to the bars, hoping someone would take pity on her, but she was owned by the king now and, unless he commanded it, no one dared even look at her. One night, she heard some soldiers talking. They said that since Pelador's daughter Chryseis had been returned to Troy, the plague had passed. Just the sound of Chryseis' name filled Sappho with excitement and, that night, as she crouched in the swinging cage, she thought of her lost friend. She fixed an image of Chryseis in her mind — naked, standing before the altar in the temple of Apollo. It was a beautiful sight — it sent thrilling shivers coursing through her confined body. Sappho pulled her shoulders down towards her bent knees and, with her fingers deeply inside her soft cunt, she made herself jerk with the ecstasy her tender touch found so easy to release.

As Sappho clung to the bars of the dangling cage, she could just see through a chink on the wall of Agamemnon's tent. One day, she watched as Ajax entered and sat by Agamemnon. Ajax clapped his hands once and, led by Master Wang, Praxis entered with some slaves for Agamemnon's approval.

'I have some beautiful Nubians for you, my lord,' said

Praxis, staring blindly around the tent, unaware of where Agamemnon sat. 'Bound as camel's toes for your delectation.'

Agamemnon furrowed his brow with interest.

Five young girls were paraded in a row. Their wrists were cuttingly bound with thin rope behind their heads. The tension of their pulled-back arms stretched their small pert breasts almost flat against their chests. The nipples of all of them were hard and prominent. Each one had a leather thong drawn tightly around her slender waist. From this, in the centre, just below their navels, another thong was attached and pulled down between the slit of their shaved cunts, before being drawn up tightly between their buttocks. There it was attached again in the small of their backs to the tight waistband.

'See, my lord,' said Praxis. 'See how the tight thong in their naked cracks forms the shape of a camel's toes. I learned this trussing from the tribes of the desert who bind all their slaves in this way. The bedouins always thrash their women bound like this. The method makes them exceptionally receptive, so they say.'

Agamemnon nodded his approval.

'And, like this, my lord, they are particularly fine for the cane. The cane has a sharpness which matches the tight pull of the thong. And this pain, though severe, always releases their greater joy. I guarantee that, like this, no woman can keep back her joy. Bound as camel's toes they are truly a pleasure to behold in their ecstasy. Shall I demonstrate, my lord?'

'You promise a lot, Master Praxis,' said Agamemnon frowning. 'But yes, I am anxious to see.'

Agamemnon waved his approval.

Already excited by what she saw, and aroused by what she heard, Sappho gripped the bars of her cage, eager to watch.

One of the girls was brought forward. She stood shaking

with fear, exposed in her nakedness, terrified by what might happen. She tried to smile, but it was hopeless. Large wet tears welled up in her eyes. She flushed with embarrassment and dropped her head. Her tears fell onto her stomach, flowed down the tight thong and into her crack.

Master Wang led Praxis forward and put a thin cane, about as tall as his waist, into his hand. Praxis flexed it and struck it with a swish through the empty air. Master Wang stood alongside the girl, facing the opposite way to her. He crooked his arm backwards around the girl's waist and bent her over. Her head dropped low as he pushed her down. Her buttocks were upturned and taut. He smoothed his free hand across them, testing their tension, ensuring their exposure. He bent her further so that the delicate shape of her cunt was revealed between her tightly stretched rump.

He reached out and guided Praxis' cane so that it lay level, and at right angles, to the delectable taut curve of the girl's buttocks. He held it there for a moment so that Praxis could fix the image of its position in his mind. When he was sure he knew exactly where it was, he nodded to Master Wang. Master Wang immediately removed his hand from the cane.

Sappho breathed in deeply as she waited for the first strike. She bit onto her lips and felt her heart beating fast. She wanted to stretch out, to lay her hand across the soft flesh of her cunt, but all she could do was watch. She breathed hard. She was gripped by the throbbing of her body and the heat that was building around the squeezed together flesh of her aching cunt.

She watched as Praxis lifted the cane away. He stopped when it was behind his head. He held it there, capturing the moment of potential, holding onto the period of expectation. The cane bent as he brought it down. It swished through the air as though it was cutting it in two. It met the girl's buttocks with a harsh crack. She winced against Master Wang's grip. Sappho saw her screw up her face. A dribble of spit ran over the girl's lower lip. Praxis drew back again, held the cane high for a second, then brought it down even harder. The girl winced again. The cane laid a thin red stripe across her smooth taut skin. Again it came down and again she winced. This time a spray of spit flew from her mouth and more dribbled onto her chin.

Sappho could only watch. She ached with the frustration of not being able to feel her cunt. She let spit dribble from her own mouth, copying the young girl, imagining herself sharing her pain. Her stomach churned with the anxiety caused by her frustrated need.

The thrashing continued. The girl began shrieking but, as the red stripes on her buttocks blended into a solid crimson daub, her screams grew less. Suddenly, she drooped loosely in Wang's grip.

'She fails us,' said Agamemnon making himself more comfortable on his huge chair. 'You have brought out no pleasure in her, Master Praxis. Show me your art. Show me how you draw out the desires of these beautiful young things. Show me what you promised. Do not show me that you can simply beat them into submission. I can do that with a dog!'

Agamemnon laughed and nodded to Ajax who was himself beginning to feel angry with Praxis.

Wang released the girl and she fell to the floor. He brought out a second girl, but again the cane only overcame her with pain. She, like the first, fell onto the floor panting, not with delight, but with exhaustion.

Sappho watched everything, and listened to the swishing crack of the cane, but she too felt unsatisfied. The beating promised her so much and gave her so little. The girl's bottoms were cut with reddening stripes, but nothing more. They looked beautiful as they were lined up for their punishment, but their beauty fell aside as they were overcome with the pain of Praxis' brutality.

Wang had one of the girls suspended by the ankles on a tripod of long spears. She spun giddily on the rope that held her. When she was thrashed she shouted out for mercy, and screamed. But again, she collapsed under the terrible thrashing before any of her own pleasure had come to the surface. Her pain inflamed Sappho, brought her to the brink, but her collapse under the strain of Praxis' harshness delivered only disappointment. Sappho needed more, and it was not available.

Agamemnon became agitated. He sat forward then sat back in his chair. He picked at his fingernails and ordered slave girls to bring him more wine. The blind Praxis sensed his king's discomfort, and was desperate to dispel it.

They had a crucifix of spears built. The next girl was tied to it with her arms outspread and her feet bound together. She was whipped across the breasts and stomach. But it was to no avail. She too, soon dropped her head, simply overcome by the cutting pain delivered by the thrashing cane of Praxis.

They hung the last girl upside down on the crucifix, facing the spears with her legs stretched wide on the crossbar. She shrieked loudly as the cane cut into her buttocks, and spit ran copiously from her mouth. Praxis caned downwards across her exposed crack, slashing at her vulnerable flesh. Still, she too faded under the penetrating pain with no sign of the release of joy that had been promised.

'I do not see the finesse you have promised, Master Praxis,' said Agamemnon angrily. 'You waste these young beauties on a simple thrashing. And now you have none left. It is lucky I am compassionate. I will let you practise on my new prize. But I warn you. I am not here to be dissatisfied. And so far that is all I have been.'

They let the cage down, released Sappho and brought her in. She looked around, fearful to find herself out of the confines of the cage — terrified to be in the presence of the angry Agamemnon. Master Wang wrapped his arm around her waist as he had done to the first girl. He held the cane across her buttocks, levelling it for Praxis so that his aim would be precise.

Sappho trembled. The cane felt so thin against her taut skin. She waited for it to be drawn away, anticipating the swish that would bring its cutting slash across her buttocks. She tightened them in anticipation. Praxis pulled the cane back. Sappho bit down hard onto her lips and waited.

Suddenly she jumped as she heard Agamemnon's booming voice.

'The binding, Master Praxis,' he shouted mockingly. 'You forget your own recommendation. The camel's toes. The trussing which brings forth such delights.' He turned to Ajax. 'Such delights as we have not yet seen. Master Praxis, you forget your own advice! Has your brain gone the same way as your sight?'

Praxis pushed at Master Wang angrily, keen to transfer the blame for his own negligence and embarrassment.

'You are right, lord,' Praxis said falteringly. 'I forgot. My assistant is trained to remind me. You can be sure he will be punished. But I promise you, my lord, the true delights are yet to be seen.'

Agamemnon waved his hand dismissively.

Master Wang took a thin thong and wound it tightly around Sappho's slender waist. She felt the cutting fineness of it as he pulled it tight. He knotted onto it another at the middle of the back. This he led down from the small of her back between her buttocks. He let it dangle as he went to her front. She felt it hanging down between her thighs. He reached between her thighs and pulled it through, bringing it up sharply between her buttocks and into the crack of her cunt. He prised the front of her slit open with his fingers. He wound the narrow thong once around her prominent clitoris and pulled it tightly into a knot. Sappho's eyes widened as he fastened it. A deep burning sensation entered her body and, as if she imagined she could somehow escape it, she rose against its pressure. She opened her mouth wide and breathed in deeply. Master Wang yanked at the thong, testing its security, then pulled it upwards into the top of her slit. She swallowed hard and the burning sensation eased. Master Wang wound the free end into the thong around her waist — in the centre a little below her perfectly shaped navel. He drew it tight and it pulled deeply into the flesh on each side of her cunt. The knot tightened hard around her clitoris and the thong settled in against the tender, moist flesh that lay inside the delicate petals of her slit.

Master Wang pushed her against two of the girls who were now standing, side by side, shivering with fear. Sappho's arms draped across each of their shoulders as she fell forward. Sappho felt the warmth of their small breasts against her own, and the smoothness of their cheeks next to hers. Their touch was light and smooth. Their skin was soft, pliant and silky. She felt their shivering bodies. She felt their fear.

'It is unbearable,' one of the girls whispered in Sappho's ear. 'His viciousness is unbearable. Nothing but pain.'

Sappho shuddered at her words.

The trembling girls were instructed to hold onto Sappho as Master Wang brought Praxis behind her. Again he positioned the cane carefully. He lined it up halfway down her buttocks and held it there until the blind Praxis was sure of its position.

Sappho felt the girls' grip tighten on her own arms as the first slashing cut came down. It stung deeply, thinly — a narrow band of burning pain. The second came down, cutting onto her skin. She jumped this time and opened her mouth. She heard the swishing sound of the third before it struck, and when it did, she shouted out. The girls held her tight. They knew what she was feeling. Sappho screamed again when the fourth came down, and louder with the fifth. Each cutting contact made her scream louder, each swishing slash preceded even more pain.

She felt nothing but pain. It spread over her like a raging fire. It scorched her, seared her, she felt as if she was consumed in flames. She heard Praxis grunting with the effort. She heard Master Wang encouraging him to strike harder, more quickly. She gripped tightly onto the girls' shoulders as she felt her legs weakening, sagging. Suddenly, her knees gave way. She dropped fully into the girls' arms. She hung limply — panting, her mouth wide open, spit dribbling from its corner, seized by pain.

Praxis was aware that now Sappho had failed him. He knew she had suffered too much. He realised he had failed to ignite her pleasure, that he had extinguished it with too much brutality. He felt desperate to redeem himself. He reached forward and gripped the thong where it disappeared between Sappho's taut buttocks. He twisted it hard, but she barely moved, she was completely overcome with the searing pain that filled her body. She was unable to sense any delights that her body contained. She was unable to detect the joy that now lay buried beneath her burning, agonised senses.

Praxis stopped. He stood staring around, holding the cane uselessly, his face filled with anger and fear. Master Wang took his arm, but did not lead him anywhere. He simply held onto him, shoring him up, as if he needed assistance to stand.

The young girls released Sappho. She fell to the ground in a heap. She lay on the ground, face down and spreadeagled, she panted hard. Her buttocks were covered in the angry red stripes inflicted by the cutting cane.

'So again you disappoint me, Master Praxis,' said Agamemnon, finally stirring in his massive chair. 'Your promises have come to nothing.' He turned to Ajax. 'And Ajax, you disappoint me too. I thought you had your slave dog from Troy much better trained. He is no better as a slave trainer than he would be as a ship's lookout. Does he not realise he must tease out pleasure from pain?'

Ajax jumped up angrily and snatched the cane from Praxis.

'You blind fool!' he shouted. 'I should have killed you

instead of only blinding you. Here. Give me this. I will show you how to thrash a woman!'

Ajax knelt behind Sappho and brought the cane down several times on her buttocks. She flinched but that was all. The pain had sunk too deeply into her for her to feel any more.

Ajax rounded on Praxis.

'You idiot! You waste a good woman too. Look! She has nothing left to offer. You have buried the pleasure that she contains. You do not deserve a position with me. Your reputation is a joke. I will have you driven out of our camp.'

Sappho started to crawl away. Ajax saw her, picked up a spear and rushed towards her. He held it above her. She cowered and covered her face with her trembling hands. She thought she had met her end. He threw the spear towards her, barely missing her head as it went deep into the ground. He pulled her to her feet and held her in front of him. He was unable to contain his anger. He shook her mercilessly.

Agamemnon got up smiling and took hold of Ajax' arm. Ajax slowly released his grip on Sappho. She dropped to her knees quaking with fear.

'This one shall not cause any more trouble here today,' said Agamemnon. 'Ajax, calm yourself. Come, we will find some other entertainment. Master Wang! Secure this "prize" to Ajax's spear. And cage her when you leave. Perhaps your Master Praxis will advise you on the bindings which will best keep her in her place! If he cannot, then decide yourself.'

He laughed loudly, and with his arm draping Ajax' shoulders, they both left.

They had barely gone before Praxis dropped his head back and roared like a bull. He struck out in every direction, flailing his arms around him, knocking Master Wang to the ground. He nearly struck Calliope, but she managed to duck away just in time. But he sensed her presence, made a grab for her, and managed to seize her by the hair.

'Wang!' he yelled in frustration. 'Tie this one to the crucifix of spears. I will teach her a lesson. She shall measure my anger by the level of her pain. She will suffer for the humiliation that Ajax has brought on me today. And he will not be free of my vengeance. I promise that. I have suffered at his hands twice now and that is too much. Next time it is Ajax who will feel the wrath of Praxis.'

Sappho lay still and watched as Calliope was bound to the crucifix of spears. Her lithe body hung to one side, tipping her shapely hips out at an angle. It furrowed the delightful creases of skin at the tops of her thighs. It squeezed the shape of her crack and accentuated its fleshy softness.

Praxis removed the spear Ajax had thrust into the ground. He felt its length and the thickness of the shaft. He cocked his head to the side and sniffed the air.

'Fetch some thin hide!' he ordered.

Some soft hide was brought and he bound it carefully over the blunt end of the heavy spear. He held it in place, with several turns of narrow leather strapping.

Master Wang led him to the bound Calliope. Filled with apprehension, she bit down hard on her lips as he got nearer. He held the leather-covered end of the spear in front of her face — knowing where it was by the sound of her panting. He cocked his head to the side and listened again. He sniffed the air and breathed in deeply.

Sappho watched as, suddenly, Praxis lowered the spear and thrust it between Calliope's legs. She reared up on her bonds, but they were too tight for her to get away. The leather-covered end of the heavy shaft squeezed between the tops of her thighs. It opened the flesh of her cunt, prising it to each side, exposing the pinkness of its inner leaves, revealing the glistening wetness of its interior.

Praxis twisted the spear between the open crack of her flesh. She squirmed on it, holding herself away. Sappho could see though, that Calliope was finding it difficult not to give in to the need to drop further onto it, to have it penetrate her more. Praxis turned the spear as he pushed it more. Straight away, her open mouth and drooping shoulders betrayed her surrender to its joyous power.

'Ajax will not make a fool of me again, I swear it! He ranted as he twisted the spear and began thrusting it rhythmically into Calliope's distended cunt. 'I will not be bettered by any slave!'

He forced the padded end of the spear into her cunt. She gasped at its bulk and depth of penetration. The leather covering glistened with her moisture as he pulled it back, and she gasped again as he forced it back in. She fell back onto Agamemnon's mighty chair, her legs wide, her arms draped on the massive clawed armrests. Praxis kept thrusting the spear and now, with Calliope against the back of the chair, the pressure from the spear was harder, the penetration even deeper.

Calliope called out, her voice rising and lowering according to whether the spear end was being thrust in or drawn out of her cunt.

'Master Praxis,' she gasped. 'Master Praxis ... I can help you ... I can help you revenge yourself ... Master Praxis ...'

Spit flowed from her mouth. She struggled for breath. She begged again, more urgently.

'Master Praxis ... I can help you ... I have learned of Ajax' greatest pleasure ... I can tell you what it is ... He could be weakened by it ... I could tell you ... If you set me free ... I could tell you ... Master Praxis ...'

Sappho, still on the ground, gripped the thong that led up from her cunt, and from its tight encirclement of her engorged, hard clitoris. She pulled at it first, testing the pain it brought. She jerked it forward to see how much it could inflict. She fixed her eyes on Calliope — her wet cunt, the thrusting spear — and twisted the ligature harder, more fiercely. But it was Calliope's treachery which excited

Sappho just as much as the sight of her suffering and of her pleasure. Sappho felt a wave of delight spread over her at the thought of Calliope's deceit. The idea of such treachery filled her with joy. She had not experienced the feeling before, and she was elated by it and by its novelty. She too wanted to deceive, to mislead, to draw someone into her own trap. She drew the thong higher. The thoughts which filled her head demanded more pain, more delight, more abuse.

Praxis suddenly stopped. He held the spear where it was. Its bound leather end glistened at the entrance to Calliope's fleshy pink cunt. He bent his head forward, breathing hard, licking his fleshy lips. He placed his ear by her mouth and listened as she explained her plan. He smiled, grabbed the spear again and began thrusting her eagerly. This time Calliope screams were screams of pleasure, of released joy, of ecstasy.

Sappho pulled at the thong that gripped her clitoris. She held it so tightly she began to cry. Tears flowed down from her eyes as, together with Calliope screeching for mercy and relief, Sappho jerked forward with a massive jolt of finally released and joyous rapture.

Sappho was pushed back into the cage. She knelt on its base, bent over, her buttocks high, her elbows squashed against her chest, her hand against her cheeks. As Praxis was led out by Master Wang, she watched Calliope getting up out of Agamemnon's chair. She was truly beautiful, her short dark hair and perfectly naked cunt adding to her lean body and high-cheek-boned face. She squatted over a bucket and urinated. The shimmering flow caused Sappho to drool. She tried to reach one of her hands away from her face, but she was so tightly fixed in the cage, it was impossible to move. She stared at Calliope, her legs bent, her elbows on her open knees, the golden flow of urine still streaming into the bowl. Sappho gulped and swallowed hard. The sensation in her throat, and the tightness of her lips as she concentrated on what she saw, allowed, at first, a trickle of joy, and then a streaming flow of unheralded ecstasy. She did not move as it welled over her, she did not need to. Simply watching the last trickles of urine splattering into the bowl, overpowered her. Silently, and without moving, she was completely overcome by the unstoppable flood of an orgasm born from deep inside her very being. It was what had been held back by the pain of the caning. It was all that had built up from her suffering and humiliation in the cage. It was a deluge. It was complete. She stared at Calliope as it ran through her, tearing at every part of her. She imagined herself lying on her back, her face peering up between Calliope's legs. She imagined Calliope's urine splashing on her cheeks, in her eyes, running into her nostrils. She opened her mouth, thinking of it being filled. Her orgasm was renewed. She shivered all over as it took control and led her into a new paradise of overwhelming rapture.

Chapter 16

Sappho's suffering continues.

Agamemnon had Sappho kept in the small cage every day, tightly confined, swinging on the chain in the glaring heat. Sometimes the constant movement made her dizzy. Sometimes she felt so hot and claustrophobic, she thought she would faint. But although she suffered from the burning heat of the sun during the day, she dreaded even more the evening and its passing. After sunset, Agamemnon allowed her to be taken around the encampment so that any soldier who wished, could use her in any way he chose. His men enjoyed her as a bonus for their allegiance, and were all the more unswerving in their devotion to Agamemnon because of it.

She was abused and humiliated in different ways each time. Sometimes she was whipped or thrashed with a cane. Sometimes she was passed from one group of men to another. They bound her and filled her cunt with their cocks, sometimes one, sometimes several at a time. They tied her to stakes, or a crucifix of spears, and stuffed their cocks into her mouth. They covered her face with semen. She was made to swallow semen collected in bowls. Often they used her for buk-ka-ke and left her all night covered in their sticky fluid. Some nights she was bound and hung from the side of a ship. Sometimes staked to the ground and doused repeatedly with buckets of water. She was tied in every way possible. Often, she was left for hours with rope contorting her body into strained and unbearable shapes.

One night, as Sappho hung, bound to a stake, soaked and dripping with water which had been thrown over her for hours, she heard some soldiers talking in whispers. They spoke of Achilles' rage. How, angered by Agamemnon's theft of his 'prize', he had returned to his tent and sworn never again to fight alongside Agamemnon. The soldiers said that without Achilles there could never be any victory at Troy. They said that the Myrmidons, disheartened by Achilles' withdrawal, were talking of leaving and, if they did, the campaign at Troy was as good as over.

Agamemnon strutted back and forth across his tent. His brother, Menelaus sprawled on a couch. Agamemnon flung his goblet to the ground and struck a naked slave girl who tried to retrieve it. She dropped to her knees and hung to his tunic, begging for mercy, asking what she could do to please him. He looked down at her. She shivered with fear, her long red hair hanging down to her small, rounded breasts. He grabbed her hair and pulled her to her feet. She shivered with excitement and her nipples hardened at his touch.

'How dare Achilles defy my call to arms like this?' he roared, shaking the petrified girl.

'He is still angry that you took his prize, the slave Sappho, my lord,' said Menelaus. 'The army thinks it wise to return her.'

Agamemnon's face reddened in fury. He lifted the young girl off the ground by her long hair. She dangled, painfully spinning in his mighty hand.

'The army thinks it wise? The army thinks it wise?' he shouted. 'Does the army consider itself wise above its king?'

He did not want an answer, and Menelaus did not give one.

Agamemnon lifted the trembling girl high, drew his free arm behind her knees and held her horizontally in front of his face. He took one of her pert nipples in his mouth and sucked at it as hard as he could. She screamed with pain and wriggled in his unbreakable grasp. He tightened his hold on her and sucked her throbbing nipple harder. She screamed again — a loud, penetrating and frightened screech of agony and terror. He pulled his mouth away and she relaxed — the tension going out of her body for a moment as she thought she was released. But, as soon as he saw her relief, he drew her breast to his mouth again. He took the same nipple — now reddened and extended to its limit — between his teeth and bit down on it fiercely. She tightened suddenly, taken by surprise, hurting, filled with anguish from the deep and shocking pain. She screamed louder, struggling frantically to free herself. But he was too powerful. She could do nothing to resist him. She was helpless in his arms and she submitted to his overpowering domination.

Her mouth dropped open and spit ran from its corners. He took his mouth away and lifted her higher. He held her across him in such a way that he could drive his hand between her legs. He forced them to the tops of her thighs and against the soft flesh of her young cunt. She gasped as he pushed his fingers inside — stretching her slit, spreading its pink edges, slipping in on its fresh moisture. She tried to beg for mercy, but it was pointless Even though her mouth opened and closed, no sound came out.

He twisted her around like a doll, holding her on her back with the vee of her open legs towards his face. He balanced her, holding her back and buttocks on his hands and forearms, and drew her towards him. Her legs opened fully against his face. Her delectable slit widened, glistening at its delicious centre. He held her there, looking at the perfection of her young flesh. He poked his long tongue out and pressed it flatly against her cunt. He licked at the delightful opening, covering it with spit. He lapped at its edges before driving the tip of his tongue deep inside. He moved her up and down in his powerful arms, sliding her slit along his penetrating tongue. He held her still for a while, and pressed his tongue hard against her clitoris. He probed its base and licked around its budding firmness. He lapped his tongue into the front opening of her slit — his irresistible intrusion parting the flesh easily and spreading it wide. He lifted her up. His tongue passed over the succulent centre of her silky flesh, licking at it, tasting it, driving between the soft edges of the luscious entrance. His tongue passed to the rear of her open fleshy slit. Again it parted the swollen leaves of flesh. Again he licked around the tender sweetness within. He lifted her higher and pressed the tip of his tongue into her anus — opening it, dilating it, entering it. He tasted the biting tang of her rectum. He kept his tongue inside as her anal muscle contracted and, when he thrust it deeper, it opened to let him in.

Suddenly, he flung her down. She lay on her back, her legs wide apart, the flesh of her cunt shimmering with a mixture of his spit and her own fragrant moisture. She did not think of drawing her legs together and, without thinking further, she ran her hand down to the crack of her cunt. She placed her fingers at its fleshy centre. She took her other hand down and slipped a finger into her anus — wet and dilated by his penetrating tongue. She drove it in and raised up supporting herself between her feet and shoulders. With only a few movements of her other hand against her throbbing clitoris, she convulsed in a jerking, shuddering and welcome release of pleasure. She kept her finger deeply in her anus as, slowly, she lowered herself back onto the ground. She bit on her lips as another jerk of ecstasy passed through her. She did not resist it as she squirmed and threw her head from side to side.

Agamemnon laughed indifferently and tossed his long hair back.

'Bring me the "prize". I want to see the one who can cause all this trouble for a king.'

Sappho struggled as they pulled her out of the cage. Although she was cramped, in a strange way, she felt safe inside it. Although she hung in the glare of the sun all day, and she was a victim of continual abuse, she still felt protected by the bars that imprisoned her. The two soldiers who released her each took hold of one of her arms and dragged her backwards. They hauled her, naked and powerless, to the entrance to Agamemnon's tent. Her heels dug out two furrows in the soft sand.

'So, our troublesome "prize" enters,' said Agamemnon, still angry, as Sappho was dropped on the ground at his feet.

'Perhaps she needs the hand of Agamemnon across her buttocks, my lord,' said Menelaus, getting up and pulling Sappho to her feet. 'And fine buttocks they are, my lord. They curve so well. And they are firm and supple. They would be a fine spring to a heavy smacking. Sometimes it is the hand that disciplines best. Even when the whip or the flogger fails, the palm of a hand can often bring success.'

Menelaus stroked Sappho's buttocks. He smoothed his hand from the small of her back, around their outward curve then back into the small crease they formed beneath them at the tops of her firm thighs. He gripped one side in his hand and tested the tension of her muscles. 'Yes, firm and springy. And youthful. She is the perfect candidate for such discipline, my lord.'

Agamemnon prowled around Sappho, still enraged by Achilles, still hurt by Achilles' petulance and the threat he posed to the venture against Troy. He kicked his sandalled feet at the ground, only half listening to what Menelaus was saying. Suddenly, he turned and grabbed Sappho around the waist. He dropped to his knee and bent her over it. She gasped as he pushed her forward, knocking the breath from her as her stomach fell heavily across his thigh. Her upturned buttocks curved perfectly as he pressed one of his hands against her back and held her head down. Her face lay against the sandy ground and she spluttered as she breathed some of it in. It made her cough and that only tightened her buttocks more.

Agamemnon flattened his huge right hand across the satiny skin of Sappho's buttocks. He parted her legs slightly, just enough to see the delectable shape of her pink slit. It showed through between her buttocks — a perfectly formed and enticing oval of flesh, split by a pink line of glistering softness. He took aim by holding his hand against the highest point of the upturned curve. He raised his arm slowly and brought it down hard.

Her buttocks sprang against the contact — shuddering, depressing, then bouncing back. The mark of his hand was inscribed precisely on her pale, taut skin. He raised his hand again and brought it down slightly to the left of where it had landed first. Again her buttocks bounced back firmly against his had. This time she tightened the backs of her thighs.

He held her firmly with his left hand and brought his right hand down again. She tightened her thighs more this time, but her buttocks still sprang back against his punishing hand. He struck her again, and again, each time slightly one side or another of all his previous contacts. Her bottom reddened all over. Each smacking strike brought the same springy, taut response from her tightly curved buttocks.

Each smack stung her. She felt it first across the surface of her buttocks but, as he smacked her more, she felt it in her breasts, between her thighs, and deep in the soft flesh of her cunt. It ached so much. She felt its flesh swelling, opening, needing. She squirmed against his restraining left hand on her back. He was overpoweringly strong, and she was pitifully helpless. She flung her arms about — desperately, pointlessly. Her face buried deeper into the sand. She choked more. She fought harder for breath.

The smacking blows rained down in a storm. Her pain increased, and soon her whole body was filled with it. But, she experienced joy as well as anguish. She knew Menelaus was watching — that he could see her cunt — and that gave her the delightful sensation of exposure. She knew that she was being punished for a reason — that she was the centre of all the problems between Agamemnon and Achilles — and that filled her with surging waves of pleasure. But she knew that the smacking was not enough. Even with the exposure and the knowledge of her wrongdoing, still it was not enough. She needed more. She had been spoiled by all the humiliations she had endured at the hands of the cruel Greeks. They had set on fire a new appetite in her. An appetite that could only be quenched by ever higher levels of suffering, more pain, deeper humiliation.

She squirmed against Agamemnon's hand, not so much to escape, but to feel the strength of the hand that held her. She needed to remind herself of his power, of his greatness. He responded to her wriggling struggle, smacking her harder, bringing his hand down faster. She writhed and threw her head from side to side. She sensed his passion, sensed his need to punish her, sensed his desire to degrade her.

She fought on, struggling frantically under his massive hand. She felt the pressure on her back increasing, pressing her down more, holding her tighter against the tops of his massive thighs. She forced her buttocks higher, exposing them to his hand. She widened them, showing more of her cunt, its softness, its wetness, its warmth. She hoped his hand would strike it. She wanted to feel the sharp, heavy smack of his hand against the flesh of her tender cunt. She wanted to feel the shock of it — the keen, piercing flavour of the sudden, slapping kiss. She lifted her buttocks as high as she could, but she was not rewarded by the smacking caress she wanted.

Sappho began shouting, pleading, begging. Her words were stifled by the sand that was in her mouth, but she did not stop. Sand stuck to her cheeks and lips. It blocked her nostrils and filled her eyes. She called out to Agamemnon, imploring him to strike her harder, more fully. Her choking shouts beseeched him to make his punishment more severe. She begged him to bring his hand down faster, to strike the soft flesh of her cunt, to fill her body with pain. But her cravings only fed her frustration. She twisted her head frantically from side to side, coughing out sand, bubbling spit, screaming hopelessly.

Suddenly the spanking stopped. Sappho listened, as if she would hear what was going to happen.

Turning her easily in his hands, Agamemnon flung her over and draped her backwards across his knee. The back of her head hit the ground hard. She squirmed her feet into the sand. Her hips lay across his thigh. Her smoothly covered hip bones reached up prominently on each side of her flattened stomach. The mound at its base rose up to the slit of her cunt. As her legs fell back slightly open, her cunt was exposed fully — open, pink, shimmering with moisture and warmed with still building desire.

Sappho gasped with pleasure at the exposure. She opened her legs more. She hoped he would continue smacking her, bringing his hand down on the soft flesh of her cunt, filling it with pain, satisfying it with the hurt of joy. She imagined the slaps coming down against it, stinging it, nourishing its hunger, feeding its frustration. She pictured the skin of his hands sticking to the flesh of her cunt. She imagined how it might pull up as he drew back. She saw it in her mind, extended until it finally broke free of its delightful stickiness. She saw herself screaming with anguish as the pain became too much. She perceived herself gulping for air as she felt the dizziness of unconsciousness overtaking her.

Agamemnon spread his right forearm across her knees to stop her lifting them. Menelaus stepped forward and stood above her gasping face. He placed his feet across her shoulders, pinning them into the sandy ground. Sappho gaped up at him, gasping, still shouting, feeling the humiliation of her captivity, straining against it as it fed her desire for more. She saw his heavy testicles hanging between his legs and the end of his cock, only half erect, which lay between them. Menelaus took his cock in his hand and held it out towards her. She watched as a stream of golden urine spouted from its end. He directed it onto her cunt and it ran around her flesh in a hot glistening flood. It burned her tender softness. It ran between the delicate petals and flowed along her slit. It streamed copiously down the insides of her thighs and down to her writhing feet. He aimed it at her breasts. Again she felt its heat as it streamed around her hard nipples, over her chest and around her neck. She felt it under her chin and then, as she looked up, she felt it on her face. It flooded up her nostrils, into her eyes and inside her wide-open mouth. She tasted its strong saltiness — like the sea — and licked at it, absorbing its aroma. She was impatient. She wanted more.

She lay beneath him as his urine streamed into her mouth. She let it flow straight in and run right down her throat. She kept swallowing it, gulp after gulp, as it came down on her in a cascade. She hoped it would never end. She wanted to drink it forever. She wanted it to be her only refreshment.

Suddenly, unexpectedly, she felt the delightful shock of Agamemnon's hand as it came down at last on her soft cunt. The smack was startling, and, for all her hoping, she was not prepared. She choked on Menelaus' urine, spitting it out as the sting of the hand smacking her cunt sent her into confusion. The urine spilled over her face and chin, into her eyes and into her ears. She licked feverishly to get it back. She did not want to waste it. She did not want to miss any of it. She threw her head from side to side, catching it if she could in her gaping mouth, sucking at it, swallowing it greedily. Another smack across her cunt, another shock, and another struggle to gulp all the urine that was offered.

Then everything blended into one. Her body felt hot, out of control, taken over. She felt the stream of urine turning into a trickle. She felt her disappointment. She felt the slapping hand on the flesh of her cunt stopping and she was filled with unsatisfied yearning. But, when she was lifted and placed onto the huge chair of Agamemnon, and soldiers were ordered to tie her backwards over it, she knew her frustration would be short lived.

They bound her tightly, her head hanging backwards off the front edge of the seat, the backs of her knees bent over its harsh wooden back. Her arms were pulled downwards until her hands reached the ground. Her wrists were bound with leather thongs to the heavy clawed feet of the mighty chair.

Now Agamemnon's urine streamed across her breasts, splashed onto the shoulders and down her neck. It covered her face in a deluge. It filled her mouth so much it overflowed from her lips before she could slurp it all down. She gulped heavily, not wanting to waste any. She felt some of it running into her eyes and hair before overflowing onto the ground. She wanted her hands free so that she could cup them and scoop it up, save every drop, not allow any to run away. She struggled against the bonds that held her wrists. But it was impossible, they were too tight, she was held fast.

Menelaus' now stiffened cock was in her cunt before Agamemnon's urine had finished flowing. She felt the penetration deep inside her aching flesh as still she swallowed heavily on the stream of urine that filled her mouth. It was too much for her. She could hold back no longer. It had built up too much. She felt Menelaus' semen running across her stomach. She started jerking with a convulsion so strong she went rigid against the bonds of her captivity. She was completely stiff. And it did not stop. Bubbles of urine exploded from her mouth as the paroxysms kept coming — heavy and strong, gripping every part of her, making her whole body rigid with the fever of her ecstasy.

Sappho was still moaning, unable to recover herself, as the two mighty warriors stood above her.

'Brother,' said Menelaus. 'I would advise you to give this "prize" back to Achilles. It would be a bad thing to keep her. The men are worried — '

'No, Menelaus, I will not return her,' said Agamemnon sprawling back onto the couch. 'But send Achilles five young girls. The best we have. I think that will bring him around. But, let him be reminded, he will not have his "prize" returned to him. She stays mine. Even the greatest warrior in Greece does not instruct his king.'

Sappho was dragged outside and secured, face forward over a round timber mast set up horizontally on trestles. Her legs were bent fully at the knees. Her ankles were bound tightly with leather thongs to the tops of her thighs. Her arms were stretched around the beam and her wrists were secured to her crooked knees. She was pulled so tightly against the timber that she could hardly breathe.

She hung over the timber spar in despair, semen running from her cunt, urine, still wet, glistening on her cheeks and around her mouth. Everything seemed hopeless. She had given up hope of ever seeing Troy or Chryseis again. She had given up hope of ever being free. All she could imagine in the future was a life of captivity and humiliation. She craned her neck up and looked at the faces of the jeering men that surrounded her. Yes, all she could see ahead of her was a life of torment and shame.

She caught sight of Master Wang hurrying though the crowd. He looked furtively from side to side, as though he was afraid of being seen. Sappho shivered at the thought he might be coming for her, that Praxis had some new torture he wanted to try on her, or some fresh degradation he wanted her to suffer. But Master Wang scuttled through the square and disappeared into a narrow alley. Sappho wondered where he was going. One of the men in the crowd approached her, grasped her cheeks and opened her mouth wide. She felt relieved that Master Wang did not give her any attention. As the man's semen poured into her mouth, and she felt the heat of her exposed cunt rising within its swelling flesh, she was filled with a strange sense of relief. She welcomed her humiliation and gulped the semen down hungrily. When she had swallowed it all, she opened her mouth for more.

Chapter 17

Praxis takes revenge

Master Wang brought the message to Ajax in the night.

'My lord,' he said kneeling down by Ajax' spartan bed. 'My master, Praxis, says he has a speciality for you. An unsurpassable speciality. He says it will make up for all your disappointment in him. He bids you hurry. To come with me and savour what he has arranged for you. An unsurpassable speciality, my lord. Unsurpassable.'

Ajax sat up, rubbed his eyes, thought for a few moments, then jumped to his feet.

'Very well, Master Wang. You have my interest. But woe betide you and your master if this should prove a disappointment. Neither of you will see tomorrow if this is another hollow promise. Lead me to this unsurpassable speciality. Quickly!'

Master Wang bowed and held his hand out as Ajax entered the great tent. The black shrouds of its roof hung low, and several heavy poles supported its massive weight. A wide ring was inscribed in the sand and, around the ring, women stood closely together, at attention, in a circle facing inwards. Their nakedness was covered only by a shield in one hand and a twin-headed spear in the other. The twin-headed spears, the type used in close combat, were held at an angle so that the spear ends were at the height of the women's shoulders. Each woman, her head shaved specially for her appearance, wore a plumed headdress of exotic feathers. The shimmering light from the torches placed near the walls of the tent, shone on the iridescent plumage of the headdresses. It reflected frantic patterns of rainbow-coloured lights on the smooth skin of the women's naked bodies.

Ajax sat himself in a huge chair placed at the centre of

the circle of women. He spread his legs wide and yawned as Praxis was led in by Master Wang.

'I have arranged such a speciality to please you, my lord Ajax,' said Praxis as he cocked his head and sniffed the soft evening air. 'A speciality fit for a king!'

'I am here against my better judgement, Praxis,' Ajax replied. 'And I shall not be tolerant of more failure on your part. Take this as a warning. Your freedom, your life perhaps, hangs in the balance tonight.'

Praxis cocked his head the other way and stared around blindly. He reached out for Master Wang who led him to the edge of the circle of young women.

'My lord Ajax. Such is the wonder of what I have planned for you, I promise, you will not leave here unchanged.'

Ajax nodded begrudgingly. He had not forgiven Praxis for his embarrassment in front of Agamemnon, and was set against letting him regain a place in his favour.

Master Wang held onto Praxis as Praxis again addressed Ajax.

'There is such a treat here for you, my lord Ajax. Not even such as you could bear to look on it without preparation. You must use your sense of touch first. By that means only will your sensations be sufficiently acclimatised for you to be able to take the sight in with your eyes.'

'Your talk of sight amuses me, Praxis. Yes, you have caught my interest. Your experiment has promise. I will undertake it as you wish.'

Ajax stood up. Master Wang took a wide red ribbon of cloth and wound it several times around Ajax' eyes.

'Praxis!' exclaimed Ajax. 'At last you have me blinded as well. You have your revenge! Now, where is this thing I cannot bear to set eyes on? Where is this speciality which, if seen would weaken even the mighty Ajax?'

'Be patient, my lord. Listen, you will hear it approaching.'

Sappho and Eva were brought in. They were both naked and strung beneath a long pole to which their wrists and ankles were bound with leather thongs. The poles were carried by naked young girls, two at the front and two at the rear of each pole. All the girls wore crowns of yellow and white flowers on their shaven heads. The poles rested on their square shoulders and they held onto them with their hands. They stood silently in the middle of the circle of women, waiting for instructions. Sappho looked around. She and Eva had both been tied to the poles hours ago. Sappho bit her lips to help contain the pain. She was terrified by the sight of Ajax standing blindfolded. She quivered when she saw the ring of women holding their shields and spears.

Ajax spun around, his arms outstretched, reaching out blindly.

'What is it you have, Praxis? Reveal it to me.'

'My lord, have patience. I need to prepare your quarry. You have two fawns to capture. But first I need to bring them out of the undergrowth.'

Ajax waited impatiently as Praxis had Sappho and Eva untied from the poles. The naked young girls worked diligently to remove their bonds. When finally they were released, the girls lifted the two women down and cradled them in their arms. Sappho relaxed as she felt the warm limbs of the girls holding her. For a moment, she thought she was back in Troy with Chryseis — enfolded in her arms, delighting in the silkiness of her skin, luxuriating in the softness of her lips.

Master Wang grabbed Sappho's arm. The leather straps that had bound her to the pole still dangled from her wrists. He pulled Eva over and forced the two of them back to back. He grabbed the spare leather thongs that hung from their wrists and bound them together. He wound the thongs around twelve times so that they were bound tightly from wrist to elbow. They both twisted and turned — anxious, unable to properly see the other, stumbling, in pain, frightened.

'Can you hear your little fawns, my lord?' asked Praxis. 'Can you hear them panting in anticipation of the chase?'

Ajax cocked his head to the side and listened. He smiled, intrigued by the scene that Praxis was painting for him.

'Yes, I can,' said Ajax eagerly. 'They sound afraid of me. When will the chase begin?'

'Soon, my lord, soon.'

Praxis stood close to Sappho and Eva. He reached out and touched Sappho's breasts, squeezing them cruelly, massaging them roughly. He pinched her hard and extended nipples. She dropped her head, suddenly aware of the exposure to the girls and all the women who surrounded them. A flush of shame ran through her. She felt her stinging nipples throb as they hardened even more between Praxis' vicelike thumb and forefinger. She pulled at her arms and felt the tension in Eva. She felt Eva's buttocks rubbing against her own — their heat, their taut curve, their pressure, their promise.

Praxis nodded approvingly. Master Wang took some long leather tapes, thin as thread, and halved them in his hands. At about the middle point of its length he wound the first around one of Sappho's throbbing nipples. She rose against the pain as he tied it hard and pulled it into a firm knot. He did the same with the other, pulling the thin leather tape sideways to get it as tight as possible before knotting it. The thin thong pulled taut between her two breasts. Master Wang took the spare ends around Sappho and Eva's shoulders and led them both across Eva's mouth. She kept it closed. He forced her to open it and slipped the two thin thongs between her lips. He pulled them tight, forcing Eva to hold her head inclined back against Sappho's as he did it. He tied off the leather tapes and knotted them firmly. Eva stood with the knotted ligature between her teeth, the sides of her mouth and her cheeks indented deeply by its cutting pressure. She gulped and tried to swallow. When she moved her head forward, the tapes pulled harshly against the tightly tied knots around Sappho's nipples. She cried out, filled with excruciating pain.

Sappho did not know what Master Wang had done with the loose ends of the threadlike strips of leather. All she could tell was that whenever Eva moved, the pain in her nipples increased. She cried out again as Eva stumbled and tried to regain her balance. Sappho's eyes filled with tears. She breathed hard, and clenched her teeth in a vain effort to keep the excruciating pain at bay.

Master Wang took some more thin thongs and tied them tightly around Eva's nipples. Before knotting the thin threads of leather firmly in place, he pulled them out between his thumbs and forefingers. This time, he led them first around Eva's shoulders and then Sappho's. He held the long ends in front of Sappho, dangling them before her eyes, showing her what was in store. Suddenly, he tugged them hard. Sappho was saturated with pain as Eva reacted to the tension of the thongs on her tied nipples. Eva dropped her head forward to try and stave it off. As she did, the strip between her teeth pulled relentlessly on Sappho's hard, bound flesh.

As Sappho opened her mouth and screamed, Master Wang forced the thin straps between her teeth. He pulled both ends tightly sideways, cutting into the sides of her mouth, notching into her pale cheeks. He tied them off at the tightest point. Eva strained against the pain and the more she pulled the more Sappho was filled with her own agony. The two of them gasped loudly. Spit bubbled from each of their mouths. It ran in sticky threads along the straining, taut strips of leather that bound them together in an unbreakable loop of mutual pain and suffering.

Sappho's nostrils flared as she struggled with the pain. She knew she was hurting Eva by her movements, but she could not stop herself. Her nipples burned. She felt on fire. The licking flames of agony penetrated every part of her body. She could not stand it. She bit into the thong in her mouth, as hard as she could, as though clenching her teeth onto it would somehow relieve her. She tried to be still, to allow the pain to ease, to bring to an end the terrible, common suffering they imposed on each other. But it was impossible. Both of them gulped and gasped for breath. Both of them shivered with the tremors of their own agony. Both of them panted in an effort to calm their pounding hearts. But they could not be still. They were trapped. Neither could prevent inflicting the terrors of her own fate on the other.

'What is happening, Praxis?' demanded Ajax. 'I am eager. What is happening?'

'A few moments more, my lord. That is all, a few moments.'

Sappho's eyes flashed from side to side. Master Wang held up a soft deer skin with leather thongs hanging from each corner. He tied it around Sappho's neck, allowing the supple skin to hang down across her breasts to the base of her stomach. He tied the bottom strings around her hips. She felt the silky smoothness of the pelt against her skin. Where it touched the sensitised ends of her agonised nipples it inflamed them more. Where it hung against her stomach, and was pulled against the sides if her hips, it sent shivers of pleasure deep inside her. She wriggled again, as if having the soft skin on her body would somehow release her from suffering, but all that was released was more pain, more anxiety, more terror.

'The quarry is ready, my lord!' announced Praxis. 'Come, touch the little fawn. Know what it is you have to hunt. Know what it is you will enjoy if you are successful in the chase. Come, feel the soft pelt of her skin. Run your hands over the smooth lines of her delectable form.'

Ajax stepped forward unsteadily towards Praxis' voice. He reached out his hands towards Sappho. Master Wang pushed her forward. She gasped with pain as Eva tightened in her own agony and sent back to Sappho as much suffering as she received. Ajax' hand touched the soft deer pelt that covered Sappho. He stroked it, moving his hand first across her breasts, then down her stomach until he felt the raised mound that announced the opening of her luscious slit.

He felt the top of the opening to her cunt through the soft deer skin. He moved it sideways, splaying her flesh. Sappho rose on his caress. It was the covering of the skin that inflamed her, the tightness of it, the disguise of it, and the sense of Ajax' arousal because of it. She bit hard onto the leather strap in her mouth. As she gripped her teeth together, she felt the tightening of the knots on her nipples as Eva responded to her own excruciating pain. Sappho tightened her buttocks and felt Eva's close to hers. Ajax' finger probed the front of her slit, opening it, pressing the supple deer skin against it, absorbing her moisture into it. The pains she felt in her nipples gave way to the pleasure that now began swelling the flesh of her heated, wet cunt.

Master Wang snatched Sappho forward, removing her from Ajax' touch — bringing the pain back into her nipples, her breasts, and the rest of her body. The pain drove her pleasure away. She widened her eyes, pleading with the blindfolded Ajax. All she wanted was to feel his hand again. She wanted it massaging the soft flesh of her cunt through the deer skin. She wanted him pressing his fingers against her throbbing slit — opening it, finding the softness of its interior, delving into it, penetrating it, inflaming it.

She stumbled and was racked with shooting spasms of pain in her breasts. She looked at Ajax stumbling forward blindly. She wanted to set herself in his path. She wanted to drive herself against his hand, to relieve herself of the pain, to fill herself with pleasure. She needed the feel of the skin pressed against her flesh. She wanted her cunt stuffed with his probing fingers.

Ajax did not know which way to turn. He reached his hands out, holding them wide and turning around, hoping to touch Sappho again — to grab her, to violate her. Sappho pulled against Eva, against her pain, against the thong that was fixed so tightly in her mouth. She felt the pelt against her skin. It set her on fire. She wanted Ajax to chase her. To run her into a corner. To set her at bay. To prevent her escape. To close in on her and take her in any way he wished. Eva pulled against her and Sappho pulled back. They both cried out in pain.

Ajax stepped forward and swung his arms around wildly. He stepped to the side and did the same. He glanced Sappho with one of his hands, touching the skin that covered her. He knew it was her. He gripped the skin. She strained towards him, drawing herself towards his grasp, yearning to be captured. He realised he had her. He stopped for a moment, sniffing the air, planning his move then, in a rush, he turned and grabbed both women in his massive, powerful hands.

In one move, he flung them over, forcing Sappho forwards onto her knees with Eva laid on her back. Sappho gasped with the strain of Eva's weight and the pain caused by Eva's struggling. But there was no delay. Ajax, dropped to his knees behind Sappho. He forced Eva's legs up high, exposing the soft pink flesh of her cunt and the darker circle of her anus. He held her legs up with the pressure of his massive body, then encircled Sappho's waist with one of his hands. He moved his hand down across the soft deer skin and gripped the flesh of her cunt through the supple pelt. He clutched the flesh hard — parting it, opening it and forcing his fingers to reach inside it. Sappho gasped again, fighting for breath, confused, overcome. She felt the shock as Ajax drove his cock into Eva's cunt. She felt the shuddering pains in her nipples as he pounded deeply inside her. But more than that, she felt his hand on her cunt. She felt the soft deer skin between her flesh and his fingers. She succumbed to the feeling of him riding behind her in his animal passion — like a beast driving himself to satisfaction. Sappho whinnied and whined, purred and screeched.

Ajax' testicles pressed against Sappho's upturned buttocks

as he continued to push his stiff cock harder into Eva. Sappho felt their heat, their potency. She lifted her buttocks as much as she could against his weight. She opened them slightly, exposing herself. She felt the draught from his movement, the heat from his body, the wetness that ran from Eva. She felt the moisture between the crack of her buttocks running down. She felt the delightful wetness encircling her anus before entering the rear of her fleshy, open crack. She lifted herself higher and the saturating dew ran freely inside the flesh of her cunt. Ajax probed at her, pulling her soft, swollen labia wide with his fingers, delving them into her, all the time driving his massive cock hard into the now screeching Eva.

Sappho panted with the strain, biting hard onto the thongs in her mouth — dribbling, gasping for breath, struggling with both the pain and the overflowing pleasure that arose in licking flames within her. Her anus dilated as she lifted higher and the moisture from Eva's cunt ran more freely, lubricating her, drenching her, making her ready. She shouted out loudly, pleading to be filled, screaming for his cock. She lifted herself higher. Spit ran in a stream from her mouth and onto the ground in front of her face.

Ajax' body stiffened as he pushed up for a last time inside Eva. His venous cock pulsated with the throb of his running semen. He filled her with it, gasping hard, letting it empty inside her. Eva struggled for breath and jerked in ecstasy, but Sappho was unfulfilled, unsatisfied. As Ajax pulled his cock out of Eva, his bubbling semen ran down onto Sappho's anus. She felt its stickiness, its heat. She felt herself using to it, as though its contact was enough to bring her pleasure out. She felt Eva's dissipation. She lifted herself more, wanting Ajax to fill her, to press his still semen-covered cock into her open, wet anus. She wanted him to hold the skin firmly against her. She wanted him to press it hard and thrust his fingers deeply into her cunt as he drenched the lining of her rectum with the flood of his searing semen.

Sappho heard Praxis calling out. It sounded as though it was in the distance, like an echo. She felt Ajax turn his attention. She felt the loss of him. He was not there. He had been distracted from her. A wave of loss built up inside her. She could not bear to hold onto her need for release. She did not know what to do. She was lost. She needed Ajax to save her from the punishing pressure of it.

Sappho cried out, begging him to return, trying to help him find his way back to her. But she could not support Eva on her back and she fell painfully onto her side. The two women struggled on the ground — each generating pain she passed to the other, each receiving pain created by the other. But Sappho could think of only one thing. She thrust her hand down to her cunt, drove her fingers inside and thrust them up and down frantically. But this was not enough — it plugged her, it did not release her. She lifted her legs high and filled her anus in the same way, thrusting three fingers inside, pulling them up and down, twisting them, desperately seeking satisfaction. But still she could not find it. Her distended anus burned with pleasure, but it was not sufficient to release all that had built up inside her.

She called again to Ajax, hopeless, driven to distraction by her desire for fulfilment, craving only for the pent-up needs to be released. She watched Ajax, his hands wide, his eyes unseeing, stumbling within the circle of women, unable to find his way to her, unable to give her the satisfaction she needed.

Suddenly, Praxis stood forward and held both his hands high. One of the women that stood in a circle around them stepped forward. Her lithe body glistened in the flickering light. She held her shield across her firm breasts. Her eyes darted towards the blind Praxis, and then to Master Wang. A glance passed between them. The woman threw herself down on the ground, crouching on all fours in front of Ajax as he ran forward in unseeing pursuit of his prey.

He could not avoid tripping over the woman and was

thrown forward with the full force of his body's weight. His covered eyes met the twin spears held by one of the women ahead. The tips pierced them and drove themselves deeply into the sockets. He hung, pinioned on the spears, the wide, red ribbon now dripping with his flowing blood. He was unable to move, unable to cry out, unable to recover. His arms hung down loosely by his side.

Sappho pulled herself towards him, dragging Eva with her, unconscious of the pain. She rolled forward onto her knees, this time Eva helping her, no longer fighting against her. Sappho knelt on all fours, Eva draped over her back, her own legs hanging down, her feet on the ground. Sappho lifted her buttocks and pushed herself back against Ajax' dangling hand. She felt it twitch against her and, as she felt his fingertips touch her dilated anus, she went rigid with a massive convulsion of ecstasy which, at last, released the flood that had been contained inside her. When she dropped back to the ground, Eva jerked with a sudden mutual orgasm. Like the pain that they shared, her ecstasy fed on Sappho's and passed back to Sappho more of what was already overcoming her.

Eva and Sappho lay on the ground. They no longer fought against their bonds, they no longer had a need to get free. Their pain had become consumed in their pleasure. They were both conquered by delight.

Sappho looked around at the confused scene. Some of the women in the circle had dropped their shields and spears. The naked young girls were on their knees with their hands clasped together in frantic prayer. Praxis was reaching out in all directions but finding no one to give him assistance. Master Wang came to his aid. He led him to the woman that Ajax had tripped over. She was still crouching on the ground. Master Wang passed Praxis' hand to the woman's. Praxis helped her up. She removed her head dress. It was Calliope.

Soldiers pulled Ajax off the twin-headed spear and carried him away. Praxis, preening himself with his victory over Ajax, was led out. This time it was not Master Wang who helped him, it was Calliope. Master Wang walked behind them as Calliope clung to her new ally's massive arm. She turned back for a moment, looked at Sappho and Eva, and smiled. The golden ring in her clitoris glinted for a second. She tossed her head back and was gone.

The soldiers came for Eva as usual and found her bound to Sappho. They unknotted and removed the thin thongs from their mouths but left them knotted and dangling from their nipples. They unbound their arms on one side but kept them both tied tightly by the other. The two women did not struggle as they were pulled out of the tent.

Chapter 18

Escape to Troy

It was a stormy night. The dark cloudy sky was filled with heavy rain and the flashing fire of lightning. Sappho and Eva were dragged from the confusion of Ajax' blinding by several soldiers. They pulled them out into the storm and hauled them off into the darkness. As Eva had promised, the soldiers took them to the edge of the Greek encampment. Here, more soldiers waited eagerly to use them for their private pleasure. Sappho did not know what to expect, and hung back nervously. Eva knew what to expect. She had been subjected to their humiliating treatment too many times before. Her fear was etched into the mysterious pools of her wide, green eyes.

The soldiers had a huge spar — the mast from a boat — set up against a tripod made from smaller spars. It reared up at a steep angle from the ground into which it had been buried so that it did not twist or turn. On the top of the tripod soldiers sat with buckets and containers. They cheered when Sappho and Eva arrived — pleased that their entertainment was about to begin, pleased that they had two victims instead of their usual one.

Alongside the heavy spar, a long ditch had been dug in the dark soil that prevailed in the area away from the beach. Sappho and Eva were brought to one end of the ditch and made to stand still. They had the leather strapping removed from their arms. Both went to rub where the leather had been so tightly bound. When they did, a burly soldier caught them both a sharp cut with a long, single tailed whip. They both shrieked, surprised and shocked, and when they turned and saw what had inflicted the shock, the shock and surprise turned to pain. It was as if the sight of the whip itself generated the pain. Sappho winced as the biting smart on her skin, held back for a few moments by the surprise and the not knowing, finally penetrated her buttocks. She squeezed them together, feeling the tightness first in her anus and then in the soft flesh that surrounded her cunt. She turned back and stood still, hoping she had done nothing else to bring about a second cutting stroke.

One of the soldiers grabbed her arms and pulled her back. At the same time, Eva was pushed forward and made to go down on all fours. Eva did as she was told — she knew that disobedience would only bring more suffering. Sappho stared at the delightful curve of Eva's upturned buttocks — their smoothness, the tightness of the crack between them, the sight of the delectable oval of pink flesh that was her fleshy slit.

Two soldiers stood behind Eva, one on each side. Each held a thin cane. One tested its flexibility by whipping it through the air, the other smacked it repeatedly against the side of his tall leather boots. They both lifted their canes and held them high — waiting, expecting, holding on to the moment of anticipation.

Sappho licked out her tongue as a dribble of spit ran from the corner of her mouth. She sucked it back, allowing its cool frothiness to slide across her tongue before she gulped it down hungrily.

One of the soldiers brought his cane down across Eva's buttocks. She tightened, and arched her back, as the smarting thwack laid a thin red stripe across her skin. She edged forward. As she moved her legs, the flesh of her cunt was exposed more, its shape altering as it was squeezed by the pressure on either side. She stopped, thinking she had moved far enough. The other cane came down, this time from the other side. It struck at a different angle, laying down a different strip of red, stinging in a new way, sensitising a new area of Eva's taut skin. Eva tightened again and moved forward. Sappho watched in fear, sharing Eva's pain and humiliation, knowing that whatever happened to Eva would also happen to her.

They drove Eva down into the end of the muddy ditch, repeatedly bringing the cane down on her buttocks to guide her and force her on. When they stopped, Eva stopped as well. Sappho felt hands on her shoulders and she was forced down onto her knees behind Eva. She stared at Eva's buttocks, covered in angry red stripes from the vicious strokes of the thin canes. She saw the swelling oval of Eva's flesh, split delectably down the centre, a glistening of moisture following the line that parted the succulent pink mounds.

Sappho shrieked as a cane struck her own upturned buttocks. The cutting pain penetrated her whole body. It burned deeply beneath her skin. It passed directly to all her senses. It jolted her with its harshness. Another sharp cut, now on the other side, sent her head reeling. She crawled forward until her face was touching the crack in Eva's buttocks. She stopped, not knowing what else to do. The cane did not come down again and she waited, shivering with fear, frightened to call out, too threatened to look up.

Sappho did not have to wait long. She felt the cane again, this time short, rapid slaps, not hard, nor forceful. She edged forward a little more and the cane was removed. Her nose and mouth now lay at the centre of Eva's taut buttocks. Sappho licked her lips and felt her tongue touch the soft pliable surface of Eva's cunt. She breathed in deeply and inhaled Eva's scent, the delectable fragrance of the moisture that glistened on the surface of her flesh. Eva rose up, opening herself to Sappho. She allowed the flesh of her slit to open — revealing its inner pinkness, its glossy wetness, its soft folds, its invitation to enter. Sappho licked more and again tasted the sweetness of Eva's dew. She lapped at it, sucking it in onto her tongue. She held it there, not swallowing, feeling the fullness of its taste at the back of her tongue before, finally, she took it down. She breathed in deeply and raised her own buttocks in response to the heat she felt growing at the centre of her own throbbing, swelling flesh.

The cane came down sharply and Sappho gasped. She leant forward, pressing her mouth hard against Eva's crack. The other cane struck hard, and again the first, and then the other. Sappho moved forward, unable to stay where she was, unable to hold back against the urgent and painful instruction from the angry canes. As she pushed into Eva, so Eva herself moved forward. But it was not far, only enough to satisfy the pressure from Sappho, only enough to respond to the need in Sappho to move on the orders of the stinging canes. As they crawled forward together, Sappho's face stayed fully between Eva's buttocks, her mouth closely against Eva's cunt.

They were both moved forward with the canes — harsh blows coming down if the soldiers thought Sappho should press harder behind Eva, short, rapid blows if she was being told to move only enough to keep herself close. They crept along the ditch. The soldiers held the canes above them all the time, ensuring they stayed together, insisting they did not part. It was muddy and their legs were covered in black soil and grime. Sappho felt the oozy slime squelching between her fingers. All the time, she kept her mouth against Eva's cunt, only slacking back when she felt the need for the cane, the pain it brought, and the encouragement it gave to her urgently mounting excitement.

By the time they were at the opposite end of the ditch, Sappho's buttocks were covered in a criss-cross of red stripes inflicted by the canes. Her face was wet with spit. It mixed with the moisture she had slurped up between the swollen, throbbing flesh of Eva's delectable crack. Her hands were deep in the mud, up to wrists, and splatters of mud covered her arms and thighs. Her own cunt ached. She had held back sometimes, raising her buttocks. She knew she would receive a hard slice with a cane to make her draw up closer. She had exposed her cunt to the slashing cane and had caught its anger several times. But that had not reduced her longing, I had only increased it. Each time she had felt the slicing bite across the soft flesh of her swollen cunt, she had not wanted to dip away but instead to rise up more, to open herself wider, to receive its anger more fully.

Eva bent her elbows and dropped her face down to the muddy bottom of the dirty ditch. Sappho licked into Eva's cunt more deeply. A soldier pressed his booted foot into the black sludge. Eva was forced to lick it. Sappho was aware only of the opening of Eva's cunt. As Eva's face went lower, Sappho responded by licking deeper, pressing her lips around the soft flesh, biting onto the hard nub of Eva's throbbing clitoris. Sappho lapped ravenously at the moist flesh, feeling her own heat growing and her own flesh throbbing. Eva licked into the mud, forcing her tongue into it, through it, until she felt the shiny leather of the boot. She drew her tongue across it, laying its full width against it, sensing its smoothness, its glossy surface, the power of its wearer.

Sappho pressed harder, and, as Eva's buttocks rose higher, Sappho pulled her tongue from Eva's cunt and laid it flat against her already dilated anus. She licked the edges, tasting the tart bitterness of its exterior, before poking it in and lapping at its delectably smooth inner surface.

Suddenly, Sappho felt herself being pulled away. She threw herself from one side to the other, looking for Eva, needing her anus, her cunt, her soft flesh, her moisture. But she was restrained. She tried again, but again she was held back. Her frustration gnawed within her hungrily. They dragged Eva out of the ditch and flung her down on its edge. Sappho was pulled forward to the end. She knelt on all fours at the bottom of the filthy ditch. She hung her head, staring down to where the soldier's boot lay buried in the muddy goo.

Sappho did not wait. She thrust her face straight into it. She pushed her tongue out, frantically licking, poking, thrusting it forward. She imagined she was still licking Eva

— still delving her tongue deep inside her anus, still savouring the delectable flavour she found there. She pressed her face down hard into the mud — seeking the boot, not caring about anything else. The soldiers pulled her back — lifting her by the shoulders, bending her backwards. Her face was covered in black mud. Her tongue hung out of her gaping mouth. She gasped for breath. She fought against them — the heat in her cunt was too much, the aching desire to find release for her own pleasure was too great to resist. She broke free of their clutches and dropped her face again into the mire. She sucked at it, taking the mud into her mouth, drinking at it, swallowing it, feeding on it. At last, her tongue felt the smooth surface of the soldier's boot and she forced herself down against it. She licked it — slowly, carefully — with the full flat of her distended tongue. She felt the shiny leather against her flesh, and drew her tongue along it. She pressed the mud out from between the two surfaces, satisfying herself with the contact, absorbed in her humiliation, revelling in the degradation her treatment had brought to her. She felt the wave of pleasure that was about to erupt.

But they would not allow her satisfaction. Even though she used all her strength against them, she could not achieve relief. She was pulled from the ditch and flung down by the side of Eva.

Sappho gasped loudly, mud bubbling from her mouth, her face covered in the black slime that dripped down her neck and ran across her breasts.

'Wash them down!' shouted one of the soldiers. 'They are both filthy!'

The soldiers threw a tent down into the muddy ditch. They bucketed water into it and formed a shallow, cold and dirty bath. Sappho and Eva were forced to kneel in the middle of it. It was soggy beneath their knees and it was difficult to keep their balance. They clung to each other, bedraggled, soiled and pitiful. They shivered as water was thrown over them from buckets. Sappho opened her mouth and drank some in as it flowed down her face. It tasted acrid, and she spit it out as she gagged and heaved.

The soldiers knocked them both over. Sappho fell on her back, thrashing in the water, choking and gasping for breath. More buckets of water were thrown at them. It splashed between Sappho's legs, fully against her exposed cunt — spreading its soft fleshy leaves, slopping inside her, making her shudder. Two soldiers stepped into the water. They held Sappho down, one pinning her shoulders with his feet, the other holding her ankles high off the ground and spreading her legs as wide as possible. Others ran up with more buckets and hurled their contents fully between Sappho's wide open legs. The force sloshed hard against the soft flesh of her splayed cunt and the tender insides of her widespread thighs. She gulped as each deluge hit her hard. She gasped with the shock of the cold water. She squirmed against the pressure of being pinned down and splayed out. She screamed out with the hurt it all inflicted.

They emptied buckets of water over both their heads. Sappho could hardly breathe as it ran down her face. It filled her mouth, and made her choke. When they were satisfied, the soldiers dragged the two women out of the water-filled bath. They pulled them over to the inclined spar that stood at an angle, fixed to the mighty tripod of timber.

Sappho looked up, her face still dripping with water, her naked body soaked and glistening in the red flickering light from flaming braziers. The massive spar towered above her. She shivered, filled with dread, not knowing her fate, only supposing the horror of it. She bit down hard onto her lips.

First, Eva was lifted up onto the massive timber spar. They dragged her almost to the top, where it was tied into the tripod. They pulled her legs around it, forcing her to straddle it. They crossed her ankles beneath it and bound them together tightly with strips of wet leather. Next, they pulled her arms around it and bound her wrists in the same way. She gaped, staring up at the tripod, gripping with the insides of her thighs in case she twisted over and was left hanging upside down on her wrists and ankles.

Sappho was hauled up next. They placed her just below Eva and bound her in the same way. The wet leather straps held her ankles and wrists completely fast — she could not move them at all. She could not see behind her as they fixed a spear with a leather cover over its blunt end to the spar. It was inclined in such a way that it lay just behind her buttocks, directed at her anus. Sappho looked up at Eva above her. If she could have reached up, she could have touched her. Eva's buttocks were widespread, and her cunt and anus were fully exposed. Sappho wished she could get closer — she wanted to feel Eva's heat, she wanted to inhale her fragrance, taste her moisture.

Several men climbed up the tripod and positioned themselves in its crook. Others passed up buckets of water to them, some climbing halfway up, forming a chain, so that they could pass more of the sloshing containers when the need arose. Sappho suddenly looked back. Something had startled her. Something was happening behind her — she felt something touching her exposed anus. At the same time, she realised her exposure. It was as if she had not noticed it until now. She recognised how exposed she was to all the soldiers gathered around. It was as though she had only just realised that they were all staring at her, looking at her cunt, her anus. She was suddenly aware of how humiliated she was before them, how precarious her predicament, how degrading her position. She felt a deep aching in her hips. Somewhere between the tops of her thighs an anxiety built that straightway melted into yearning. She felt a dribble of spit in the corner of her mouth. She breathed out through it, frothing it, adding more spit to it, making it run in a stream down her chin. She sucked back at it, cooler and more sticky now, drew it into the mouth and slowly swallowed it. She wanted to push her hand down and drive her fingers into her cunt. The frustration of her captivity and the overwhelming delight that had come with the sudden realisation of her exposure, sent a sharp shock of overpowering joy through her whole body. She tightened in a quick jerk of transfixing ecstasy.

She turned again, this time to the other side. Still she could not properly see what was going on. She felt confused, giddy. She started panting hard, not knowing what to do, not knowing if she could do anything, feeling as if everything was spinning out of control.

She did not see the first bucket of water emptied from the top of the tripod. The first she knew of it was the loud splashing sound it made when it hit Eva. Eva tightened against the spar, desperate not to swing upside down. Sappho saw Eva's buttocks clench, her anus contract, the flesh of her cunt tighten. Then the water came again. This time it barely glanced Eva before it hit Sappho. It was cold and hard. She closed her eyes and tightened her body. She felt it washing around her and she felt her grip on the spar weaken. She clenched her arms and legs as tightly as she could to prevent herself from slipping. Another massive slosh and another bucket was emptied over them. Eva slid back, and her exposed cunt came closer to Sappho's face. Sappho choked as the water hit her — filling her eyes and nostrils, running into her mouth, soaking her. She felt herself slipping back and gripped even harder with her arms and legs. But, she could not stop herself sliding. She felt something hard against her anus. She clenched herself and pulled back but the spar was too wet and her grip on it too weak. She could not move away from the object that pressed against her — the blunt end of the leather-covered spear.

More water came down. Eva slipped some more and so did Sappho. Sappho tried to hold back, to stay in place. She wanted to feel Eva's flesh against her lips again. She wanted to delve her tongue into her anus. But, each time more water splashed down, she slid back. Each time she slid back, the leather-covered spear pressed harder against her anus. Suddenly, with only another slight movement towards it, Sappho's anus dilated and let it in. Each time she slid back more, it entered a little further, a little deeper. Her anus opened more to receive it, she could not prevent it. And she opened herself to it as well — she could not resist it. She was dizzy with confusion. She reached up her face towards the delectable sight of Eva's cunt and anus. She dropped back, sliding on the wet spar, as her own anus was gradually filled by the leather-covered spear that, little by little, was stuffing her full.

She managed to tighten the insides of her thighs against the wet spar and pull herself up slightly. The contraction of her muscles tightened the grip her anus had around the leather-covered spear. She licked out her tongue. Spit dripped from its end as she strained to reach Eva's beckoning, dilated anus. Sappho squeezed her legs tighter, pressing her thighs hard against the unforgiving timber spar. Another deluge of water splashed down on them. Eva struggled to keep her balance. Sappho stayed as she was, gripping the beam between her legs, her tongue licking out, her objective clearly in her sight. Another heavy splash of water and, this time, Eva slipped back. Sappho's tongue touched the object of its desire — Eva's anus. Sappho tasted its tart fragrance. She closed her eyes in delight, letting the fragrant contact soak into her — mix with all her senses, flow through her completely. More water poured down on them. Eva slipped back further and Sappho's tongue went fully against the rim of Eva's anus — the tight circle of delight that promised so much. Sappho extended her tongue fully, stretching it out, forcing it further, keeping it in contact.

Another smack of water hit Sappho's face. She slid back more onto the leather-covered spear. She gulped with the penetration. It could go no further — she was full of it. It stuffed her rectum. It filled her completely. Still she kept her tongue in place, just at the entrance of Eva's anus. One more splash of water knocked them both back. But Sappho could not slip any further, she was pinioned on the spear, and Eva slid back onto her.

Sappho's face squashed between Eva's open buttocks and her tongue drove into Eva's anus. Straight away, in a sudden frenzy, Sappho sucked hard. She drew the aroma from her tongue into her mouth. The pressure of Eva above her forced Sappho hard onto the leather-covered spear. She tightened herself onto it, holding it in her rectum, feeling her bowels filled with it, pinioned by it. She sucked harder with her lips, lapped more frantically with her tongue. Her eyes rolled up. She was overcome by a heavy, slow and pounding heave which started a seemingly never-ending surge of unstoppable joy.

Sappho tightened against the spar, sucking with her mouth, squeezing her anus hard, tightening all her muscles, keeping herself fixed on it. She overflowed with pleasure. A soldier climbed onto the spar behind her, straddled the spear which penetrated her and started thrashing her with a long leather strap. She jerked as it fell across her buttocks. She tightened more onto the spear, and forced her tongue even further into Eva's rectum. Another splash of water and another smack of the strap and she tightened again. Her ecstasy spun out of control. She could not restrain anything within her — she was completely taken over by rapture. She lifted up her buttocks for the beating, and dropped back heavily onto the spear which then drove even further inside her.

Sappho and Eva were cut down from the spar and thrown onto the ground. Sappho clawed after Eva, forcing her legs wide, licking at her cunt, driving her tongue again into her anus. The soldiers threw buckets of water over them, but they did not stop. Sappho was out of control. All the time, she kept her tongue in Eva's anus. She could not release herself from it. She was dizzy with the heavy throbs of her orgasm — unrelenting, unstoppable, unending.

One of the soldiers knelt down and thrust his cock into her anus and others took their turn after he had filled it with his semen. Sappho was beaten again, this time with a cane. They were both strung up by their ankles with their legs wide apart. The soldiers dribbled spit and ejected their semen onto their exposed cunts. It ran down their bodies, onto their faces, and into their eyes.

Finally, after everything, the braziers burned down and, one by one the soldiers left. Sappho and Eva were thrown onto the ground and left alone. The soldiers did not think them capable of escape. Even if they had, they could not have imagined how they could find their way out of the camp. But they did. Eva had watched so many soldiers making their way out of the enclosed camp to seek prostitutes — the route was firmly fixed in her mind. She led Sappho by the hand, weaving between standing piles of armour, spears set in the sand, sleeping soldiers, and ravaged women. Eventually, they found themselves at the mighty gates of Troy.

They stood, still hand in hand, before the huge entrance to the city. High walls led off at each side into the distance. The massive buildings within reached towards the sky. Sappho felt dizzy with a sight she thought she would never see again.

Eva fidgeted nervously. She had never seen anything like it before.

'Do not be afraid Eva,' Sappho said, squeezing Eva's hand. 'You will be safe with me now. You will be rewarded as I promised. We will live together like sisters. You will never have to suffer again. I give you my pledge. You have suffered too much. Now, it is all over.'

Chapter 19

Troy at last

Sappho and Eva wandered between the crowds of beggars, thieves and foreigners who gathered around the gates hoping for entry to the city. They were held back on two sides of the path reserved for those allowed to enter, by thin copper wires strung in close pairs between spears set in the ground. Several soldiers were posted in front of the gates, occasionally granting access to those who had a right or, if they had no right, to those who could satisfy their eager lust.

Slave traders brought lines of girls to the gates. They were naked, chained into rings attached to iron collars around their necks. Only the Africans had their pubic hair, all the rest were shaved. They waited with their heads hung as purchasers bargained and argued over prices. The buyers checked the girls in turn. They opened their mouths wide and looked closely at their teeth. They fondled their breasts and forced their fingers into their cracks. They bent them over and pushed the stubby ends of their whips into the frightened girls' anuses. When deals were struck, the girls were marched over to braziers into which were stuck the branding irons of different owners. They were made to bend down and hold onto their ankles as they were branded on their buttocks. If they jumped up in pain they were forced down again and, this time, tied. Sometimes the branding iron slipped between the crack of their squirming buttocks. After they were branded, they were dragged away — some screaming, some holding their heads in their hands, some struggling to walk. As the lines of girls were led along the passage between the copper wires and in through the gates, more appeared, brought by ever greedy traders to the gates of this, the richest city in the world.

Sappho finally plucked up enough courage to approach

the gatekeepers. She leant against the copper wires. The pair at chest height first pressed against, and then snapped around the hard tips of her breasts. She shivered as the two wires tightened against her sensitive nipples. They hardened more under the pressure and pressed out further between the cuttingly thin wires. She tried to pull back but she was caught fast. The wires tugged at her nipples, pulling them, stretching them, drawing at her breasts. The gatekeepers laughed at her predicament.

Tears welled up in Sappho's eyes.

'My name is Sappho. I have escaped from the Greeks,' she said falteringly. 'I was their slave. I am the friend of Chryseis, daughter of the high priest Pelador himself. Please let me into Troy, my home.'

She managed to part the pair of wires that bit into her nipples. She sighed as she relieved herself from the pain and humiliation they imposed.

'And you do not know the great Pelador is dead?' they jeered, kicking out at her and picking up dust in their hands and throwing it over her face.

Her nipples, still throbbing and indented from the pressure of the wires, were now covered in smears of dust. She shrank back and clung to Eva. They huddled together not knowing what to do.

A small pony trap drew up, two beautiful women harnessed between its ivory embellished shafts. They were naked except for plumed, multicoloured headdresses. A young prince stood proudly on the painted platform built between the decorative wheels. Black leather reins led from his hands and into silver bits pulled tightly into the women's mouths. He carried a long whip and thrashed out at the women as they drew up. It cracked painfully across their red striped buttocks. They dropped their heads, sweat dripping from their noses and chins, spit dribbling from the sides of the silver bits. He pulled back on the shiny leather reins and brought them to a halt.

The young prince called over to the gatekeepers, still laughing at Sappho, as they checked the tension of the copper wires that had trapped her.

'Have you no entertainment for your prince?' the young man asked disdainfully. 'Have you not provided for Polydorus, youngest son of King Priam himself? When I pass through the great gates of Troy, I expect to be entertained! And I see nothing prepared!' He lifted his whip and held it ready to crack it this time across the women's backs. 'Perhaps you have been in your posts too long,' he said menacingly. 'I shall speak to the King.'

The gatekeepers looked at each other fearfully. They obviously knew the young prince and had been both surprised, and caught out, by his unheralded appearance. They were not going to allow disappointing him to ruin their prospects of the easy jobs they enjoyed. One of them rushed forward keenly, bowed and held onto the sides of the trap.

'Of course we have something prepared for your highness,' he fawned. 'How could you think otherwise, sire? Of course, my lord Polydorus. Please step towards the wire that keeps back the unwanted from our beautiful city. We have something we know will please you. We are so glad you are here at last. We have been awaiting you.'

The haughty young man stepped down from the trap. The shafts lifted as he got out. The women were pulled sideways. He raised his whip high and brought it down hard across both their backs. They cowered down but could not avoid the punishment. The silver bit fell from the mouth of one of the women. She struggled to put it back in but the prince thrashed her so hard she could not.

'See what I have to put up with,' he said petulantly, still beating the harnessed woman.

Sappho winced at his cruelty.

The whip cracked fiercely and the woman was soon screaming as she twisted and squirmed beneath the fiery leather lash of her ruthless master.

The gatekeeper's eye fell on Sappho. She looked down as his eyes met hers. Her stomach filled with anxiety. She knew she had made a mistake in looking at him. He strode across to her purposefully.

'See, my lord Polydorus. We have kept this beauty for your entertainment.'

He grabbed Sappho by the arms, pulled her away from Eva, and pushed her against the copper wires. Her sensitive nipples again felt the sharpness of the two thin wires. They pressed against her soft skin and cut a line deeply into her firm yet pliant breasts. She gasped as she grabbed the wires to steady herself. One of the other gatekeepers ran forward and grasped her arms. He pulled them behind her and held them fast in the small of her back.

The first man stood in front of Sappho and flexed the wires apart, about the width of two fingers. The man behind her pushed her forward until her nipples poked between the two thin wires. They lay against her lightly pigmented areola squeezing into it, forcing it proud of her rounded breast.

Polydorus came closer and bent to look.

'Here, my lord,' said the first gatekeeper. 'This is for your pleasure.'

He took Polydorus' hands and placed them on the wires in such a way that his fingers held them apart. Polydorus nodded and smiled.

'Now, my lord,' the gatekeeper continued. 'Allow the wires to come together. See how you can regulate the pain this poor beggar receives.'

Polydorus held the wires. Sappho looked down, she was too afraid to meet his gaze. She saw the two thin wires, one above and one below her extended nipples. The man behind her pushed her slightly forward and the wires dug deeply into her breasts. Her nipples hardened and throbbed. She could not stop them.

'Now, when you are ready, my lord, allow the wires to come together. I think you will be rewarded.'

Polydorus brought his fingers together and allowed the wires to close onto Sappho's nipples. She tried to pull back as she watched them closing around the pink hardness of sensitive flesh, but the man behind her kept her firmly in place. He squeezed her wrists together in the small of her back and, using his shoulder and other hand, he pulled back her shoulders so that her breasts were thrust forward even more. As the wires closed, they touched the sides of her nipples. She felt their heat — warmed by the searing sun — and she felt their piercing thinness. Polydorus allowed them to close together more and the pressure increased. The two wires pinched down on her nipples, cutting into them, sending a sharp penetrating pain into both her breasts. Sappho gasped. She could not move. Polydorus withdrew his fingers and allowed the wires to come completely together.

She shrieked as they crimped her erect flesh — the pain was excruciating. The hot wires pinched her hard nipples at their base. They clenched onto them and sent heavy jolts of pain deep into her body. She twisted herself against the grip of the man who held her wrists. The movement caused her more pain as her nipples stretched out from the tips of her aching breasts. Her hard nipples were now firmly fixed between the wires.

Polydorus released the wires completely and they closed together as one. Sappho screamed and a froth of spit sprayed into the air from her gaping mouth. She did not stop, the pain was unbearable. When she breathed in, she still screamed. Spit ran freely from her mouth. It dribbled down her chin and onto her pain filled breasts. It flowed down onto her nipples but its bubbling coolness brought no relief for her pain.

'And now, my lord,' said the first gatekeeper. This will bring out this pitiful pauper's ecstasy.' He held up a short dagger. 'I will place my dagger between the wires on this side of the woman. You, sir, place your dagger in the same way on the opposite side. When you are ready, sir, we will turn our daggers and tighten the wires as if we were twisting hemp for a rope.'

They both pushed their daggers between the two wires and then twisted them in opposite directions. Sappho screeched. Everyone watched, everyone saw her pain, her humiliation. She knew her exposure to their stares. She knew her hopeless vulnerability. But there was no chance of her pleasure escaping — the pain was too great to bear, her joy could not find a way out. She screamed louder, but now she could barely hear the sound that came from her own mouth. Her head was spinning giddily. Her ears were buzzing. She seemed to be falling. She felt a trickle of warm urine running down the insides of her thighs. She closed her eyes and was consumed.

Suddenly, Eva was by her side, standing by the wires, pushing her own nipples against them.

'I will save you, my dear Sappho,' she whispered hurriedly in Sappho's ear. 'I will take your place. You can escape. I will wait until you return for me. I know you will. Be ready to go. To go quickly.'

Polydorus' eyes widened as he watched Eva pressing herself against the taut wires. She looked beautiful — still proud, her shapely form erect and smooth, her wine red hair falling in coiled tousles around her shoulders. He was transfixed. He took his dagger from between the wires and so did the gatekeeper. Eva took the wires in her hands and calmly opened them. Sappho moved back, releasing her nipples from the piercing vice of the cutting wires. Tears ran from her eyes, spit streamed from her mouth, mucus dripped from her nostrils. Eva moved forward and pressed her hard nipples between the wires. She released the wires and let them close. She showed no sign of pain. A trickle of spit started to run from the corner of her mouth. The man holding Sappho's wrists let go. Sappho dropped to the ground and crawled away into the crowd.

Sappho crawled between the legs of the crowd. Straight away, she was surrounded by a group of beggars and vagabonds. They stood over her, leering, pointing, prodding at her with their feet, picking at her with their dirty, long-nailed fingers. She tried to get up. She felt so threatened. She had to escape. They pushed her over and she fell on her back. Her legs spread wide, exposing her cunt to them, laying bare her naked flesh. Without thinking, she tried to pull them together. She felt she needed to protect herself from their gaze but, even as she struggled to bring her knees together, she found herself dropping them further apart.

A dirty beggar in rags knelt down on one side of her and took one of her sore nipples between his teeth. He bit hard onto its base and she yelled. Another bit onto the other one. Sappho wriggled and squirmed, her legs wide, screaming with pain. She felt a finger inside her cunt, and one in her anus. She opened her mouth to shout out. She felt it held wide as a cock went into it. She sucked hard onto it — she could not stop herself — she was filled with confusion and fear. She sucked harder hoping the bulk in her mouth would distract her from the pain in her breasts. The end of a hard cock was pressed against one of her nostrils. She sealed her lips tightly around the venous shaft of the cock in her mouth. She dropped her knees as wide as possible and felt the stinging surge of hot semen squirting into her nose. She felt it bubbling inside. It ran into her throat. As she gulped at it, the one in her mouth also filled her with its creamy liquid. She swallowed the semen in her throat hungrily — gulping it down, feasting on it. She breathed in the semen in her nostril as if it was air — inhaling it deeply sniffing it in.

Suddenly, she heard Eva's screams — loud and penetrating, filling the air, demanding everyone's attention. Sappho felt alone, abandoned, as everyone turned to the sound of Eva's pain. Semen dripped from her nose and from her mouth. Her cunt was wet and her anus hot and dilated. She lay for a moment on her back — breathing hard, fearful, expectant. She wanted to drop her hand between her legs, to feel her cunt. She wanted to rub the semen that ran from it around her flesh. She wanted to grasp her clitoris, to pull it, pinch it hard. She wanted to thrust her fingers deeply into her anus. She wanted to release the joy that the terrible pain she had suffered had been masking.

Eva screamed again and Sappho jumped to her feet. Now, she could think of only one thing — escape.

She did not even look back as she darted though the unguarded crack in the mighty gates. Her head rang with Eva's continuing screams. Her mind was filled with Eva's desperate appeals for mercy. Sappho clasped her hands over her ears to block it out. She could not bear the sound of Eva's pain.

Sappho ran along the narrow streets until, at last, she saw the temple of Apollo. She stood before its imposing steps and massive columns. She gasped with relief. She climbed the steps and stopped at the top. She inhaled deeply. Her nostrils filled with the scent of incense. Her ears rang with the sound of chanting. One voice was raised above the dirge, proclaiming to Apollo, seeking his advice, offering him sacrifice. It was Chryseis — at last.

Chapter 20

The temple of Apollo

The great priest Pelador was dead. Chryseis, his beautiful daughter, was now the priestess of the temple of Apollo. Her power was second only to the king, the ageing Priam, father of brave Hector and his brothers, the handsome Paris and the cruel Polydorus.

Chryseis stood in front of the massive altar, naked except for the ram's fleece across her back. Her face was painted with daubed flashes of red and yellow. Sappho crept into the back of the temple, unsure what to do. Since Chryseis had been given back to Troy, Sappho had thought of nothing else except being with her again. But now, seeing her like this, resplendent before her followers, Sappho was struck with fear and apprehension. Would Chryseis welcome her, she wondered? She was so powerful now. Would she even recognise her?

Sappho looked down onto the sunken floor of the temple. She stood behind the same statue of Aphrodite she had crouched behind when she had first seen Chryseis. She squatted down, as she had done then, opening her knees, dropping down on her haunches, allowing her cunt to splay open. She watched Chryseis and, without thinking, found her hand slipping down to the front of her warm slit. She ran a finger around its soft edges and pressed it against the moist, satiny centre. The tip of her finger entered, it took no pressure — her silken flesh simply parted beneath her delicate touch.

Suddenly there was a young man in a robe behind her.

'I have found a spy!' he shouted down into the main part of the temple.

He grabbed Sappho roughly and led her down towards the altar. Worshippers gathered around. Some grabbed at her. Some pinched her. Some spat on her. Pulling at her roughly, they brought her before Chryseis.

Sappho stood gasping for breath and shaking with fear. She dropped her head, too afraid to look at Chryseis, thinking only that her escape, her coming back to Troy, had been a terrible mistake. Chryseis reached out and lifted Sappho's chin. Sappho looked up anxiously.

'Bend her over the altar!' shouted Chryseis.

Sappho's stomach churned with panic.

They forced Sappho to kneel and bent her face down onto the cold marble altar where once before she had been humiliated. Her breasts squashed against its shiny surface. Her nipples hardened under the unforgiving pressure of her own weight against it. Her arms were pulled forward and held tightly by two men in robes. She looked to the side and saw Chryseis parading around her — chanting, holding her arms up high, evoking her gods.

Chryseis flung the ram's fleece from her back and draped it over Sappho. Sappho felt the sudden heat of the fleece, its smooth suede lining warming her skin, clinging tightly to it. Chryseis stood behind Sappho, facing away from her, then, opening her legs wide, she sat back onto Sappho's upturned buttocks. She called one of the young men over. He came to her straight away. He bent before her, half kneeling, and presented his stiff cock. She took hold of it and directed its swollen glans towards her exposed and glistening cunt.

Sappho felt the heat of his testicles against her buttocks as he drove his cock deeply into Chryseis' hot wet flesh. She tried to lift herself, to bring herself closer, but Chryseis' weight would not allow it. Sappho, looked to each side. All the worshippers in the temple were staring at her, watching her. She felt a thrill inside her at the realisation of their penetrating glare. She managed to lift herself slightly. But, instead of the heat of the man's testicles, as Chryseis pushed the man back and again took hold of his throbbing cock, she felt coolness against her buttocks. Chryseis pressed the end of the man's cock against Sappho's anus. She drew the man forward and his wet pounding cock went deeply inside. As soon as it was inside the tight muscular ring, it swelled and his semen filled Sappho in a hot, pulsating stream.

Another followed. This time, as the first man's semen still dribbled between Sappho's buttocks, Chryseis took the next man's cock from her own cunt and pushed it into Sappho's anus. It slid it on the silky cream that already filled it and, as it squirted deeply into her, Sappho felt herself brimming over with its heavy flow. The next and the next were taken in the same way. Each filled her with their copious stream — each already wet from Chryseis' cunt, each throbbing with the delight of Sappho's tight, wet anus. Semen ran down and covered her cunt. It poured down the insides of her thighs, lay in pools in the hollows at the backs of her knees, and dripped in sticky strands onto the ground. Still more came. Chryseis took every one into her cunt first, then, when they were throbbing with the pent-up stream that lay within, each one filled Sappho's anus with its creamy, flowing semen.

Chryseis turned around. She lay face forward over the ram's fleece that covered Sappho's back. Now she took the men's cocks into her own anus. Just before they released their pouring flow, they drove the shafts into Sappho's cunt and filled her with it. Sappho waited for each one, feeling their pounding thrusts in Chryseis' anus, and the tightness of their stiff bulk as they pounded in as deeply as they could. She felt the increasing tension as the flow of semen built up in its urgency for release. She felt the swelling thickness of their cocks tighten as they drew out of Chryseis' contracting anus. And she felt the relief as, on the first thrust inside her cunt, the hot stream of semen flooded into her like a deluge.

When it had all finished, Sappho lay gasping for breath. Chryseis lay on top of her, her naked body glistening with gleaming droplets of sweat. She dropped her mouth against Sappho's ear and licked her lips before she spoke.

'Dearest Sappho,' she said, her voice still trembling with excitement. 'Dearest Sappho. I knew you would come back to me. I have prayed to Apollo. I have wished for it every day.'

Sappho could hardly believe what she was hearing. A wave of relief passed over her.

Chryseis got up and took Sappho's hand.

'Now, my dear Sappho, you will stand with me as a priestess of Apollo.' Sappho stood up, still with the ram's fleece on her back. 'Behold, your new priestess, Sappho!' screamed Chryseis. 'In her honour, we will celebrate the buk-ka-ke!'

A roar of excitement went up. Naked girls ran forward and lined up around the altar. More were brought in. Some of them, girls Sappho hand seen traded outside the gates to the city.

Young men gathered around a square of patterned tiles near to the altar. They dropped their robes and stood naked. A young man with a leather crop in his hand, selected a girl from the line. He brought it down viciously onto the girl's pert buttocks. She squirmed with the sharp pain it delivered and a smudged red line was imprinted where it had fallen. Using the crop, he drove her forward until she stood within the circle of naked men. He ordered her to kneel and, when she was on her knees, he bound her wrists behind her back with a thin leather strap.

Sappho watched excitedly as Chryseis stepped forward and held the dagger high in the air.

'See your new priestess, Sappho. She wears the fleece of Apollo. She has shared semen with me, your high priestess. Now you will honour her as you honour me. As you honoured my father before me.'

The young girl pulled back her shoulders and tightened her knees together. Sappho could not see the line of her naked slit, only the two beckoning creases that led into it. The girl's eyes were wide and inviting as she looked up at the men who surrounded her. They held their cocks in their hands — all were stiff, all were throbbing and venous, all were ready to cover her with their flowing semen. The young girl opened her mouth. She wanted to take the cocks one by one between her lips but, as she edged forward slightly, the crop came down on her back and she stayed where she had been placed.

Sappho's mouth felt dry and she licked her lips as the first cock deluged the girl with its hot, creamy semen. It spurted onto her nose and cheek and ran down into the corner of her mouth. Another sprayed her other cheek, and another one of her eyes. Still she kept looking up, her eyes wide and appealing. Another streamed into her other eye and filled it. It dripped from her eyelashes and onto her cheek. Two poured their semen onto her shaved head and it ran in two streams down into her ears. One shot straight into her ear and dripped from its lobe. Another squirted into her nostrils and she breathed in deeply to suck it up.

Sappho found her hand seeking out the top of her crack. It was wet and silky, and still dripping with semen. She had only to press against it slightly to gain entry. Chryseis looked at her. The glance set a shock of pleasure through Sappho. She wanted Chryseis to watch her feeling her cunt. She wanted everyone there to see her. She wanted to bend down and exhibit her buttocks. She wanted to show the soft oval of her cunt. She wanted spanking, thrashing. She wanted to be opened up — exhibited, displayed. She wanted the man with the leather crop to drive her into the circle of men.

The men moved back and more replaced them. The girl was kept where she was. Another drenching followed. She was saturated in semen. It dripped from her mouth and nose, it ran in her eyes, it dripped from her ears and flowed over her shaved head. It ran down her neck and onto her pert breasts. It streamed down her stomach and into the creased wedge that pointed towards her unseen slit.

Sappho pulled her finger deeply into her cunt. She lifted

herself on it, opening her legs, turning around, displaying herself, making herself vulnerable to every gaze. Chryseis took hold of Sappho's arm. She pulled her hand away from her slit and placed it, with the other, by her side. Sappho felt an ache in her cunt. Having to hold it back caused her to want more. She stood waiting, hoping, expecting.

Chryseis caught the eye of the man with the leather crop and he walked over. Chryseis nodded to him. She turned her eyes to Sappho, now standing to attention, her hands clasped in fists, her thumbs pointing down and pressed against the sides of her hips.

The man lifted the leather crop to shoulder height then brought it down sharply on Sappho's buttocks. The sting penetrated her deeply and the shock made her gulp. She flinched but not enough to move or to shift her hands from her sides. The man brought the crop down again. Sappho swallowed hard as the cutting pain sunk into her shapely buttocks. She knew what she must do. She walked towards the men. With a flick of the crop on her shoulder, the man stopped her outside the circle they described. He beckoned the young girl. She crawled out of the circle, semen still dripping from her face and breasts. She looked up at him, her dark, doe eyes filled with white stickiness. The man thrashed her sharply on the buttocks as she crawled past. She stopped at the side of the marble altar. She waited, still on hands and knees, glistening with the gluey cream that had flowed over her so copiously.

The man brought the crop down again on Sappho's buttocks. She crawled forward into the circle of men. She was aware that all eyes were on her. She was overwhelmed with her nakedness, her humiliation, and her degrading exposure. She felt the soft flesh of her cunt squeezing between the tops of her thighs as she crawled forward. She lifted her buttocks to meet the crop as it came down again on her taut, delightfully curved, skin. She bit onto her lips as a shiver of joy penetrated her. It stiffened her already hard nipples, tightened her throat and made her head spin.

She knelt at the centre of the circle of men. She could feel the heat of their hard cocks around her. She looked at them, each throbbing and hard, each venous and swollen at the end, each held tightly, each directed towards her. She pushed her hands behind her, clasping them together and pressing them down into the top of the crack of her buttocks. She did not need them tying. She squeezed her knees together, pushed her shoulders back and lifted her chin. She opened her mouth — moving the tip of her tongue onto her bottom lip — and waited for it to be filled.

The first came as a hot stream across her cheek. It stuck to her skin and dripped down onto the line of her jaw. She felt a spot on her mouth, only a taste, but its salty tang sent shivers of expectation coursing through her trembling body. The next fell on her forehead and ran down straight away into her left eye. It flowed into the corner, lubricating it, sticking her eyelids together, blurring her vision. She felt it on her shaved head, splashing on her skin and running down behind her ear. More came into her other eye, and more on the other cheek. Then, at last, her mouth was filled by a sudden, gushing flood that hit the back of her throat and covered her tongue in a creamy pool. She lapped at it, sucking it in as it ran around her mouth. More came in her mouth, and overflowed onto her chin and down her neck. Her breasts were covered, and a stream of semen ran down the front of her stomach and into the creases that pointed to her hidden slit. Strands dripped from her hard, throbbing nipples and reached down to the tops of her thighs. She bathed in it, languished in it, wished for it to continue for ever.

More men came, more semen flowed and still she knelt, still she bathed, still her thirst was not quenched. She was drenched in it, swamped by its stickiness, soaked by the flood of it. She wanted to feel her cunt. She wanted to be thrashed and whipped. She wanted to be rolled over and exposed to all who stood around and watched. But she waited for more — obedient, still, needy.

Semen inundated her. It overflowed from her mouth and completely filled her eyes. It ran from her nose — foaming in a froth as she breathed out, sucking back in collapsing bubbles as she breathed in. Her body was covered in it. She was saturated. Still she did not dare move. She knew that moving would release the pleasure that was shut up inside her. She knew that if she squeezed her thighs together even slightly her joy would come out, flood through her, take her over. Even as she blinked her eyes, she felt it welling up inside. Even as she breathed, she felt the heat of her own delight beginning to boil over. She pressed her hands against the top of her buttocks — she could not help it. She needed to wait, she knew that, but she could not — it was hopeless. She started to breathe hard, to gasp as it began. She blinked her blurred eyes. She opened her mouth as wide a she could. She sucked at the semen that spurted around her. She gulped it in. She swallowed it down. She could not quench her insatiable thirst.

Her head started spinning as she rocked forward. She could not help herself. It was too much. She tightened her buttocks and the pressure against the throbbing swollen flesh of her cunt was enough to release it. She gasped loudly, choking as more semen poured over her. She jerked in a sudden and devastating convulsion. She stayed on her knees as it ran through her. She rocked forward and back. Her stomach contracted and tightened. Her breasts rose and fell. Her thighs squeezed hard against each other. She drowned in it. She suffocated beneath it. She was overcome by it. She sucked it up and she felt as if she herself had been swallowed by it.

When the last man left, she dropped forward onto her knees. She hung back, waiting for the whip on her buttocks, before she moved away. Even when the thin leather cut across her skin, she moved only slowly, delighting in the pain of the harsh blows on her taut buttocks, not letting them pass without absorbing the delight of every one. She licked at the semen around her mouth, allowing it to drip from her nostrils and over her top lip. She squeezed it from her eyes with slow, determined blinks.

She crawled forward and she stopped by the young girl who was still waiting, her buttocks upturned and smeared with red smudges from the leather crop. Sappho waited with her, filled with joy, warmed throughout her body, still jerking with the ecstasy of her orgasm.

They remained on all fours as water was sluiced over both of them — washing the semen from them, cleansing them, purifying them.

Chryseis stretched her hand down and touched Sappho on the shoulder. Sappho shivered with delight at the feel of Chryseis' fingers. Another shock of orgasm ran through her. She bit down on her trembling lips. She turned her face towards Chryseis.

Chryseis smiled.

'Sisters,' she said, helping Sappho to her feet. 'Sisters!' she shouted to the worshippers as she held Sappho's hand and stretched it high in the air. 'Sisters of Apollo!'

Sappho and Chryseis lay naked in each other's arms. Sappho kissed Chryseis softly on the neck. A line of naked young girls with flowered crowns waited for any instructions the two priestesses of Apollo might wish to give. Sappho beckoned one over. It was the girl who had taken part in the buk-ka-ke with Sappho. The girl ran forward and knelt down, smiling, waiting, hoping to be allowed to favour her mistress by fulfilling any of her wishes. The others watched, their hands at their sides.

'Bend over, girl,' said Sappho. 'Take my toe into your mouth. I want to feel your lips around it. I want to feel the pressure encircling its base as you suck at it. I want to feel your spit enveloping it, warming it, lubricating it. And when

I feel ready, you can lick my cunt. I will let you press your tongue in as deeply as you can. I will let you lap at it. I will let you cover it with your spit. And then you can lick my anus, slowly, all around it. When I am satisfied, I will let you push the tip of your tongue inside. I want to feel you tasting it, lapping at it. I want to feel as if you are completely inside me.'

The young girl went down on all fours. Her smooth, slender buttocks described a delectable curve as she bowed her head. She took Sappho's toe slowly into her mouth. Her smooth-skinned cheeks dished in as she sucked. Her spit-covered lips glinted as they tightened around the base. Sappho rolled her eyes back and moaned.

'Then, when I am ready,' she continued. 'When I feel I need to release my pleasure, I will thrash you. As I feel my heat swelling over me — suffocating me — I will thrash you so hard you will scream. You will be grateful for the ecstasy of pain I will bestow on you. And even at the height of your suffering, even when you think you are at your limit, you will beg for more, and I will reward you with it.'

Chapter 21

Humiliation at the Walls of Troy

Many new women had been brought into the temple, gathered from the alleys and brothels of the town. One of them was Eva. She stood proudly erect, her tattered clothing hanging in rags from her supple body, her flame-red hair tangled and knotted, hanging over her forehead and sticking to her soiled and dirty cheeks. Chryseis ordered her onto all fours. Eva did as she was told. She waited, her buttocks upturned, her head hung, her hair hanging to the ground. As she was thrashed with a multi-tailed leather flogger, she slowly drooped. Her back bent lower, her elbows collapsed, her face touched the ground. Spit dribbled from her mouth and, finally, her face fell into it. Young men came forward and began flogging her with leather straps. Her buttocks dropped down under the weight of pain they inflicted. She fell flat against the marble floor, her arms stretched out, her legs wide apart.

On Chryseis' command, the beating was stopped. Eva crawled forward, hardly daring to move in case the heavy leather straps were brought down on her buttocks again. She looked up, as if she was appealing to her own gods. She gaped as she saw Sappho standing above her. She could not believe it. At last, she would be saved. Her heart lifted and she reached out her hand. Sappho bent down and took it.

'You are safe. I thank my gods,' she said weakly. 'I waited for you. But you never came. Am I safe at last?'

'You are,' said Sappho, kneeling down beside Eva and waving away the men with the straps in their hands. 'I promised you a reward, and I will honour that. But, dear Eva, we must wash you first. You are so dirty. Here, come this way.'

Eva tried to get up, but winced with pain — the flogging with the straps had left her bruised and agonised.

'I cannot ... ' she started.

'Do not speak. Do not try to get up. Here, follow me. Stay on your hands and knees.' Sappho led Eva out of the temple and into a large square filled with people. 'Go across this square. I will arrange for you to be received and cared for. Dear Eva, you have suffered so much. And I owe my new life to you.'

Chryseis walked up behind Sappho and they watched together as Eva crawled on into the crowd that now surged around her. Suddenly, they turned away and looked at each other. They giggled like spoiled girls as, abandoning Eva in the dirty square, they ran back onto the steps of the temple.

Eva looked back, her tear-stained face covered in mud and dirt.

'Help me,' she called plaintively. 'Sappho, you said we were like sisters. That you would reward me for helping you escape, for suffering so much. Please.'

Sappho did not reply and Eva suddenly realised what was happening. There was only one place for her to go, back towards the gates.

Sappho and Chryseis laughed and punched each other playfully as Eva, pushed and kicked at by the herd of ruffians that surrounded her, crawled pitifully towards the city gates.

As she watched, Sappho felt a wave of excitement running through her. The pleasure of seeing Eva on her hands and knees was only enhanced by the excitement caused by her own act of treachery. She looked again at Eva. How misled she had been. How she had begged for her bargain to be honoured. How she had been humiliated by Sappho's rejection of her. Sappho felt the hot moisture of her cunt. Its swelling edges told her, with every throb of her soft flesh, that she had discovered a new and magnificent way of releasing her joy.

Eva felt the full weight of Sappho's treachery — how she had been abandoned, tricked, humiliated. Sappho had never intended to honour her promise — she realised that now. Eva had been living a false hope of returning home. She glanced back at Chryseis and Sappho for one last time. Her stomach filled with anxiety as she soaked up their mockery, contempt and scorn. She crawled on all fours, her tattered rags barely covering her body, her buttocks completely exposed and still heavily striped from the strapping she had received at the hands of Chryseis' servants.

'Open the gates,' shouted Chryseis triumphantly. 'Let the foreign dog crawl out. Perhaps she will find her own way home!'

Sappho watched as the heavy gates of the city creaked open.

Eva looked up at the slaves that drew them back on heavy ropes. Several of them spat down at her. It ran across her face and into her mouth. She wanted to shout out for help but she knew it was hopeless. One of the slaves ran forward and started flailing her across the buttocks. The thin strips of leather wrapped around her thighs and cut into her skin. She tried to duck away. Her legs parted and, as the flail came down again, the soft flesh of her cunt was stung by its lacerating cut.

Outside the gates, dirty beggars leered at her. One of them ran up holding his cock in his hands and urinated onto her. She crawled on and, to the screams of the slaves and the giggling of Chryseis and Sappho, she fell into the hands of a new set of torturers — torturers with no taste for the higher pleasures, only base eagerness for the ugliest delights of all. She felt their greedy hands around her body, pulling at her skin, pinching her nipples, clawing at the flesh of her slit. A finger penetrated her anus, another her cunt. She tasted semen as it ran down her face. She licked it away, and tasted the dust and urine that mixed with it. She swallowed it. It ran down her throat and she felt the heat of expectation building inside her. She turned her head and opened her mouth for more, wishing only that the desires of the animals around her would be many and their demands almost too difficult to bear. She looked up and saw Praxis standing before her, with Calliope at his side, and she knew her future held only pain.

Sappho was again behind the pillar set above the sunken floor of the temple of Apollo. She crouched down and pulled her robe up around her waist. She looked down as Chryseis, resplendent in her finery, her breasts bared, her dark hair oiled, her acolytes attending her, naked girls tossing flowers around her feet. She held up a dagger above the altar and chanted to her god.

A fresh young girl appeared alongside Sappho. She was beautiful, slim and small breasted. She crouched down and opened her legs wide, exposing her delectable slit, its pink edges and its glistening, moist centre.

'You are Mistress Sappho, the priestess,' said the young girl nervously.

'I am,' said Sappho.

The young girl ran her fingers down to the top of her crack and opened it slightly. Its moisture gleamed.

'Can you help me to be a maiden in the temple?' the young girl asked.

'Yes,' said Sappho. 'Of course.'

Sappho slid her fingers between her own thighs, finding the soft flesh of her cunt and probing into its moist sweetness. She rolled her eyes up in pleasure as she delved into the dark entrance. She opened her mouth as she pressed the palm of her hand against the hard nub of her throbbing clitoris.

She glanced at the young girl — her open legs, her glistening cunt, her sweet smile. She moved herself slightly, exposing herself to all that were gathered in the temple. A wave of vulnerability ran through her. She thought again of all that had happened before she had again found safety in Troy. She watched the young girl lifting her narrow hips. A jerking shock of ecstasy gripped her and she screamed her joy out loud.

Dark Slave

Lee Ash

"As the darkness vanished every exciting aspect of the moment was snatched away from her. Instead of being a desired submissive in the throes of elation, Laura realised she was only a bound and naked woman, caught in a forbidden act by three strangers.

Two men and a woman stepped into the room, each regarding Laura with expressions of distaste, surprise and curiosity. She didn't recognise any of them and silently returned their inquisitive gazes."

Laura's nights are spent in tormented ecstasy, but who is it who commands her and makes her submit to his will? Three people, a private investigator, a hypnotist and a psychologist, receive a summons to try and unravel the mystery of the 'Dark Slave'. All three are involved in the world of SM but the revelations that await them are stranger and more erotic than they could ever have imagined. A tangled web of domination over beautiful submissives is slowly revealed and acted out while Laura's fate hangs in the balance.

A Slave's Desire

Kim Knight

Mel, recently freed from slavery, is determined to win her lover's freedom. But Natalie is still a slave and has been sold into slavery in Russia. Helped by the mysterious Claudia, Mel tracks her but is foiled at the last minute.

The vicious mistress called 'Faith' has had the beautiful Natalie taken to a training camp in Algeria. Here her torment seems never-ending and she sinks into complete submission.

Inventive, cruel and clever; Kim Knight's second volume in the 'Unchained' series is as absorbing as it is highly erotic.

The Roman Slave Girl

Syra Bond

'Magnus smacked her hard, each time bringing his hand down more firmly. The loud smacks caused Bec to tense her body until it was rigid, but she did not cry out, nor did she squirm or try to avoid the blows. Caristia looked at Bec's taut body and listened to the regular rhythm of Magnus's smacking hand. She leant back against the wall — almost hidden by the shadows — and allowed her hand to drift…'

A beautiful, flaxen haired Saxon girl, captured and enslaved, is bound to cause a stir in Pompeii. And once she arrives at the house of Rufo the slave dealer and comes under the discipline of Magnus, his trainer, Caristia has no choice but to experience every aspect of their brutal world; a world that demands complete submission from her.

Controlling Catherine

Elena Gregory

A minor burglary leads Catherine into a meeting with a very dominant policeman and before she knows what's happening, she finds herself falling under his spell. But she doesn't slip easily into the role of submissive and some strange adventures lie in store for her before she finally comes to terms with being controlled.

Elena Gregory gives her readers a fascinating glimpse into the secret world of the submissive woman in this, her second Silver Moon novel.

There are over 100 stunningly erotic novels of domination and submission in the Silver Moon catalogue. You can see the full range, including Club and Illustrated editions by writing to:

Silver Moon Reader Services
Shadowline Publishing Ltd,
No 2 Granary House
Ropery Road,
Gainsborough,
Lincs. DH21 2NS

You will receive a copy of the latest issue of the Readers' Club magazine, with articles, features, reviews, adverts and news plus a full list of our publications and an order form.